WATCH YOUR BACK!

Donald E. Westlake

WATCH YOUR BACK!

NEW YORK   BOSTON

Copyright © 2005 by Donald E. Westlake
All rights reserved.

Mysterious Press
Warner Books

Time Warner Book Group
1271 Avenue of the Americas, New York, NY 10020
Visit our Web site at www.twbookmark.com.

The Mysterious Press name and logo are registered trademarks of Warner Books.

Printed in the United States of America

First Printing: April 2005

10 9 8 7 6 5 4 3 2 1

Library of Congress Cataloging-in-Publication Data

Westlake, Donald E.
    Watch your back! / Donald E. Westlake.— 1st ed.
        p. cm.
    ISBN 0-89296-802-8
    1. Dortmunder (Fictitious character)—Fiction. 2. Bars (Drinking establishments)—Fiction. 3. Organized crime—Fiction. 4. New York (N.Y.)—Fiction. 5. Criminals—Fiction. 6. Robbery—Fiction. I. Title.

PS3573.E9W17 2005
813'.54—dc22   2004061064

To Susan Richman, who wasn't sure it was such a good idea,
but who marched forward anyway. God bless.

WATCH YOUR BACK!

1

WHEN JOHN DORTMUNDER, a free man, not even on parole, walked into the O.J. Bar & Grill on Amsterdam Avenue that Friday night in July, just before ten o'clock, the regulars were discussing the afterlife. "What I don't get," said one of them, as Dortmunder angled toward where Rollo the bartender was busy with something far over to the right end of the bar, "is all these clouds."

A second regular put down his foaming beerglass to say, "Clouds? Which clouds are these?"

"That they're sitting on!" The first regular waved an arm dangerously, but did no damage. "You look at all these pictures, Jesus sitting on a cloud, that other God sitting on a cloud, Mary sitting on a cloud—"

"A little lower down," suggested a third.

"Well, yeah, but the point is, can't Heaven come up with *furniture?*"

As Dortmunder approached Rollo, he saw that the beefy bartender in his once-white apron was deeply absorbed in making five very complicated drinks in glasses Dortmunder had never seen before and would not have suspected the O.J. of possessing: curled, twisted, wider than deep, they looked mostly like crystal hubcaps, though smaller. But not much smaller.

Another regular, meantime, was objecting to the concept of furniture in the beyond, saying, "Whadaya want with *furniture*? Heaven isn't Westchester, you know."

A fifth regular weighed in, saying, "Yeah? What about all those fields of plenty?"

"Land of milk and honey," added the third regular, as though it were an indictment.

The first regular lifted a skeptical glass and a skeptical brow to say, "Do they give out overshoes?"

What Rollo was doing with those glasses was just about everything. He had already sluiced in some crushed ice, and now he was adding some red liquid and some yellow liquid and some brown liquid and some clear liquid, all of them channeling around through the shards of ice and combining to form pools that looked like a lab test you didn't want the results of.

The second regular was now saying, "What gets me is this fruitcake Muslim Heaven with the seventy-two virgins."

"There *aren't* seventy-two virgins," the first regular objected.

"Well, no," the second regular conceded, "not all at one time, but still, what kinda Heaven is *this*? It would be like being assigned to an all-girls' high school."

"Ouch," said the third regular.

"Can you imagine," the second regular said, "what it sounds like in the cafeteria at lunchtime?"

The fourth regular, the one with something against Westchester, said, "Would you have to learn volleyball?"

This introduction of sports stymied everybody for a minute, as Dortmunder watched Rollo slice up a banana and drop the chunks into the glasses like depth charges. Next he reached for a lime, as Dortmunder looked around and saw what must have happened. It was summertime in New York City, late July, and the sluggish tide of tourists had washed up on this unlikely shore five ladies who did each other's silvery wavy hair, and who were seated now at one of the booths on the right. They perched very straight on just the front edge of the seat, their backs not touching the seatbacks, like freshmen in military academy, and they gazed around the unlovely precincts of the O.J. with an anthropologist's guarded delight. Their clothing combined many of the colors Rollo was injecting into their drinks. One of them, Dortmunder saw, had a cell phone–camera and was sending pictures of the O.J. to the folks back home.

Well, being a free person and not on parole was all well and good, but there was no point in overdoing it. Hunching a shoulder against the spy-cam, Dortmunder said, "Whadaya say, Rollo?"

"With you in a minute," Rollo said. Inside each glass now, it looked as though an elf had blown up, but Rollo was not done. To cap it all, he dropped a shiny red spheroid on top of each; could those be related to cherries somehow?

Surely that was all even these glasses could stand, but no. Turning to a little-used drawer under the backbar, Rollo came up with five Oriental pastel parasols and plopped one onto each drink, as though some poor shipwrecked son of a bitch were marooned on each of them.

And now they actually were done. Since apparently total concentration was not necessary while loading glasses onto a tray—not even glasses like these—while Rollo did that operation he said, "You already got the beer and salt back there."

"Good."

Tray full, Rollo reached under the bar and came up with a bottle of sluggish brown liquid behind a label reading,

Amsterdam Liquor Store Bourbon
"Our Own Brand"

Placing this bottle on the bar before Dortmunder, he said, "The other bourbon and ice? He coming?"

"Yeah."

"I'll get you two glasses," Rollo said, and while he did, Dortmunder told him, "Also the rye and water, the one that tinkles his ice cubes all the time."

"Haven't seen him for a while." Rollo knew everybody not by their name but by their drink, which struck him as the professional way to go about things.

"He's the one called this meeting," Dortmunder said. "Let's hope it's good news."

"I'll drink to that," Rollo said, though he didn't. Instead, he carried the tray of weirdness toward the five tourist ladies, who filmed his approach.

Picking up the bottle and the two glasses with their own discrete burdens of ice cubes, Dortmunder made his way around the regulars, who were still gnawing the same bone, the third regular now saying, "What if you *can't* play cards in Heaven? What if you *can't* dance?"

"Big deal," the second regular said. "I can't dance on Earth."

Leaving the theologians, Dortmunder made his way down the hall, past the doors defined by neat dog silhouettes labeled POINTERS and SETTERS and past the phone booth that was now a helplessly gaping unofficial portal to cyberspace, and into a small square room with a concrete floor. The walls were fronted, floor to ceiling, by beer and liquor cases, leaving just room for a battered old round table with a stained green felt top and half a dozen armless wooden chairs, at one of which—the one most completely facing the door—sat a carroty-headed guy with a glass of beer in front of his right hand, a salt shaker in front of where his left hand should be, and his left hand actually holding a cell phone to his ear. "Here's John now," he said into it. "I'll tell him."

"Hello, Stan," Dortmunder said, and sat to his left, so he, too, could have an unobstructed view of the door.

Hanging up and secreting his cell on his person, Stan said, "I think the Williamsburg is gonna be all right."

"That's good," Dortmunder said. Stan Murch was a driver, and as a result he gave more than the usual consideration to the routes he chose.

"For many years," Stan said, "the Williamsburg Bridge was where you went if you wanted to sleep in your car. Only now the construction's done, turns out, that humongous express-way Robert Moses wanted to put across Manhattan from the Williamsburg to the Holland Tunnel, slice the island in half like the Great Wall of China, only he didn't get it, that's fine, turns out it didn't have to happen anyway. Canal Street's a great run across, the West Side Highway's a snap coming up, I'm here so early this is my second saltshaker." Being a driver, Stan liked to pace his alcohol intake, but he hated it when his beer went flat; hence the salt. Every once in a while, a judicious spray, the head comes right back.

"That's nice," Dortmunder said.

"However," Stan said, "that was Ralph on the phone, the meet is off."

Ralph was Ralph Winslow, the rye-and-water-in-a-tinkling-glass. Dortmunder said, "He called the meeting, now he calls to say it's off."

"Some cops found something in his car," Stan explained. "He couldn't go into details."

"No, I know."

"In fact," Stan said, "he's got me on his speed-dial, so the cops think he's still on his one permitted call to his lawyer."

"Call Andy," Dortmunder suggested. "He's on his way, save him some time."

"Good idea. He's on *my* speed-dial. You don't have one of these, do you?" Stan asked, unleashing his cell.

"No," Dortmunder said simply.

As Stan made the call to warn off the final attendee of the non-meeting, he and Dortmunder walked back down the hall and around the regulars and over to where Rollo was firmly wiping with a dirty rag the part of the bar where he'd made all those strange drinks. At the booth, the ladies were gone and those glasses were all empty except for some dirty ice. That was fast. They'd taken the parasols with them.

"Sorry, Rollo," Dortmunder said, returning the bottle and glasses. "Change of plan."

"You'll be back," Rollo said.

As Dortmunder and Stan headed for the street, the first regular was saying, "You want *my* idea of Heaven? You go there, you take a nap."

The third regular veered half around on his barstool to get a better look at things. "Yeah? Then what?"

"What what? It's over. The Last Nap. Can you think of anything better?"

Into the profound silence that followed upon that, Dortmunder, on his way out the door, said, "I was counting on this. I could use something."

"Me, too," Stan said. "I'll give you a lift home."

"Thank you. Maybe," Dortmunder said, "I'll get another phone call."

2

DORTMUNDER! JOHN DORTMUNDER! ARE YOU THERE, JOHN DORTMUNDER?"

"Aack!" Dortmunder recoiled, flinging his telephone hand as far from his body as he could without surgery.

"JOHN DORTMUNDER! IS THAT YOU?"

"Don't shout!"

"What?"

"Don't shout!"

The phone muttered something. Cautiously Dortmunder allowed it to approach his head. The phone muttered, "This is it? I come back and the phones don't work?"

"Arnie?" This was three weeks since the non-meeting at the O.J.

"There you are! Hello to you, John Dortmunder!"

"Yeah, hello, Arnie. So you're back, are you?"

"Not ten minutes since I finished unlockin the door."

"So it didn't work, huh?" Dortmunder was not surprised.

But Arnie, not quite shouting, cried, "Whadaya mean, it didn't work? A *course* it worked! I graduated with honors,

John Dortmunder. What you see before you is a changed man."

"Well, I'm not *seeing* you," Dortmunder pointed out, "and I have to say, you don't *sound* that different."

"Well, it's a makeover, that's all," Arnie explained, as Dortmunder's faithful companion, May, came into the living room with a pen in her hand (she'd been doing a crossword puzzle in the kitchen) and an expression of concern on her face, wondering what all the racket was about. "It's not like they slid a new chassis in," Arnie went on. "I'm still the same physical plant like I was before, except my skin is all this khaki color."

"Well, you been in the tropics," Dortmunder said, as he showed May an elaborate combined shoulder shrug, head shake, eyebrow waggle, and torso twist, to indicate that he didn't know so far exactly what was going on, but it didn't seem to include any imminent threat.

"That's it, all right," Arnie agreed. "I don't know *when* I'll be able to leave the house again. But listen to me, what I'm saying, I never leave the house anyway."

"That's true," Dortmunder said.

"In fact," Arnie said, "the reason I'm calling, fresh offa the plane, I want *you* to come *here*."

"There? Your apartment, you mean?"

"That's where I'm gonna be, John Dortmunder, and that's where I'm gonna put before your eyes a proposition so good you'll fall right over."

"What do you mean, a proposition?"

"Dortmunder, not to go into details on this public instrument here, this telephone—"

"No no, I follow that."

"But you know," Arnie said, "in our transactions, me and you, I always give top dollar."

"That's true."

"I always *had* to give top dollar," Arnie reminded him, "because if I gave medium dollar like that goniff Stoon, nobody would ever come to do business with me, because of my basic unpleasantness."

"Yrm."

"Which is in the past, John Dortmunder," Arnie promised him. "Wait'll you see. You come over, I'll lay it out, you're never gonna even *thought* about a dollar as large as this one. Come over, I'm here, until I get my pallor back I am not leaving the apartment. Come over any time, John Dortmunder. And I'll tell you this, it's good to be back. Good-bye to you."

"Good-bye," Dortmunder told the phone after Arnie hung up. Then he also hung up, and shook his head.

"I've been patient," May reminded him.

"Let's sit down," Dortmunder said.

So they sat, and May looked alert, and Dortmunder said, "I mentioned, from time to time, a character called Arnie Albright."

"A fence," she said, and put her pen on the coffee table. "You sell him things sometimes. You don't like him."

"Nobody likes him," Dortmunder said. "He doesn't like himself. He told me once, he finds himself so disgusting, he shaves with his back to the mirror."

"But you sell him things."

"He makes up for his personality," Dortmunder explained, "by paying a better percentage than anybody else."

May said, "Is he really that bad?"

"Well," Dortmunder told her, "he just came back from the intervention."

"Intervention? He's a drunk, too?"

"No, he's just obnoxious, but it's enough. Turns out, his family couldn't stand it any more, it was either drop him out of an airplane or intervent. I don't think any of them had a plane, so they went for the other."

"John," May said, "when a group of people do an intervention, they go to the drunk or the druggie or whatever he is, they tell him you have to go into rehab now, or detox, or whatever it is, or nobody wants you around here any more. If they did an intervention for obnoxiousness, where would they send him?"

"Club Med," Dortmunder told her. "Down in the Caribbean somewhere. They figured, all the good weather, all the smiley faces, maybe it'd soak in. He called me once when he was there, he hated it. I figured, it's not gonna work, but now he's back and he says it *did* work, so go know."

"Did he sound like it worked?"

Dortmunder thought back to the recent conversation. "Gee, I don't know," he said. "Could be. He was still loud, but maybe he didn't grate quite so much. Still and all, he wants me to go over to his place, he's got a proposition for me, he called me as soon as he got home, but I dunno about that."

May said, "Did you say you'd go?"

"I don't think I said one way or the other."

"But he called you right away when he got home. I think you've got to do it."

Dortmunder sighed, long and heartfelt. "I don't think I can go over there by myself, May."

"Call Andy," she advised.

He nodded, slow and heavy. "That's what it comes down to," he agreed.

3

WHEN HIS VIBRATOR went off, Andy Kelp was standing in an elevator with a bunch of people he didn't know. He was on his way to an upscale furrier whose display space was on the eleventh floor of this midtown Manhattan building, and he was going there today because, this being a Tuesday in mid-August, the entire staff of that exclusive boutique was away on vacation, as he'd verified this morning by listening to their answering machine. A good day, therefore, to shop.

Now, riding the elevator, feeling the vibration against his leg, he thought, this is a bad time for this, but on the other hand, in the hall in front of Gogol's Sables would be even worse, so he pulled the phone from his pocket, opened it, and murmured into it, "Yes?"

Around him, all the other people put that face on that pretends they're not listening, the way they always do, while they leaned in a little closer just the same.

"You doing anything?"

"Naturally I'm doing something," Kelp said, having recognized the voice as belonging to his sometime associate, John Dortmunder. "I'm usually doing something."

"Oh." Voice now reeking with suspicion, Dortmunder said, "On your own?"

Meaning, of course, was Kelp freezing him out of something good. "Sure, single-o," he said, while around him the other people began to clear their throats and rub their noses and move their feet around on the floor to express their dissatisfaction with the interest level of the phone call so far. "It happens."

Two people coughed so loudly, Kelp had trouble hearing Dortmunder's response: "So call me when you get a little time off."

"Hour, maybe maybe."

"I'll be home," Dortmunder said, he being someone who, Kelp knew, very often did nothing at all.

"Done," Kelp said, and hung up as the elevator stopped at 11. He got off, and the elevator continued on up, full of sneezing, nose-blowing and elbow scratching, and fifty-five minutes later Kelp walked into his own little apartment in the west Thirties, carrying a big shopping bag from Wal-Mart, full but not too heavy, with a polyester sweater in lime green on top. He went through into the bedroom, and his close personal friend Anne Marie Carpinaw looked up from the computer, where she was lately in frequent hyperspace correspondence with history freaks who wanted trivia answers about her daddy, who had for a long time been a congressperson from the greatish state of Kansas.

"Shopping?" she asked, fingers still on the keys. "At Wal-Mart? *You?*"

"Not exactly," he told her, as he put the shopping bag on the bed. "I was more hunting for the pot." Tossing the sweater into the wastebasket, he reached into the bag and brought out a short silver sable coat of a style that's never out of fashion. "I think this one's your size."

She leaped up from the computer. "Sable in August! How appropriate."

"I got three of them," he told her, admiring the way she snuggled into the coat. Taking two similar trophies from the bag, he said, "One for you and two for the rent."

"Well, this is the best of them," she said, smiling as her hand smoothed the fur down her front.

"John wants me to call, I'll do it in the living room."

"These people," she said, with a dismissive wave of the hand at the computer. "They want to know where Daddy stood on the Cold War. As though Daddy ever stood on anything. He was a politician, for God's sake."

"Tell them," Kelp suggested, "your daddy felt the Cold War was an unfortunate necessity and he prayed every night that it would come out okay."

He left her standing there in the sable but with a sudden fraught expression on her face, as though wondering if she'd wound up with her father after all, and in the living room he sat on the sofa, looked at the television set, and called John.

Who answered on the fifth ring, sounding out of breath. "Ern?"

"You hadda run from the kitchen."

"It turns out, snacking's a good thing. Many small meals all day long, easier on the system."

"Still, you hadda run from the kitchen."

"You aren't going to," Dortmunder said, "talk to me about extra telephones."

"I am not," Kelp agreed. "I gave up on you long ago. Besides, you're the one wanted to talk, so you get to pick the subject."

"Good," Dortmunder said. "Arnie Albright."

Kelp waited, then said, "That's the subject?"

"It is."

"He's down south, for the intervention."

"He's back, he called me, he says it worked."

"I'll want a second opinion."

"You can have one," Dortmunder offered. "Your very own opinion. He wants to see us, he says he's got a great proposition for us."

"Us?" Kelp watched Anne Marie walk through the room toward the kitchen, smiling. She still wore the coat. Into the phone, he said, "Arnie didn't call *me,* John, he called you."

"But he knows we're a team."

"Arnie Albright didn't call me," Kelp said, "so I don't need to go over there."

"He says it's a really great offer."

"Fine," Kelp said. "You go over, if it turns out it really is a really great offer, *then* you call me. You can even come here and describe it to me."

"Andy," Dortmunder said, "I'm gonna level with you."

"Don't strain yourself."

"I just can't do it alone," Dortmunder admitted. "I'm afraid to know what Arnie is after Club Med. Either we go together, or I'm not going."

Kelp was beginning to feel trapped. "Look, John," he said, and Anne Marie walked through the room again, from the kitchen toward the bedroom, still smiling and still wearing the sable coat. She stopped midway and opened the coat, and she didn't have anything on underneath it. "Uuuuu," Kelp said.

"So you'll meet me there," Dortmunder said.

It was unfair; life was too full of distractions. How could a person figure a way to weasel out of a thing? Anne Marie walked on to the bedroom, the coat twitching behind her legs, and Kelp said, "Only not right now. Later on today, say four o'clock."

"I'll meet you there," Dortmunder said. "Out front."

"I can hardly wait," Kelp said, and hung up.

4

"ANOTHER BEAUTIFUL DAY in paradise."

"You say that every day."

"Well, of course I say it every day," Preston said, flicking sand off his belly. "That's the point, isn't it? The unchanging sameness, the lack of surprise, the loss of suspense, the eternal undifferentiated pleasantness of it all, of *course* I have to respond in the character of the setting, with the same hackneyed phrase every single pointless, drifting, inane day. The wonder of it is that *you* don't say it every day."

Alan frowned. Preston suspected, not for the first time, that Alan had not been paying strict attention. "Say what every day?"

"'You say that every day.'"

Alan scrunched his monkey face into a walnut, a walnut wearing a Red Sox hat and sunglasses. "I say *what* every day?"

"Oh, Lord," Preston said. Should he try to get back to the beginning of the thread, untangle the snarl? What for? Instead, he said, "You're not quite the thing as a paid companion, are you?"

"I'm every bit a companion," Alan insisted. "I'm here at your beck and call, I engage in conversation with you, I fetch and carry, I completely subordinate my own preferences and personality, and I never argue with you."

"You're arguing with me now."

"No, I'm not."

Another dead end. Preston sighed and looked out over his own supine form on the chaise longue, past his mounded pink belly cresting at the waist of his scarlet swimming trunks, past the tops of his toes, just visible way down there this side of the white wood rail enclosing the porch, past the bit of sand and neat plantings and brick path that paralleled the shoreline, past the shoreline out there and then to the green and foamy sea, speckled with snorkelers, whizzing with windsurfers, caroming with canoes. It was exhausting just to watch all those people exercise. "I hate this place," he said.

Alan had no doubt heard that before as well. "We could go somewhere else, if you'd like," he said.

Preston snorted. "Where else? It's all the same, except most of it is even worse. At least, here there's no weather."

Alan waved a hand at the view. "It's August, Preston," he said, "the whole northern hemisphere's like that at the moment. No snow, not even much rain. You could go anywhere you like."

"You know perfectly well," Preston told him, beginning to become really annoyed, "the only place I'd like to go is the one place I certainly can*not* go, and that is home. New York. My apartment. My clubs, my city, my theaters, my restaurants, my board of directors' meetings, my five-hundred-dollar hookers speaking French. *That's* where I cannot go, as you full well know. And you also know why, because that's something else I talk about often, because it preys on my mind."

"Your wives, you mean."

"To have ex-wives is the normal state of affairs," Preston

explained. "It's merely the end product of lust. But ex-wives are not supposed to band together, pool their resources, set themselves to strip their former benefactor to his skivvies, and then set fire to the skivvies."

"You probably jeered at them," Alan suggested.

Preston spread his hands. "Well, of *course* I jeered at them. Ex-wives are *meant* to be jeered at. Tiny little grasping brains, greedy little pigs."

"Driving them together."

"Well, they weren't *supposed* to be together, they were supposed to hate each other too much. If those four women had remained solitary soreheads, as they were supposed to do, I wouldn't be on the run the way I am, hounded to the ends of the earth by the baying of the world's most rapacious divorce attorneys."

"Club Med isn't exactly the end of the earth," Alan informed him.

"It's one of them," Preston said. "It isn't your *hub,* your *beating heart,* your *nerve center,* in short, your New York. It isn't, Alan, New York."

"I agree," Alan said.

"Thank you." Preston brooded, then said, "If I *could* go home again, Alan, I would go there in a shot, as you very well know, and I would have absolutely no further use for a paid companion, and you would no doubt starve to death in a gutter somewhere. And deserve it, too. Is there anything more otiose than a paid companion?"

"Probably not," Alan said. "Of course, pleasant people get companionship for free."

"And worth every penny of it. What do you mean, pleasant people? I am pleasant. I smile at the waitstaff, I josh with the other guests."

"You taunt and tease," Alan told him. "You like to hurt people's feelings—mine, if I had any—and use big words they won't understand and just be so superior it's amazing you're not in a toga."

"Don't forget the laurel leaves," Preston said, and laughed, and said, "Do you know who I miss?"

Alan seemed mildly surprised. "You miss somebody?"

"That little Albright fellow," Preston said. "The crook, whatever he was. The fellow out of the Bowery Boy movies."

"You miss him," Alan said, the words as flat as a skipping stone.

"I do," Preston said, and smiled at the memory. "You talk about teasing people, he was the best subject I ever had in my life. Albright—*there's* a misnomer. And when he got to drinking!"

"You got to drinking yourself," Alan told him.

"Oh, a bit, here and there," Preston acknowledged, and waved the idea away. "Just enough to keep him company, so he could tell me things I could make fun of."

"You told him a few things yourself," Alan said.

"I did?" Preston tried to remember something he might have told the little Albright fellow. "What on earth could I possibly have told Arnie Albright?"

"Oh, I don't know," Alan said. "Personal details, when you were in your cups together. He's probably forgotten it all. But you know, I almost had the feeling sometimes that he came around so often mostly because he was trying to pump you."

"Pump? Me? Don't be foolish. Arnie Albright was about as crafty as that scuba instructor you inveigled me into going to."

"If you'd gone back," Alan said, "he might have drowned you."

"One of the reasons I didn't. But Arnie Albright. To pump *me*. He came back, day after day—"

"Because he had nowhere else to go, like you."

"Paid companions do not interrupt," Preston said. "He

came back because, in his pitiful little brain, he had dreams of someday one-upping me. It was wonderful to watch him, tongue-tied, nose turning bright red, trying to find a *snappy retort*."

"No, he didn't have a lot of those," Alan agreed.

"I should think not." With another laugh, Preston said, "Wherever he is right now, back up there in the city, I wonder if he thinks sometimes of me."

5

DORTMUNDER WAS FIVE minutes early and Kelp five minutes late—par for the course. Dortmunder was well aware that Arnie's nasty little apartment, up on the second floor, had no street-facing windows but was wrapped like a dirty scarf around an unpleasant airshaft, but nevertheless he felt exposed out here on West 89th Street between Broadway and West End Avenue, as though Arnie might be able somehow to see through the front apartment and down to the street, where Dortmunder was not rushing to come up and see him.

But then Kelp did get there, whistling up the street with his hands in his chino pockets, wearing a light blue polo shirt with the ghostly echo of a panther on the left front, where Anne Marie had removed the manufacturer's logo. "Waiting long?" he wanted to know.

"Nah, I just got here," Dortmunder said, to give him no satisfaction. "Let's go."

He turned toward the building, but Kelp said, "Shouldn't we discuss it first?"

Dortmunder frowned at him. "Discuss what?"

"Well, what the plan is, what's our approach, like that."

"Andy," Dortmunder said, "he hasn't told us the proposition yet. We discuss *after* we got something to talk about. You're just trying to stall here. Comon."

Dortmunder turned toward the entrance again, and this time Kelp followed. The ground floor of Arnie's building was a storefront, at the moment selling video games, with the most astonishing posters about sex and violence in the window and with a tiny vestibule to its left. Dortmunder and Kelp crowded into the vestibule; Dortmunder pushed the button next to the dirty card that said *Albright,* then gave a fatalistic look at the metal grid beside it, knowing what was coming next.

Which it did. *"Dortmunder?"*

"That's right," Dortmunder said to the metal grid, sorry he couldn't deny it, and the nasty buzzer sounded that would unlock the door.

Inside, a narrow hall was filled with the fragrance of old, damp newspapers, and the steep stairs led up to the second floor, where Arnie Albright himself stood and gazed down, a very strange expression on his face that he might have intended for a welcoming smile. "So," he called. "Two of you."

"I *knew* he didn't mean me," Kelp muttered as they went up the stairs. Dortmunder did not dignify that with a reply.

When they reached the top, Arnie turned away toward the open door of his apartment, saying, "Well, come on in, but try not to look at me, I still look like an army uniform."

Well, it was slightly worse than that, in fact. The way a tan manifested itself on Arnie Albright's city-bred skin was to look like the kind of makeup the mortician uses when there's going to be a viewing. If anybody wanted to know what Arnie Albright would look like in his coffin, this was the chance.

Otherwise he seemed unchanged, a grizzled, gnarly guy with a nose like a tree root. He was dressed in a Soho Film Festival T-shirt, bright blue cotton shorts, and Birkenstocks that looked as though they came from the same tree as his nose.

Arnie's apartment, small underfurnished rooms with big dirty windows showing the airshaft, was decorated mostly with his calendar collection, walls covered with Januarys of all times, combined with pictures of leggy girls, icy brooks, cuddly kittens, and classic cars. Here and there were the ones he called incompletes, years that had apparently started in June or September.

"Sit down at the table by the window there," Arnie offered. "It's the only place in the apartment where you don't get that smell."

So they sat on opposite sides of a kitchen table with incompletes laminated onto it, and Arnie dragged over another wooden chair to join them. Dortmunder said, "It doesn't smell so bad in here, Arnie."

"Not here," Arnie said. "But try the bedroom. Lemme tell you about the intervention."

"Sure, if you want to."

"It's what you call the background to the proposition," Arnie said. "I went down there, because my nearest and dearest made it pretty plain the alternative was sudden death, and believe me, it was not an experience I would wish on anybody."

"Sorry to hear that," Dortmunder said.

"In the first place, sun." Arnie scratched an ecru arm reminiscently. "It's overrated," he assured them. "You can't look at it, you can't get away from it, and it makes you itch. Or anyway, me. Then there's the ocean."

Kelp said, "You were on an island, I hear."

"Boy, was I. Any direction you go, ten feet, splash. But the thing I never got about the ocean, you think it's water, it isn't."

Kelp, interested, curious, said, "It isn't?"

"Looks like water, sounds like water." Leaning in close, Arnie half-whispered the secret: "It's salt."

"Sure," Kelp said. "Salt water."

"Forget the water, it's salt." Arnie made a face that did not improve his looks. "Yuk. I couldn't believe how much beer I had to drink to get *that* taste outa my mouth. Then somebody said, 'You don't want all that beer in the sun, you want a margarita,' so I took a margarita and *that's* salt. Come *on.* All the salt down there, you could curl up like a mummy."

"This is a lotta background, Arnie," Dortmunder said.

"You're right," Arnie said. "Now that I'm not so obnoxious any more, I'm garrulous instead. You know, like an old uncle after he goes straight. So let me cut to the chase, and the chase is a guy called Preston Fareweather."

Dortmunder repeated the name: "Never heard of him."

"Well, he isn't a movie star," Arnie said, "he's a venture capitalist. He's got more money than the mint, he invests in your up-and-coming operation, when the dust settles, hey, look, you got a partner, he's even richer. The reason he's down there, he's hiding out from lawyers and process servers."

"From the people he screwed?" Kelp asked.

"In a way," Arnie said. "But not the businesspeople. Seems, one way or another, Preston Fareweather married most of the really good-looking women in North America, and they banded together to get revenge. So he went to this island where nobody can get at him, waiting for the wives to get over their mad, which is not likely. But the thing about him is, his personality's even worse than mine used to be. Everybody down there hates him because he's so snotty and in your face, but he has all this money, so people put up with him. He insulted me a couple times, and I shrugged it off, he's just another bad taste, like ocean, but then a couple people there told me about this place he has."

"A place," Dortmunder echoed. "I have the feeling we're getting somewhere."

"We are," Arnie agreed. "Preston Fareweather has a big luxury duplex penthouse apartment on top of a building on Fifth Avenue, views of the park, all that, and in that apartment he's got his art collection and his Spanish silver and all this *stuff*. Well, you know, I'm interested in stuff, that's been the basis of our relationship over the years, so I went back to this guy. I hung around with this guy, I drank with him, pretended I was drunk, pretended his snotty little remarks got under my skin, and all along I'm getting the details of this apartment, because it occurs to me I know some people—namely, you people—who might be interested in this apartment."

"It sounds possible," Dortmunder agreed.

Kelp said, "Depending on this and that. Like getting in and getting out, for instance."

"Which is why I hung around the bastard so much," Arnie said. "He has this guy with him, personal secretary or assistant or something, I dunno, named Alan Pinkleton, and he's actually pretty sharp, I thought once or twice he might have piped to what I was doing, but it turned out okay. And by the time I had everything I needed to know, I realized this Preston son of a bitch had cured me, can you believe it?"

Kelp said, "*Preston* cured you?"

"I watched him," Arnie said. "I watched the people around him, how they acted, and I suddenly got it, those are the expressions I used to see on the faces of people looking at *me*. I was never obnoxious in the same way as Preston, on purpose to hurt and embarrass other people, but it all comes down to the same place. 'I don't wanna be Preston Fareweather,' I told myself, 'not even by accident,' so that was it. I was cured and I come home, and I called you, John Dortmunder, because here's my proposition."

"I'm ready," Dortmunder allowed.

"I'm sure you are. I despise that Preston so much, I put up with so much crap from that guy while I'm casing his apartment long-distance, that *my* reward is the thought of the expression on his face the next time he walks into his house. So what I'm offering is this: Anything you take outa there, I'll give you seventy per cent of whatever I get for it, which is way up, you gotta know, from the well, uh, twenty-five, thirty per—"

"Ten," Kelp said.

"Well, even if," Arnie said. "Seventy this time. And not only that, the thing's a piece a cake. Lemme show you."

Arnie jumped to his feet and left the room, and Dortmunder and Kelp exchanged a glance. Kelp whispered, "He *is* less obnoxious. I wouldn't have believed it."

"But this place does smell," Dortmunder whispered, and Arnie returned, with a kid's black-and-white composition book.

"I did all this on the plane coming back," he told them, and sat down to open the book, which was full of crabbed handwriting in ink. Following his route with a stubby fingertip, he said, "The building's eighteen stories high, at Fifth and Sixty-eighth. There's two duplex penthouses on top, north side and south side, both front to back. He's got the south side, views of the park, midtown Manhattan, the east side. His neighbor's probably got just as much money, what's his view? Spanish Harlem. And don't think Preston didn't chortle over *that*."

"Nice guy," Dortmunder said.

"In every way. Now, here's the wrinkle that makes the difference. Behind this building, on Sixty-eighth street, there's a four-story town house converted to apartments. Preston bought that building, rents it out, keeps getting richer. In the bottom of that building, where it's against the back of the big corner building, he put in a garage. Out of the garage, going up the outside of the bigger building, he put an elevator shaft and an elevator. His own elevator, just from his garage to his apartment."

"Not bad," Dortmunder acknowledged.

"Not bad for *you* guys," Arnie assured him. "Everybody else in that building, they've got this high-tech security stuff, doormen, closed-circuit TV. What Preston's got is a private entrance, a private garage, a private elevator."

Dortmunder said, "Who's in this apartment now?"

"Twice a month," Arnie said, "on the first and the fifteenth, building security does a sweep, spends maybe two hours. Twice a month, on the tenth and the twenty-fifth, a cleaning service comes in, spends seven hours. The other twenty-seven days of every month, the place is empty."

Dortmunder said, "Arnie, you're sure of all these details."

"I paid for them, John Dortmunder," Arnie assured him. "With emotional distress."

Kelp said, "You know, I gotta admit it, it does sound possible. But we'll have to look it over."

"Of course you gotta look it over," Arnie said. "Now, if I was you guys, I know what I'd do. I'd ease into that garage—there's alarms, but you know how to do with that—"

"Sure," Kelp agreed.

"In there now," Arnie said, "is Preston's BMW, top of the line. If I was you, I'd go in there, take out that car, sell it, put a truck in there, take a ride up in the elevator."

Dortmunder had been interested in the story, but now it was over, and he was beginning to realize that the smell Arnie had mentioned was more insidious than he'd thought. It really was not to be borne, not for very long. Maybe it was the last lingering trace of Arnie's former obnoxiousness, or maybe it was just August, but the time had come to leave. Pushing his chair back from the table, he said, "Is that it, then? Any more details?"

"What more details could there be?"

Kelp stood, so Dortmunder stood, so Arnie stood. Kelp said, "We'll look it over."

"Sure," Arnie said. "But it looks like we've got a deal, right?"

Kelp said, "You wanna know, should you offer this to any other of your clients, I'd say, not yet."

"We'll call you," Dortmunder promised.

"I'm looking forward," Arnie said, "to your call."

6

WALKING THROUGH CENTRAL Park, away from Arnie's place and toward the potential harvest on Fifth, Dortmunder said, "Did you ever hear from Ralph Winslow again?"

"What, after the non-meet?" Kelp shrugged. "Believe it or not, I was three blocks from the O.J. when Stan called."

"There was no reason to hang around."

"I know that." Kelp ducked a passing Frisbee and said, "A couple days later, Ralph's brother called, he said Ralph talked himself out of the problem later that night, but then he decided to take his attorney's advice, which was to move to a location for his health, which happens to be not in New York State."

"So whatever Ralph had," Dortmunder said, "it's gone now."

"Seems that way. The brother didn't know what it was." This time, Kelp caught the Frisbee and tossed it back, then called, "Whoops. Sorry."

"The brother didn't know what it was."

"Well, the brother's a civilian," Kelp said, and nodded toward Fifth Avenue. "Maybe this'll make up for it."

"Let's hope."

The building, up ahead, taller than its neighbors, built in the real-estate flush of the 1950s, when details and ornamentation and style and grace were considered old-fashioned and unprofitable, hulked like a stalker over the park, a pale gray stone structure pocked with balconies. Dortmunder and Kelp studied it as they waited at the light, then crossed over to it and walked down the side street, past its hugeness. Then they stopped, in front of the smaller town house back there, and looked up at the tall black box running up the back of the apartment building.

"You can't get up the outside," Dortmunder pointed out. "No ladder rungs or anything."

"John," Kelp said, "would you want to go up seventeen flights of ladder rungs?"

"I'm just saying."

Deciding to let that go, Kelp turned his attention to the smaller building behind the big apartment house, the one either from which the elevator shaft rose like a postmodern tree trunk or into which it was sunk like a sword hilt, depending on your general view of life. This twenty-five-foot-wide building, on the wide side for New York City town houses, was four stories high, with large windows and with the lowest floor halfway below sidewalk level. It was faced with the tannish-gray limestone New Yorkers call brownstone, and was probably older than the monster on the corner. In fact, the monster on the corner had probably replaced another half-dozen town houses just like this, from a lower-horizoned age.

The facade of this structure had a broad staircase centered, flanked by wrought-iron railings and leading up half a flight to an elaborate dark wood front door with beveled windows.

Under the staircase a more modest staircase led from left to right, down half a flight to the ground-floor apartment.

On the right front of the building, the symmetry was destroyed by a recent addition, a featureless metal overhead garage door, painted a little darker tan-gray than the building. A driveway indentation lay in the curb fronting this door, and there appeared to be two locks above the simple brass handle at waist height in the middle. Above the right corner of the door was an unobtrusive dark green metal box, one foot high, six inches wide, three inches deep.

"Pipe the alarm box," Kelp said.

Dortmunder said, "I see it. We seen boxes like that before."

"You just have to be a little careful, is all," Kelp said.

"On the other hand," Dortmunder said, "an alarm like that, you gotta get in there with foam, if you're gonna muffle the bell and short the wires."

"Naturally."

"Which means a ladder."

"Not necessarily," Kelp said.

"Well, let's just say necessarily," Dortmunder said. "A ladder, in this neighborhood, whadawe gonna do? Wear Con Edison coveralls and helmets? To lean on an alarm box?"

"What I was thinking, John," Kelp said, "instead of a ladder—"

"You'll fly."

"No, John," Kelp said, not losing his patience. "I think Arnie's right, what we should do to begin with, and that's take the BMW outa there and put a truck in. Now, this truck's gonna be a little tall."

"Oh," Dortmunder said. "I get it."

"Drive around the corner with one of us on the roof—"

"One of us."

"We'll figure that out later," Kelp said, and did hand gestures to demonstrate his thought. "Back it up to the garage door, do the alarm box. Truck drives away, around the corner, time he's back, the BMW's outa there, truck goes in."

"Maybe," Dortmunder said.

"Everything's a maybe," Kelp told him, "until you do it."

"Well, that's true."

"Have we seen enough?"

Dortmunder looked up at the long elevator shaft one last time. "For now."

For protective coloration, by tacit agreement they walked to the corner and back across Fifth Avenue and into the park, this time strolling southward instead of back toward Arnie's place. In the park you were anonymous, just two other guys among all the other citizens enjoying the summer air: the joggers, the skateboarders, the bicyclists, the stroller pushers, the dog walkers, the Frisbee tossers, the unicyclists, the tree worshippers, the Hare Krishnas, and the lost Boy Scout troops. But back on Fifth Avenue in the Sixties, they couldn't have been anything but what they were, which was not a good fact to advertise.

Strolling along southward, they both contemplated what they had heard and seen today, until Kelp said, "So we need two drivers."

"You can be one of them."

"No, I don't think so," Kelp said. "How about we call Stan Murch?"

"He isn't two drivers. He's good, but he isn't that good."

"He has a mom," Kelp reminded him, "and she's been known to drive."

"Mostly that cab of hers."

"But for us, too, sometimes. Anyway, I feel my own talents, with locks and suchlike, would be better availed of inside the building."

"You may be right," Dortmunder said. "So us two and Stan and his mom. There's gonna be heavy lifting."

"You're talking about Tiny."

"I am."

Kelp said, "You wanna call everybody? We'll make a meet at the O.J., tomorrow night."

"Good."

They walked a bit more in the sunshine, among the happy crowds, and then Dortmunder said, "Who knew? That Arnie's intervention would turn out to have an upside."

7

IT WAS JUST simple woolgathering, that's all. Stan Murch had been driving for twenty minutes across the original-equipment neighborhoods of Brooklyn and Queens, enjoying the massive delicacy of this dark green Lincoln Navigator, equipped with everything, when it suddenly occurred to him that if this vehicle came with everything, that meant it came with *everything*.

Yes. Unobtrusive on the dashboard, because it wasn't at the moment in use, was the little screen of the Global Positioning System. This was a car, unfortunately, that knew where it was. And would tell.

That was the snag lately. If you grabbed some old clunker, it didn't have enough resale value to be worth the risk involved in taking it away from its former owner, but a shiny new, valuable piece of tin was more than likely to be leashed to a satellite. And there was no known way to jam a satellite.

That's the problem, Stan thought. The law's got all the labs.

How long had he been in possession of this bigmouth? Twenty minutes by the dashboard clock—no, twenty-one.

He'd picked up this untrustworthy beauty at a seafood restaurant in Sea Gate at 1:27, and it was now 1:48. Was the original purchaser of this vehicle an early luncher or a late luncher? Once he completed his piscatory blowout and moved from restaurant to parking lot to find an empty space where his wheels were supposed to be, how long would it take to get the law on the case? And then how long before that nosy satellite up in the sky, the one whose weight on the top of his head was now giving Stan a migraine, would be telling every cop in the five boroughs that the dark green Lincoln Navigator they all so much wanted to meet was at this very instant eastbound on the Belt Parkway, just past Aqueduct racetrack, with JFK Airport coming up on the right? Thirty seconds.

I gotta get outa here, Stan informed himself, even though he knew he already knew that. I do not want to be on a highway, he advised himself. Yeah, yeah, shut up, he snapped at himself, getting a little edgy, here comes Lefferts Boulevard.

Slow damn traffic around JFK all the time. Nobody wants to take a train to the plane, that's the problem, one form of tubular transport a day is enough. Still, the exit ramp did creep closer on the right; Stan signaled—always be law-abiding, when possible—and onto Lefferts Boulevard he swung, headed north into South Ozone Park. Three minutes later, he pulled to a stop next to the yellow curb of a bus zone, pulled two tissues from the Navigator's dispenser, wiped the steering wheel and whatever other parts he might have touched, and exited.

And just in time, too. He'd walked barely two minutes farther along Lefferts when a cop cruiser pulled in beside him as he waited for traffic to stop or the light to change, whichever came first. The passenger cop, a blonde woman who got her iron supply by eating nails for breakfast, said, "You. Sir." The "you" was a little more believable than the "sir."

Stan kept an innocent look for just such occasions as this. Strapping it on, he said, "Yes?"

"D'jou park that car back there?"

Stan frowned, looking back toward but not directly at the Navigator. "Car? What car?"

"That isn't your car?"

"What, that Lincoln?" Stan chuckled, which was part of the innocent look. "Don't I wish. I'm on my way up to the subway."

"I thought you were the one just got outa that car," the cop persisted.

All right, he'd have to give her more. He said, "Wait a minute, do I look Chinese?"

"No, you don't," she said. "So what?"

"Just before I got there," Stan told her, "there was a Chinese guy stopped that car, got out, went up this way. I remember thinking, 'He's gonna get a ticket, that's a bus zone.'"

"That wasn't you." Still skeptical.

"He passed me," Stan explained. "Moving fast. Listen, the light's with me now, okay?"

"Go on," she said, but she wasn't happy about it.

So he went on, headed for the subway as he'd said, because maybe today wasn't a good day for private wheels, and damn if, three minutes later, she wasn't back again, pulling in next to a fire hydrant, both cops getting out of the car, hitching their gunbelts, the driver male, skinny, bored.

It was still the woman doing the talking: "You. Sir."

"Hello, again," Stan said. "Still on my way to the subway," he said, and pointed up the boulevard. Just a couple blocks to go.

"Tell us more about this Chinese guy," she said.

So then he understood he'd made another mistake. He'd given her the Chinese guy to distract her, throw a little fairy dust in her eyes, and now the Chinaman was coming back to bite him on the ass, because guess what? The first time, they were only interested in an illegally parked car, but since then the satellite has been at its busybody work, and now they've got a stolen car, and Stan has already declared himself a witness who saw the perp. Crap—a double scoop, please.

"Well," he said, picking his words carefully now that it was too late, "I don't know he was Chinese, exactly. Oriental, though. I think. Could be Japanese, Burmese. Maybe Thai."

"Dressed?"

"Oh, sure."

"Dressed *how*?"

"Oh." This part he could get right. "Kind of like me," he said. "You know, normal. Chinos and a light T-shirt. I don't think his T-shirt said anything." Stan's, in fact, said NASCAR, with smoke coming out of tailpipes on all the letters.

The woman cop gave this shirt a flat look, then said, "And which way did this Oriental person go?" She was still skeptical about the existence of the Oriental person, but so long as she contented herself with sarcasm, Stan didn't care.

"Up to the corner and turned right," he said, and pivoted to point back to where he'd come from. "Back there, that would have been."

"How old—"

The cell in Stan's pocket ripped off the race-starting jingle, and the woman cop gave him a severe look. "Sorry," he said, took out the cell, and managed to button it before it announced the second race. "Yeah?"

It was John Dortmunder's voice—Stan recognized it right away—saying, "You wanna make a meet tonight? You and your mom."

"Oh, hi, John," Stan said, with a bigger smile than he'd usually offer John, put on mostly for the cops' benefit. "Oh, you wanna play poker again, huh?"

"No, I—"

Stan wasn't sure whether the cops could hear what John was saying, so it would be better if he didn't say it. Interrupting, he said, "Wanna win your money back, huh? Fat chance. Listen, I'm here helping a couple cops with a car in a no-parking zone—"

"Nk."

"—so maybe we could talk later."

"You gonna be in jail tonight?"

"I don't see why, John."

"O.J. at ten," John said, and broke the connection.

So did Stan. "Friendly game," he assured the cop. "Nickel-and-dime."

She nodded. "May I see some ID?"

Stan frowned, honestly sorry not to be more helpful. "Gee, I don't think so," he said.

"No?" Skepticism doubled, she said, "You got something to hide?"

"Not that I know of," Stan said. "But I don't believe I have to show ID to walk on the sidewalk, and what else am I doing?"

"You're a witness."

"To a car in a no-parking zone?"

"To a *stolen* car in a no-parking zone."

"Oh," Stan said, showing surprise. "In that case, I'm not a witness at all. I forget everything. Sorry I can't be more help. Listen, I don't wanna miss my subway. You probably want to get back to your evidence before it's towed."

And he walked very briskly indeed to the Ozone Park–Lefferts Boulevard subway station, end of the A line, which, before it reaches its other terminus, in the Bronx, burrows through four of the five boroughs. But we don't have to go there.

8

THE ADDRESS WAS the Avalon State Bank Tower on Fifth Avenue, near St. Patrick's Cathedral. Nineteen-year-old Judson Blint, hot inside his light gray Gap sports jacket, JC Penney summerweight necktie in aquamarine, Banana Republic short-sleeve white button-down shirt buttoned down, Wal-Mart black cotton socks, and Macy's lace-up black dress shoes, none of which he was used to wearing, had walked up the twenty-some blocks from Penn Station under the August sun, having ridden the train in from Long Island to start his real life, now that the vacation he'd given himself after finally getting out of high school had come, by his own decision, to an end.

Yes, there was the Avalon State Bank Tower, looming up ahead of him, bleak and gray and stern; but he would not be deterred. He was a winner, and he knew he was a winner, and he was about to prove he was a winner. Stepping through the glass entry doors to the lobby, he looked left and right, found the building directory, and went over there. Allied Commissioners' Courses, Inc.—712.

Good. He was about to turn away when another familiar name snagged his eye: Intertherapeutic Research Service—712. Also room 712?

Suddenly suspicious, he cast an eye over the rest of the business names arrayed before him, and there, at the far end of the alphabet, was another name he knew: Super Star Music Co.—712. What was going on here?

Judson Blint had come to the city today thinking he'd solved the biggest mystery in this equation, which was where to find the offices of Allied Commissioners' Courses, Inc., so he could meet the company's owner, one J. C. Taylor. Mr. Taylor did not want to be found—he'd made that clear enough—but Judson had used many of the techniques he'd learned in the Allied Commissioners' mail-order detective course, plus a few techniques from old private-eye movies and a couple extra he'd made up himself, all of which had led him here. To Intertherapeutic? To Super Star?

Madly curious, Judson took a 5–21 elevator, got off at seven, walked down to 712, and found painted on the door the three names he recognized, plus, beneath them, a fourth he didn't know: Maylohda, Commercial Attaché.

Maylohda. What was that, a country? Who *was* J. C. Taylor, anyway?

Only one way to find out. Taking one last deep breath, Judson turned the knob and entered suite 712.

What a mess. This was a small, cluttered receptionist's office in which the reception desk almost disappeared into the accumulation of *stuff*. All the available wall space was taken up by floor-to-ceiling gray metal shelves, stacked to bursting with small brown cardboard cartons. The computer and printer on the battered gray metal desk were the only neat things in the room, but they were upstaged by stacks of labels, piles of books, and leaning towers of what looked like most of the world's unpaid bills. Columns of liquor store boxes, some empty, some full, obscured and jammed most of the space. And in the middle of it all, stacking books into another liquor store carton, was what had to be the receptionist.

Oh, my God. She was something out of Judson's dreams, but not the more soothing ones. No, more like the ones inspired by video games. In her thirties, she was a hard-looking brunette with gleaming eyes that caught the light, and a mouth that looked born to say no. Only louder than that.

She looked over at him when he entered, and what she did say was, "You want something?"

"I'm here," Judson said, deciding that boldness was the only strategy, "to see J. C. Taylor."

Hefting a book in one hand, she looked him up and down. "I'm afraid he isn't in right now," she said. "Did you call for an appointment?"

"Oh, sure," he said.

She didn't believe him. "Yeah?"

Reaching to his inner jacket pocket, bringing out the white legal-size envelope, Judson pressed on, afraid to move forward but even more afraid to stop. "I'm supposed to give him my résumé," he said.

"Oh, you are, are you?" Cold eyes were not on his side.

"I'm hoping to get a job here," Judson said. "With the Commissioners' Courses. I took the course, you know."

"No, I didn't know."

Judson frowned over his shoulder at the door, with all those company names on the other side. "Is he really *all* of those?"

Now a wintry smile did appear. "Why? You sent in for them, too?"

"Well . . . yes."

"To Super Star," she said. "Did you send in lyrics to have music written, or music to have lyrics written?"

"Lyrics. I sent in lyrics."

"Most of them do. And the fuck book before that, I suppose."

"Yes, ma'am," Judson said, and felt his cheeks grow hot. No woman had ever said "fuck book" to him before. Or "fuck" anything, come to that.

The wintry smile again. "Lied about your age for that one, didn't you?"

He had to smile back. "Yes, ma'am."

She put a hand out. "Let me see this résumé."

"Yes, ma'am."

He handed the paper to her, and she walked around the desk with it, saying, "Sit on some cartons, the chairs are all full."

They were. He sat on a stack of liquor store cartons and she sat at the desk to open his envelope and read his job résumé. The room became very silent. He could hear himself breathe.

She looked up. "How old are you?"

"Twenty-four."

She nodded. "You lie pretty good," she said. "Maintain eye contact, all that."

"Ma'am?"

"I wouldn't give you the time of day," she informed him, "if it wasn't for this résumé." And she waved the three sheets of computer printout he'd done at home in his bedroom.

"Thank you, ma'am."

"Very impressive."

"Thank you, ma'am."

"A beautiful tissue of lies."

"Tha— Ma'am?"

She smiled more fondly at his résumé than she had so far smiled at Judson. Running a finger down the list, she said, "What have we here? Bankruptcies, deaths, mergers. Every bit of this job history is compelling and makes you the very highest level of job applicant, and yet not one of these claims could be verified." She transferred her smile to Judson, adding some ice to it. "You must have worked long and hard on this."

The mixed signals Judson was getting from this woman were driving him crazy. She was accusing him of being a liar, but she didn't seem to be angry about it. Was his being a good liar supposed to be something positive? An asset for the job? Not knowing whether he'd do better to acknowledge his duplicity or deny it, he just sat there and stared at her, knowing full well he was the bird and she the snake.

She dropped the résumé on her messy desk with a flip of disdainful fingers. "We aren't hiring."

"Oh."

"As a matter of fact—" she said, and the phone rang. It took her until the second ring before she could find the phone in the jumble on her desk, and then said into it, "May-lohda, Commercial Attaché. Oh, hello, John." She smiled much more warmly into the phone, liking this person John. Judson seethed with envy and listened closely. "Sure, I'll tell him. Ten tonight at the O.J. He's due to come over here soon, help me move some of this shit out. Talk to you later." She hung up and frowned at Judson. "Where was I?"

" 'As a matter of fact—' "

"Oh, right. Thank you. As a matter of fact, I'm just now in the process of shutting down all those lines. The Maylohda number's working so well, who needs the hassle of all the rest of it?"

Judson said, "Ma'am, what *is* Maylohda? Is it a country?"

"Of course it is. Do you know there are almost two hundred different separate nations in the United Nations?"

"No, I didn't."

"No, and I bet you couldn't name more than twenty of them. Maylohda's just as good as Lesotho."

"I'm sure it is."

"Just as good as Malawi."

"Why wouldn't it be?"

"Just as good as Bhutan," she said, and the door opened and a man monster walked in.

Could *this* be J. C. Taylor? Judson prayed not. It was horrible. It was as though he had fallen asleep in a video game and woken up in a fairy tale, the kind with ogres in it.

This fellow absolutely filled the doorway when he entered. His head was like a rocket's nose cone, with nasty curled-up ears on the sides. His body appeared to be the size and softness of a Hummer, in broad brown slacks and a green polo shirt, as though he were trying to disguise himself as a golf course. This behemoth looked at Judson without love and said, "What's this supposed to be?"

"We're still working on it," the woman said. "He came in with a cocked-up résumé, but a goddamn clever one, and said he wanted a job."

"You're shutting down," the monster pointed out. "Devote your time to the Maylohda scam."

"I know, Tiny," the woman said, and Judson lost a word or two while trying to encompass the idea that *this* person might be known as Tiny. When he tuned back in, she was saying, ". . . gonna miss this old stuff. I know I don't have the time for it. But then there's this infant here."

Judson thought, Does she mean *me*? Yes.

The woman looked at him. "You're eighteen, nineteen, am I right?"

These people were out of his league. He'd come to the city from Long Island today not knowing there were people who were out of his league, and now he would just dwindle and dwindle on the train all the way back, until he was so small you wouldn't be able to find him. "Nineteen," he said, and sighed, and got to his feet, and reached for his résumé, even though he knew he'd never have the boldness to flash it ever again.

"Hold on there," she said.

Surprised, he stopped where he was, bent forward slightly over the desk, holding the résumé. He looked at her, and she offered him a sunnier smile than before, a sort of encouraging smile, and said, "Sit down a minute."

"Yes, ma'am."

He sat down, and she turned to the man-mountain, Tiny, and said, "Before I forget, John called, he wants a meet at the O.J. tonight at ten."

"Good," Tiny said. But then he pointed at Judson and said, "Whatcha keeping this around for?"

"He made me realize," she said, "if I get an office manager, he can take care of all the old stuff, so I don't have to give it up after all, and I can still concentrate on Maylohda."

He considered, then nodded that massive head. "Not bad," he agreed.

She stood and came around the desk, smiling much more welcomingly, hand stuck out, saying, "Welcome to the firm, Judson."

He leaped to his feet. Her handshake was very hard. He said, "Thank you, ma'am."

"I'm J. C., of course," she said, astonishing him yet again. "Josephine Carol Taylor. But you're a bright kid, you figured that out, didn't you?"

He could recover fast, which was a good thing, because, he now realized, he was often going to have to. "Oh, sure," he said. "Nice to meet you, J. C."

9

WHEN DORTMUNDER WALKED into the O.J. Bar & Grill at ten that night, the regulars were clustered, as usual, down toward the left end of the bar, while Rollo, whose apron was well on its way to becoming a regional cuisine all by itself, stood some way to the right, doing nothing in particular as he leaned against the high-tech cash register he never used, preferring to operate it with its till jutting open until all advanced technology should someday retreat out the door.

Dortmunder aimed himself at Rollo, and was halfway there from the front door when he realized something was wrong. It was silent in the joint. Not just quiet—silent. Not a regular was stirring. Apart from them and Rollo, there was only one occupied booth, over on the right—two guys in satin-bright polyester shirts, one emerald and one apricot, with wide contrasting collars, and except for their shirts those two were silent as well.

What was going on? Was it a wake around here? Nobody wore a black armband, but the faces on the regulars were long enough. They, all of them, men and the women's auxiliary, too, were hunched over their drinks with that thousand-yard stare that suggests therapy is no longer an option. In short, the place looked exactly like that section of the socialist realist mural where the workers have been utterly shafted by the plutocrats. Dortmunder looked up, half-expecting to see top hats and cigars in the gloom up there, but nothing.

Nothing from Rollo, either. He stood against the cash register with his meaty arms folded, and gazed at his domain with what had to be at least a hundred-and-fifty-yard stare of his own. Dortmunder made sure to get directly into the line of sight of that stare, and then said, "Rollo?"

Rollo blinked. "Oh," he said. He could be seen to recognize Dortmunder, but whatever welcome was rising toward the surface never made it. Instead, he shook his head. "Sorry," he said.

"We thought we'd meet," Dortmunder told him, "in the back room." And he pointed generally toward the back room, in case Rollo had forgotten its existence.

"No can do," Rollo said, and shook his head again.

This was unexpected—in fact, unprecedented. Dortmunder said, "You got other people back there?"

"No, it's in use," Rollo said, which sounded an awful lot like a contradiction.

Dortmunder was baffled. When the time came to get the string together, to discuss the situation and work out the possibilities, the place to do it was the back room at the O.J., always had been. The room was secure, the management minded its own affairs, and the drinks were priced with repeat business in mind. So this is where they would come. This is, in fact, where they were all coming tonight, summoned by Dortmunder himself.

Trying to get around this sudden bump in the road, Dortmunder said, "I suppose we could wait a while, you know, till it frees up, sit in one of those—"

The Rollo headshake again. "Sorry, John," he said. "Forget about that room."

Dortmunder stared at him. The entire world had gone mad. "*Forget* about it? Rollo, what's—"

"Any problem here, Rollo?"

Dortmunder looked to his right, and it was the emerald shirt from the booth, with its pterodactyl collar. The man with it was short but strong-looking, as though his body were made of one hundred percent gristle, with a head on top full of outsize parts, so that he could only look reasonable in profile. Sideways, he could have been somebody on a Roman coin, but head-on he looked like a hawk that had gone through a windshield.

This person didn't actually look at Dortmunder, but he made it clear he was aware of Dortmunder's existence and wasn't made particularly happy by the fact. "Rollo?" he asked.

"No problem," Rollo assured him, though he sounded very gloomy when he said it. To Dortmunder he said, "Sorry, John."

Dortmunder, still trying to find the old terra firma, said, "Rollo, couldn't we—"

"He said he was sorry, John."

Dortmunder looked at the emerald. "Do I know you?"

"I don't think you want to, my friend," the emerald told him, and without actually moving anything he seemed to suggest that Dortmunder look past his emerald left shoulder to where, back at the table he'd come from, the apricot now watched Dortmunder with the fixed ferocity of a cat watching a chipmunk.

What Dortmunder might have said or done next he would never know, because movement farther to his right attracted his attention, and here came Andy Kelp, cheerful, smiling in sunny ignorance, saying, "We're the first? Hey, there, Rollo, whadaya say?"

"No," Rollo said.

"John, you got the bottle? We gotta—"

"Rollo told you no," said the emerald. "Politely. I heard him."

Kelp reared back to look the emerald up and down. "What flying saucer did *this* come out of?" he wanted to know.

The emerald wore his magnificent shirt outside his pants, and now his quick move toward his waist at the middle of his back did not suggest a sudden lumbar distress. Kelp cocked an eyebrow at him, interested, half smiling.

"Andy," Rollo said, with a kind of muffled urgency, and when Kelp turned toward him, still smiling, still bland, he said, "We don't want any trouble in here, Andy. Believe me, we don't want any trouble in here."

The emerald was still in position, hand at his back, eyes fixed on Kelp. And here came the apricot, saying, "Some kinda problem, Rollo?"

"Everything's fine," Rollo said, though not as though he meant it. Then he said, "John, listen, wait a minute," and both his hands dove under the bar.

Everybody tensed. Even the regulars rustled slightly. But then Rollo came up with a quart bottle of *Amsterdam Liquor Store Bourbon—"Our Own Brand,"* holding it in both hands like an abandoned baby, which he thrust toward Dortmunder, saying, "On the house. Sorry for the inconvenience. Thank you for your patience."

Dortmunder found himself holding the bottle. He'd never gotten a freebie bottle in here before, but somehow the circumstances clouded the gift. "Rollo," he said, "is there anything I can do?"

"Go home, John," Rollo suggested, but then he leaned

forward, lowered his voice so that only people in the bar could hear him, and said, "Do me a favor. Don't let Tiny get upset."

Kelp said, "He will, you know."

"Please," Rollo said.

Kelp looked at Dortmunder. "John?"

There was nothing to be done. Dortmunder sighed. "He did say please," he said, and turned toward the door.

All the way out, they could feel those eyes on the backs of their heads.

10

"IF YOU DON'T like the route I'm taking," Murch's Mom snarled at her only child, "why don't you steal a car, find your *own* way to the O.J.? We'll see who gets there first."

"No matter who's driving," the ungrateful pup replied, "or how many cars we're in, I wouldn't try to drive up inside Central Park at ten o'clock at night in the summer. Do you *see* all these hansom cabs, all these horses crapping all over the place, all these tourists getting the experience of the *real* New York by riding around in a horse and buggy?"

"They're not even *going* anywhere," his Mom complained. Her right thumb hovered over the horn button but didn't quite touch it.

"Sure they're going someplace," her son corrected, never agreeing with anybody. He shifted a little, trying to get his knees farther from the air conditioner wind here in the front seat of his mother's cab, and said, "They're going all around in a great big circle inside Central Park at, what, seven miles an hour? And back down to Fifty-ninth Street, and thank you very much, and *walk* back to the hotel and call Aunt Flo back home, guess what, we just had a real New York experience, forty minutes through Central Park behind a farting horse. Making *unwary* people late for their appointments."

"It isn't the *tourists* that bother me," his Mom informed him. "It isn't the *horses,* the *carriages.* It's the cop on my tailpipe. Don't look around!"

"Why not?" Stan asked, twisting all the way around to gaze at the patrol car that was, indeed, traveling so close behind their cab he could see a bit of spinach caught in its grill. "I can rubberneck just as well as anybody else out for a mosey through the park." Facing front again, he said, "How did you let that happen?"

"I was committed to the turn into the park," she said, "nobody behind me, and all of a sudden he was there. I think maybe he U-turned. Believe me, Stanley, I do not choose to be followed through the city of New York by a cop."

"Bad luck," Stan said, which was probably meant to make peace.

Accepting the offer, at least a little, his Mom said, "These horses and carriages and tourists aren't going to get in my way, Stanley, not if I can use my horn. But with that cop behind me? They *love* to hassle the cabbies, especially when there's tourists around to watch."

"Well, here comes Seventy-second Street," Stan said, "slower than I've ever seen it arrive before—"

"Enough."

"When we do get outa the park, I think you oughta go—"

"I'll pick my own route, Stanley."

"Fine," Stan said.

"Good."

"You're the driver."

"That's right."

"The professional driver."

"That's right."

"Years of experience behind the—"

"Shut up, Stanley."

So he shut up, and when they finally got shut of the park, the horses, the tourists *and* the cop, he didn't even tell her she was making a mistake when she took the right onto Central Park West. He didn't mention that the better way was to run west past Amsterdam to Columbus, *then* make your right, so you're on a one-way street with staggered lights, and to get back to Amsterdam it's all right turns. No, fine, let her do it her way, up a two-way street, no staggered lights, and all left turns at the end of it. Great.

Eventually, though, they did get onto Amsterdam, but just as Murch's Mom was pulling in next to the fire hydrant down the block from the O.J., out the door of the place came Dortmunder and Kelp, Dortmunder carrying a bottle. Surprised, Stan said, "The meeting's over already? We can't be *that* late."

"Watch it, Stanley."

"I'm only saying," Stan said, and got out of the cab to say, "John? Andy? Whassup?"

Dortmunder gestured with the bottle. "Something screwy at the O.J."

"What, it's closed?"

"There's some guys there," Kelp said, "they seem to want privacy right now."

Murch's Mom, joining them on the sidewalk, said, "Closed for a private party?"

"Kinda," Kelp said, and a horn sounded.

They turned to look, and Tiny was just buttoning open the rear window of a stretch limousine. Since he found regular taxis too form-fitting, Tiny tended to whistle up a limo when it was necessary to go somewhere. Now, window open, he said, "Everybody's on the sidewalk."

Dortmunder, walking toward him, said, "We can't use the back room tonight, we gotta go somewhere else."

Stan said, "Somewhere else? There isn't anywhere else."

Kelp said, "John, is May at the movies?" because usually that's what she did when Dortmunder was out and about for one reason or another.

Lowering a suspicious brow, Dortmunder said, "So what?"

"So it looks," Kelp said, "like we gotta convene at your place."

"Why my place? Why not your place?"

"Anne Marie's home, and she wouldn't go for it, John."

From the limo, Tiny said, "Josey wouldn't go for it in spades."

Stan said, "You don't want to come all the way down to Canarsie," that being where he and his Mom lived.

Dortmunder muttered and growled and scuffed his feet around. "I don't see why everything's gotta get screwed up."

"John," Kelp said, "it's hot out here on the sidewalk. You got a nice air-conditioned living room."

Stan called, "Tiny, we'll meet you there. The rest of us will take Mom's cab."

"Done," Tiny said, and spoke to his driver as he buttoned the window back up.

"Come on, John," Kelp said. "You know it's the only answer."

"All right, all right," Dortmunder said, still surly, but then he said, "At least I got this bottle."

"Sure," Kelp said. "Climb aboard."

As they all did, Murch's Mom said, "You know I gotta throw the meter, I wouldn't wanna get stopped by a cop."

"Fine," Dortmunder said. "Stan can pay the fare."

"No meter, Mom," Stan said.

She sulked all the way downtown.

11

EVERYBODY HATED DORTMUNDER'S living room. Dortmunder hated it himself, under the circumstances. They couldn't sit all together around a table, everybody at the same height, the same distance from one another. There was nobody to bring drinks, and not that much variety of drink anyway. The only thing Tiny could find to mix with his vodka was cranberry juice, which was a comedown from the red wine he was used to. Stan and his Mom did have the beer they preferred to harder stuff when driving (and backseat driving), but neither of them liked Dortmunder's salt shaker. "It comes out too fast!"

The first ten minutes were spent going back and forth to the kitchen, which was actually quite far from the living room, a fact Dortmunder had never noticed before. Finally, though, they all settled down, Dortmunder in his regular chair, Murch's Mom in May's regular chair, Tiny on much of the sofa with Kelp on the sliver of sofa that was left, and Stan on a wooden chair he'd brought from the kitchen.

"Now," Tiny said, "I know we're here because you

people got something, but first I gotta know, what's with the O.J.?"

Dortmunder said, "Rollo wouldn't let us use the back room. He didn't look happy."

"He looked morose," Kelp said.

Dortmunder nodded at him. "The very word I was thinking."

"Also," Kelp said, "the regulars weren't saying anything."

Stan said, "What? The loudmouths at the bar?"

"Not a peep," Kelp told him. "They looked like they didn't wanna attract attention."

"That's the only thing they *ever* want to attract," Stan said, and his Mom said, "When Stan is right, he's right," and Stan said, "Thanks, Mom."

"Also," Dortmunder said, "there were two guys in the place, throwing their weight around."

With a little purr in his voice, Tiny said, "Oh, yeah?"

Kelp said, "Those were mob guys, John. You could smell it on them."

Tiny shook his head. "Mob guys in the O.J. Why don't they stick to the Copacabana?"

Dortmunder said, "I think something's going on in there that's linked up with the mob."

Kelp said, "You know how they like to kill one another in restaurants and bars? Maybe those guys were in there waiting for Mickey Banana Nose to walk in, and bang-bang."

"Then I'd like them to get it over with," Dortmunder said. "And not do any stray bullets into Rollo."

"That could be why he was morose," Kelp said, then held up the jelly glass into which he had poured from Dortmunder's freebie bottle. "You know, John?" he said. "Not to badmouth your apartment, but this stuff doesn't taste as good here as it does at the O.J."

"I noticed that myself," Dortmunder admitted. "I guess it doesn't travel."

Tiny said, "Whadawe gonna do about the O.J.?"

"Tomorrow afternoon," Kelp told him, "John and me, we'll go over, see what the story is, are they finished whatever they're doing over there. Right, John?"

"Sure," Dortmunder said. "Could we get to the actual topic now? The reason we're here?"

"If I'm gonna get back to Canarsie before my bedtime," Murch's Mom said, "we better."

"Good," Dortmunder said. "This opportunity comes to us courtesy of Arnie Albright."

"He's off in rehab," Stan said.

Dortmunder sighed. "No," he said, "he's back." And he then related, with footnotes from Kelp, everything Arnie had said to them in his apartment.

When he finished, Stan said, "This elevator goes up the outside of the apartment building?"

"Right," Dortmunder said. "And it's only got doors at the top and bottom."

"Something goes wrong up top," Stan said, "that sounds like maybe you're trapped."

Kelp said, "Stan, that's not the only way in and out. That's the best way, for us. But the apartment's got a front door, too, and a hall, and other elevators, and even staircases."

Murch's Mom said, "That part's okay, Stanley. What I wonder about is this seventy percent."

"That's not natural," Tiny said. "For a fence to take the light end of the seesaw."

Murch's Mom appealed to Dortmunder: "So what do you think, John? Did he mean it?"

"Well, in a way," Dortmunder said. "I think he meant he was that mad at the guy owns the apartment. He's still that mad at the guy, so that right now what he thinks he wants is revenge."

"I agree," Kelp said. "But this is before Arnie has paper money in his hand."

"Green beats revenge," Tiny said, "every time."

"The thing is," Stan said, "seventy percent of *what*? We give him, I dunno, a silver ashtray, he says I got a hundred bucks for it, here's your seventy. Whadawe know what he got for it? He doesn't deal with people where you're gonna have invoices, receipts."

"If Arnie ever saw a paper trail," Dortmunder said, "he'd set fire to it."

"So what it comes down to," Murch's Mom said, "we do the work, we take the risks, he gives us whatever he wants to give us."

"Like always," Kelp said. "It's trust makes the world go round."

"Tomorrow," Tiny said, "I'll go look at this place." To Stan and his Mom he said, "You wanna be there?"

They looked at each other and both shook their heads. "We just drive," Stan said. "You guys say it's good, we'll show up."

"Right," his Mom said.

"Fine." Tiny looked at Dortmunder and Kelp. "You two are going to check on the O.J.?"

"That's the plan," Kelp said.

"So where do we meet after?"

"Not the O.J., I don't think," Dortmunder said. "Not until we know for sure what's what." He looked around his crowded living room. "And maybe not here."

"It's daytime," Tiny said. "We'll meet at the fountain in the park. Three o'clock?"

"Fine," Dortmunder said, and they all heard the apartment

door open. The others looked at their host, who stood and called, "May?"

"You're home?"

May appeared in the doorway, gazed around the room, and said, "You're all home."

Everybody else got to their feet to say hello to May and get likewise back, and then she said, "How come you didn't go to the O.J.?"

"It's a long story," Dortmunder said.

"We've all heard it," Tiny said, moving toward the door. "Night, May. Three o'clock tomorrow, Dortmunder."

12

JUDSON BLINT ENTERED names and addresses into the
computer. He printed out labels and affixed them to the
small cardboard boxes of books, along with appropriate
postage from the Pitney Bowes stamp machine. He stacked
the labeled boxes on the tall-handled metal cart and, when it
was full, wheeled it out of the office to the elevator, then on
down to the postal substation on the Avalon State Bank
Tower lobby level. After turning the boxes over to the United
States Postal Service, he used the tagged keys J. C. Taylor had
given him to open Box 88, Super Star Music Co.; Box 13,
Allied Commissioners' Courses, Inc.; Box 69, Intertherapeutic Research Service; and Box 222, Commercial Attaché, Republic of Maylohda. Back upstairs, he put all the mail on his
desk except the few items for Maylohda, which appeared to
come from real countries and official organizations connected with the United Nations. After a discreet knock on
the door to the inner office, he then brought the Maylohda
mail in and placed it on the desk in front of J. C. herself, who
was usually on the phone, sounding very official and occa-

sionally foreign. Back at his own desk, he next entered the newly hooked customers into the database and prepared a deposit of their just-received checks into one of J. C.'s three bank accounts in the Avalon Bank branch, also on the lobby level, having first forged *J. C. Taylor* on each check, a skill he had picked up in no time.

If everything he did didn't happen to be breaking some law or another—mail fraud, misuse of bulk rate, identity theft of the endorsements, plagiarism, sale of inappropriate material to minors, on and on—all of this activity would be very like a job. But it was better than a job. It was a world, a world he'd always believed had to exist somewhere, but hadn't known how to find. So it had found him.

When he had assembled his fake job résumé out on Long Island, he'd thought he was being brilliant, and in a way he was, though not in the manner he'd thought.

No wonder J. C. had caught on so immediately. When Judson, with his eyes freshly opened, studied J. C. Taylor's businesses, she had done exactly the same thing for references. The police chiefs and district attorneys who'd endorsed the detective course, all dead or retired or otherwise unavailable. And the same for the music publishers, disc jockeys, and songwriters boosting Super Star, and likewise the psychiatrists, "medical professionals," and marriage counselors urging the purchase of Intertherapeutic's book of dirty pictures. (Was that J. C. herself in some of those pictures? Couldn't be.)

Ultimately, though, what made the routine in office 712 of the Avalon State Bank tower so much better than an actual job was that the job hadn't existed until he'd come along. J. C. had planned to shut down all three of these operations and had changed her mind only when she'd seen his brilliant résumé—seen *through* his brilliant résumé, in a New York minute—and realized he was the perfect person to pick up the torch.

He would not fail her. She has faith in me as a con artist and a crook, he told himself, and I will not let her down.

At just after ten in the morning on the second day of his illicit employment, he was at his desk, busy with labels and Pitney Bowes, when the hall door opened. This was the first such occurrence, but he'd already been told what to say in such a circumstance—J. C. Taylor isn't here, did you make an appointment, leave your name, go away—so he was already opening his mouth before the door was fully open, but then it turned out to be the man improbably called Tiny, who was presumably J. C.'s boyfriend, though the word had never seemed more inadequate.

"Oh, hello," Judson said, since his mouth was open anyway.

"That's a better getup, kid," Tiny said, closing the door and waving a hand at Judson's polo shirt and slacks, which were, in fact, a much better getup than the costume he'd worn while job hunting.

"Thank you," Judson said, pleased. "Am I supposed to tell J. C. you're here?"

"I'll tell her myself." Tiny seemed to consider for a minute, then said, "You got a credit card?"

Surprised, Judson said, "Sure. A couple."

"One will do. This afternoon, rent a car. A full-size one, you know?"

"For you, you mean."

"That's right. Two o'clock, meet me at Lex and Seventy-second, northwest corner. When you get your credit card bill, I'll pay you back in cash."

"Oh, sure. No problem."

"Don't be *too* trusting, kid," Tiny advised him. "I'll square your absence with Josey. Two o'clock."

"Seventy-second and Lex. I'll be there."

"So will I," Tiny said, and advanced into the inner office, closing the door behind himself.

Whatever it is that's happening, Judson thought, I'm getting in deeper. The thought made him smile.

13

S ILENT AS THE tomb. When Dortmunder and Kelp walked into the O.J. a little before two that afternoon, even the floor didn't creak. There seemed to be fewer regulars than usual, huddled together at the left end of the bar, as silent and miserable as kittens in a sack with the bridge getting close. The two watchful guys in the booth on the right were not the same as the two from last night, but they weren't that different, either. Rollo had a newspaper folded open on the bar at the right end, far from the immobile regulars, and was bent over it with a red Flair pen in his hand.

Approaching the bar, Dortmunder felt the eyes of the guys in the booth on him, but ignored them. Then he saw that Rollo was not reading the *Daily News,* like a regular person, but the larger paper, the *New York Times.* And then he saw that what Rollo was reading in the *New York Times* was the want ads.

Rollo didn't raise his eyes from the columns of jobs awaiting the qualified when Dortmunder and Kelp bellied up to the bar in front of him, but he was not unmindful of their presence. "Sorry, fellas," he said, eyes down, pen poised. "Still no go."

"Rollo," Dortmunder said, "all's we want's a beer."

"Two beers, in fact," Kelp said.

Now Rollo did look up. He seemed wary. "Nothing else in mind?"

"What else?" Kelp asked him. "It's a hot August day, the time seems right for a nice beer."

Rollo shrugged. "Coming up," he said, and went away to draw two.

While they waited, Kelp said, "I think it's my round, John."

Dortmunder looked at him. "What are you up to?"

"What up to? I feel like I wanna buy you a beer. It happens, we have another one, then *you* buy for me. That's how it works, John."

Dortmunder said, "What if we only have the one?"

"My feeling is," Kelp said, whipping out his wallet and putting cash money on the bar next to the glasses Rollo was putting down in front of them, "some day we'll be in a bar again."

Dortmunder could only agree with that. "You'll keep track, I guess," he said, as Rollo took Kelp's money away to his open cash register and rummaged around in there a while.

"No problem," Kelp assured him, and lifted his glass. "To crime."

"Without punishment," Dortmunder amended, and they both drank.

Rollo came back to put crumpled bills on the bar in front of Kelp, who took a few, left one, and said, "Thanks, Rollo."

Rollo leaned close over the bar. Very softly he said, "I just wanna say, this isn't the best place right now."

"We noticed that, Rollo," Kelp said, and nodded, and smiled in an amiable way, inviting confidences.

"The thing is," Rollo said, more sotto voce than ever,

"there are people around here right now, what they are, they're criminals."

Dortmunder leaned very close to Rollo over the bar. "Rollo," he murmured, "*we're* criminals."

"Yeah, John, I know," Rollo said. "But they're organized. Take care of yourselves."

"Everything okay, Rollo?" demanded a nasty voice.

It was one of today's organized men, come from his booth to stand at the bar in front of Rollo's *Times*. His strange shirt was off-puce.

"Everything's jake," Rollo assured him. Scooping the loose dollar from the bar, he went back to his newspaper, while the puce, after one quick, dismissive look at Dortmunder and Kelp, headed back to his booth.

Dortmunder said, "You think everything's okay in life, and then something different happens."

Kelp gave him a look. "John? On one beer you're turning philosophical?"

"It's the environment," Dortmunder told him.

Meanwhile, returning to his want ads, Rollo called toward the entrance, "Just put 'em in back," and when Dortmunder turned to look, a blue-uniformed deliveryman was wheeling in a dolly piled five-high with liquor cartons.

"Right," the deliveryman said, and wheeled the dolly on by. The regulars didn't even turn to watch.

Dortmunder and Kelp exchanged a silent glance as they sipped their beer. Soon the deliveryman returned, pushing his empty dolly, and Dortmunder stepped back from the bar to say, in a normal volume of voice, "I gotta hit the gents."

"I'll watch your beer," Kelp offered.

"Thank you."

Dortmunder circled the clustered regulars and went around the end of the bar and down the hall past POINTERS and SETTERS, noticing that beneath SETTERS was a thumbtacked handwritten OUT OF ORDER notice, and past the entry-to-the-universe phone booth, and stopped at the open green door at the very end of the hall.

And there was the back room, where so often they had met in the past, and which was now transformed. It was so jam-packed full of *stuff,* you couldn't even see the round table in the middle of it any more, let alone the chairs around it. The bare bulb hanging from the center of the ceiling was partially blocked by all the matériel that had been introduced into the place. Liquor cartons were stacked everywhere, along with new barstools with their plastic wrapping still on them, at least half a dozen cash registers, a complete mini pool table, and boxes and boxes of pretzels and Slim Jims.

"Help you, Mac?"

It was Puce, following Dortmunder down the hall. He had an aggressive swagger in his shoulders, as though he felt it was a little past time to start sparring with somebody.

"Gents," Dortmunder told him, calm about it.

"Pointers," Puce told him, and pointed at it.

"Thanks," Dortmunder said, and went into POINTERS, where the aroma immediately reminded him why generally he did not go into POINTERS. He stayed the minimum time plausible, flushed, washed his hands as the grimy sign said, and went out to the hall, which was now empty.

It wasn't a surprise that the door to SETTERS was locked. Dortmunder headed for the bar, and on the way he passed the deliveryman, wheeling another quintet of cases, this one all rum.

Puce was back in his booth, muttering at his pal in plum, and Kelp was where he had been, at the bar. Dortmunder joined him, and Kelp raised an eyebrow as Dortmunder raised his glass. Dortmunder shook his head, drank, and the deliveryman came back, the dolly empty. This time he went around to extend a clipboard toward Rollo and say, "Sign it there, okay?"

"Sure."

Rollo, in the manner of someone signing his own commitment papers, signed the form on the clipboard, and the deliveryman and his dolly went away.

Dortmunder finished his beer. "Maybe," he said, "I'll buy you that round next time."

14

M AKE THE LEFT on Fifth," Tiny said from the backseat.
"Okay," Judson said, stopped the rented black
Lexus Dzilla at the traffic light, and signaled for the left.

This was their third time around the block, over Sixty-
ninth Street, down Fifth, over Sixty-eighth, up Madison, over
Sixty-ninth, on and on. And Tiny never said, "Circle the
block"; he always just gave the next turn, as though he hoped
Judson wouldn't notice or remember the route.

Well, Judson did notice and remember the route, and he
had even figured out what it was they were looking at. "Very
slow here," Tiny would say every time they made the left turn
from Fifth Avenue to Sixty-eighth Street, and every time Judson watched in the rearview mirror to see what Tiny was fo-
cused on, and every time it was the first house on the right
after the big apartment building on the corner. There was
something about that house that interested Tiny a whole lot.

"Make the left on Sixty-eighth."

"Okay."

Waiting for the green light, Judson could look diagonally

across at that house, an old town house with what looked like a more recent garage cut into it on the right. Glancing once more at Tiny's reflection in the mirror, he could see Tiny frown at the house, as though something about it troubled or baffled him.

Green light. As Judson made the turn, Tiny said, "Stop on the right. At the driveway."

Directly in front of the house, in other words. So this was something new.

Judson had to watch what he was doing when he parked, because this SUV was really big, but once he'd stopped, he could do his own frowning at the house. What was it Tiny was trying to figure out?

"I'll get out here," Tiny said, opening the right-hand door. "Go around the block and pick me up."

"Okay."

Driving on, Judson saw Tiny just stand back there, head cocked to one side as he looked upward at the house. Upward. At what?

By the time he'd circled the block once more, he'd worked it out. Tiny was on the other side of the street now, looking not at the house but at his watch. Fortunately, there was a fire hydrant on that side, so Judson slid in there, and as Tiny got back into the car, Judson told him, "You could boost me up."

Tiny finished entering the car, shutting the door, adjusting himself on the seat, and only then did he look at Judson's right ear and say, "To what?"

"The alarm box. That's what you're trying to figure out, isn't it? How to reach the alarm box."

"Drive on down and make the left."

"Okay."

It wasn't until they'd made the turn onto Madison that

Tiny spoke again: "Go up to Seventy-second and take the left. Why would I wanna reach any alarm box?"

"I don't know," Judson said, stopping for the light at Sixty-ninth. He was beginning to think maybe he'd been just a bit too much of a smart-aleck. "I could be wrong."

"You think so?"

"I dunno."

The light turned green, and as Judson drove on, Tiny said, "One time, in the can, I knew a guy, said he knew how to break out, we could use the ductwork from the main boiler. I was too big and I didn't like the idea, but this other guy said it sounded great, he'd go first, so he went first, only he went the wrong direction."

"Did he get back?"

"Some ash did."

Judson thoughtfully made the left on Seventy-second, and Tiny said, "We'll go into the park."

"Okay."

"We wanted to get into a museum one time," Tiny told him, as he drove slowly through the heavy two-way traffic of Seventy-second Street. "One of the guys said he'd go there in the afternoon, hide himself in the mummy case, come open up for us at four in the morning. We get there at four in the morning, he doesn't show. Turns out, there's no air in the mummy case, so first he falls asleep, then he falls dead."

"Gee, that's too bad," Judson said, and stopped at the red light at Fifth.

"Wasted a night," Tiny said. "I was with some people once, we were in a penthouse, the owners weren't home. There was a power outage, that whole part of the city, this one guy said he could find the fire escape, he already counted the windows."

With gloomy foreboding, Judson said, "He counted the windows wrong?"

"No, the floors."

Judson nodded. "Mr. Tiny," he said, "do any of your stories have happy endings?"

"Not so far. The light's green."

So they crossed Fifth Avenue into the park, with a stream of traffic. "Stay on the transverse," Tiny said, when the option came to angle right northward toward the boathouse. They kept westward instead, Ramsey Playfield and then Naumburg Bandshell on their left, Bethesda Terrace with its fountain on the right. "Pull over to the right."

"I don't think I can," Judson said, looking in the mirror at the traffic behind him.

"I think you can."

So he did, and stopped half off the road, angry drivers detouring around him. Swarms of people walked around the park in the August sun, many of them going up and down the broad stone steps leading down to the fountain and the lake beyond.

Tiny rolled his window down as he said to Judson, "Honk."

So Judson honked, and two men who'd been loitering off to one side of the steps suddenly looked their way, then waved and walked over.

"One in front, one in back," Tiny told them when they arrived, and after a brief, silent, unmoving struggle of some kind out there, the cheerful, sharp-nosed one got into the front seat next to Judson while the gloomy one got some of the seat next to Tiny.

"Drive on," said Tiny. So Judson drove on, and Tiny said, "Dortmunder," meaning the one in back, "and Kelp," for the one in front, "this is Judson Blint. He's Josey's office manager now."

"Harya."

"Hello."

Tiny said, "He says I can boost him up to the alarm. I didn't ask him, he just says it."

Judson felt many eyes on him, but didn't dare look back at anybody. I'm being taken for a ride, he thought. No, I'm taking myself for a ride.

Kelp, the one in front, with a pleasant manner Judson didn't at all believe, said, "Judson? You like to volunteer?"

"Oh, no," Judson said. "No, I just thought— I don't know, I must have been wrong."

"I knew a guy wanted to volunteer once," Tiny said. Judson sighed, and Tiny went on, "We were in a thing together where the cops took an interest, and he thought it would be a good thing if he rolled over first."

Interested, half-turned around in the seat, Kelp said, "What happened?"

"He rolled off a roof instead," Tiny said. "Keep going across Seventy-second," he told Judson.

The red light at Central Park West was ahead. "As soon as the light changes," Judson promised.

"Maybe he's some kinda burglar." That was the other one back there—Dortmunder.

"You think so?" Tiny asked. "Judson, is that it? You a burglar?"

"Not me," Judson said, and drove forward under the green light.

He could sense Tiny looming behind him, larger than ever, but refused to look in the mirror. Lots of traffic to look at, two-way traffic. Very dangerous out here.

"Or maybe," Tiny said, "it's your idea *I'm* some kind of burglar."

"Oh, no, sir."

The one called Dortmunder said, "Tiny? What does J. C. think of him?"

"What, this driver here?" Tiny chuckled. "She thinks he's a good scam artist."

Kelp, still friendly and amiable, said, "That doesn't make him a good burglar."

Dortmunder said, "But what you're saying is, J. C. trusts him."

"In *her* business." To Judson he said, "Head up for the Boat Basin."

"Yes, sir," Judson said, and over the next several minutes, while they kept on with their conversation, he traversed West Seventy-second Street, Broadway, and West Seventy-ninth Street, headed for the West Seventy-ninth Street Boat Basin, where you could launch your boat, or some people kept their yachts or their houseboats, or conceivably you could drop an unwanted volunteer into the river and let him drift out to sea. Judson drove well, breathed shallowly, and didn't say a word.

"So I looked at this thing," Tiny said, "and maybe so."

"Good," Dortmunder said.

"But first I wanna know," Tiny said, "about the O.J."

"Well," Dortmunder said, "it's a bust-out joint."

"Shit," Tiny commented.

"You should see it in there, Tiny," Kelp said.

"Maybe I should."

"No, you shouldn't," Dortmunder said. "It's too late for anything like that. Tiny, they're already muscling the customers out. The back room is *full* of merchandise. The ladies' room is locked, so it must be full, too."

"If they're busting out," Tiny said, "how come they don't just do it?"

Dortmunder said, "You know those guys, Tiny, they're greedy. One way or another, they got control of the O.J.—"

"Usually," Kelp said, "the owner's some kind of dumbass gambler."

"Something like that," Dortmunder said. "But they got their hands on this legit business, good line of credit, they're not just gonna bounce in, bounce out, Tiny, they're gonna use up that credit until it's *gone*. Buy buy buy, fill the booths up next, lock the men's room—"

"Not too soon for that one," Kelp commented.

"No," Dortmunder agreed. "But the thing is, Tiny, they're not gonna move the stuff *out* until the bills start to come in."

Kelp said, "They might not even have all the customers lined up yet."

Tiny said, "But they will."

"Sure," Kelp said. "When your cost of doing business is zero, you can give real deep discounts."

Tiny said, "So that's it for the O.J."

"Goddamn it," Dortmunder said. "I don't want it to be."

Kelp said, "John, nobody wants it to be, but if they're that far along, if they've already burned the credit rating and the customer base that much, there's no getting it back, you know that. They're in there now, they'll strip the place, sell everything they ordered, disappear, the owner goes into bankruptcy, end of story."

"There's gotta be a way," Dortmunder insisted. "If only we could make a meet. But we need the O.J. to do a meeting!"

Kelp, being kindly, said, "John, you're pretty good at thinking things out. Think about this problem. We've still got maybe a couple days before they pull the plug. You come up with something to save the O.J., we're with you. Right, Tiny?"

"The kid, too," Tiny said. "If we decide to keep him."

A very small moan escaped through Judson's clenched lips. He drove slowly and carefully. He hoped he'd never reach the Seventy-ninth Street Boat Basin.

Dortmunder said, "All right, I'll try. But I don't know."

"If anybody can do it, John," Kelp said, "you can."

"Here's the Boat Basin," Tiny said. "Kid, park some-where."

"Okay."

There were parking places below the West Side Highway, with views over the Hudson toward New Jersey and, closer at hand, boats of various kinds, many of them occupied. I'll be safe with all those people around, Judson thought, but didn't believe it for a second.

Tiny said, "Leave the engine on, kid, for the A/C."

"Okay."

Kelp said, "I guess next on the agenda is this youth here."

Tiny said, "I wanted you two to take a look at him. Josey thinks he's okay, but that's in her area. Us, I don't know."

"Let's find out a couple things," Kelp said, and offered Judson his untrustworthy smile. "Let's just say," he said, "batting these ideas around here, let's just say Tiny *did* boost you up to that burglar alarm. Then what?"

"I dunno," Judson said. "I figured, Mr. Tiny'd tell me what he wanted."

Kelp cocked his head, the smile turning quizzical. "No idea? What, you figured you'd go up with a screwdriver, open the thing up?"

"Well, whatever," Judson said. "I don't know how those things work."

Dortmunder said, "What's in it for you?"

Judson blinked at him. Dortmunder at least wasn't smiling. In fact, he didn't look optimistic at all. "Well, sir," Judson told him, "I thought you people would want to share with me or something."

Dortmunder nodded. "And you'd leave it up to us, the de-tails and all that."

"I never did anything like that," Judson explained, "so I don't know how it works." Then, desperate, reaching down deep inside himself for the truth, he said, "What it is, I don't know *anything,* and I just want to get along until I figure out what I should be doing out here, so when I realized Mr. Tiny was interested in that alarm box I just offered to help, like, on the spur of the moment kind of thing."

Dortmunder said, "What you should be doing *out here*? What's 'out here'?"

"Well, out of high school."

I shouldn't have said that, he thought, as they all looked at one another. Then Tiny said, "Up to you two."

"Up to Andy," Dortmunder said. "He's the one would have to teach him."

Kelp laughed. "I was thinking," he said, "I don't think I'd like Tiny to boost *me* anywhere." Turning his smile on Judson, he said, "Judson? You got any close friends at home? High school buddies?"

"Oh, no," Judson assured him. "I said good-bye to all that."

"Live with your folks?"

"Until I find a place in the city, yes, sir, but I don't talk to my parents. Never did."

"Ever been in trouble with the law?"

"Not real *trouble,* no, sir."

Again Kelp laughed. "You mean, you got away with it."

Judson couldn't help a sheepish answering smile. "A few times, yes, sir."

Kelp nodded at the two in back. "I'll give him a try."

Judson said, "Thank you, sir."

Still with the unchanging smile, Kelp told him, "If I'm making a mistake, Tiny can always drop you from a high place."

"Yes, sir."

"Let me know," Tiny said, and opened his door, saying, "I'll walk it over to Riverside from here. Kid, drive these two home."

"Yes, sir."

Tiny left, and Kelp said, "I'm west Thirties."

"East Nineteenth," said Dortmunder.

"Yes, sir."

Relieved, amazed, giddy, Judson drove up around, out of the Boat Basin, onto the West Side Highway south. Driving along toward the ship terminal and the USS *Intrepid,* he said, "And if it turns out you could use some help on that bust-out joint, I'm up for that, too."

Well, they didn't have to laugh *that* much.

15

W HEN DORTMUNDER WALKED into the O.J. Bar & Grill at two-thirty on the morning of Friday, August 13, the place had been closed for three hours, and the only illumination inside, other than faraway streetlight glow through the time-grimed windows, was the amber tube over the space-age cash register. Closing the door as silently as he'd opened it, putting away the spatulas and doohickeys that had steered him safely through the locks and alarm system, Dortmunder made his way across the empty tavern and around behind the bar, into Rollo's realm.

The first thing he noticed back there—and a lucky thing he did—was that one section of the duckboards Rollo was wont to tread on had been pulled back over the rest, and the long trapdoor beneath had been left in its upraised position, leaning against the shelves under the bar. That could be a nasty fall if you didn't watch yourself, particularly since the stairs started down from the far end of the rectangular opening.

Whether it was sloppiness or a snare for unwary burglars, Dortmunder didn't know, but he knew he needed to move around back here, so he found the hook that held the door open, unhooked it, and eased the door back down where it belonged. He didn't move the duckboards, though—no need to.

Standing on the closed trapdoor, he opened the first of three drawers in a row under the backbar beneath the cash register, and found it was full of officialdom: fire inspections, coil cleanings, health code violations, water meter bills. Nothing that would explain why this terrible fate had struck the O.J.

The other two drawers were equally useless from a mystery-solving point of view, though it was interesting to note that one of the drawers contained a gun, a Star Model F automatic, very dusty but also very loaded; the safety, however, was on. It lay next to some Oriental parasols.

Closing the drawers, Dortmunder looked around and saw nothing else that might be of help. What about correspondence, gaming chits, threatening notes? Why wasn't there anything useful in here?

Well, there wasn't. He was just about to give the whole thing up when a sudden metallic skritching noise, like a robot mouse gnawing on a copper carrot, came from the front door.

Keys! Somebody with keys, coming in.

Where to hide? Nowhere. The bar could not be more open, and both POINTERS and the back room could not be more closed cul-de-sacs.

Where? Where? Up front, several locks had to be dealt with, which Dortmunder had just recently learned, but time wasn't the problem; space was. He had to have space in which to disappear.

The basement! The trapdoor he'd closed. Quickly he hopped onto the duckboards and bent to lift the door, while up front that other door was about to open. Should he close the trapdoor after himself? No, too awkward. Also, there was nothing he could do about the duckboards.

Hook the trapdoor open, *skitter* down the stairs, his furrowed brow sinking below bar level just as the street door opened and several guys trooped in. At least several.

"Dark in here."

"There's lightswitches behind the bar. Hold on a second."

The basement was absolutely black. With hands splayed out in front of himself, eyes uselessly staring, Dortmunder inched across the unseen floor into the unseeable black.

"*Jesus* Christ! Look at *this*!"

Dortmunder froze, fingers twitching at the end of his outstretched arms.

"What is it? Manny? What's the problem?"

"This goddamn trapdoor's open! I just about dropped myself into the cellar."

"Holy shit, close that thing."

"How? I can't *see* in here."

"Wait, don't move, I think I know where the lightswitch is. That Rollo's getting too damn careless."

"I think he's lost his job satisfaction."

"He can lose all he wants to, we gotta keep him on until we're done in here, because we don't want him opening his yap to some of these wholesalers. *Here's* the lightswitch!"

Sudden light flowed down the basement stairs, swaddled Dortmunder, and streamed on to give faint yellow-gray light to his surroundings. A rough stone wall stood directly in front of him, less than a foot from his outstretched fingers, which he now dropped to his sides. A long rectangular room extended to his right, under the main room of the bar. To his left, a doorway in a wooden wall suggested a corridor beyond. Afraid his feet could still be seen from certain angles upstairs, Dortmunder turned left and tiptoed toward that corridor.

Darkness. Almost as total as before, except that when he looked back, he could see a rectangle of thin yellow lines up above in the black, outlining the trapdoor that had just been lowered.

A sound of voices came from up there. Saying anything useful? In movies and on television, people are always just happening to be hid someplace when other people have a conversation that explains the whole thing. Could that be happening here?

Dortmunder tiptoed back to stand beneath that thin yellow rectangle overhead. What were they saying?

At first, nothing; they seemed to have stopped talking just as he got there. And then all at once there came a painful irritating screech and scrawk, which of course had to be the duckboards being slid back into position—a problem to think about a little later. But then at last, the duckboards were in their proper place, almost the entire yellow line of the rectangle had been blotted out, and people up there began again to speak, muffled but legible:

"Remember, only the Russian."

"Gotcha."

"And the gen-u-wine French."

"I got some Polish here."

"Forget that. We bring back Polish, he'll hand us our heads."

"Well, I'll take a bottle for myself."

"This cash register's empty."

"Sure, they empty it every night."

"What's with this safe here?"

"Forget that, we'll take care of that later."

"Is this French?"

"*No!* What'sa matter with you? What you want is *Dom* Perig-none."

"*Dom* Perig-none."

"There should be more in back."

"Remember, when a boss's daughter marries, only the best Russian vodka, only the best French champagne. Or they'll find us in the Meadowlands."

"Stoli, right?"

"Now you're talking."

The voices faded, moving into other parts of the bar, but Dortmunder could follow their progress by the dull thuds of their shoes on the floor. From here and there, from everywhere, the feet moved toward the front door and away from it again, as the soldiers up there carried the cases of Russian and French out of the place, to prepare for the celebration of the fact that one of their major scumbags was going to replicate himself.

Well, it had sort of worked. They hadn't known he was hiding here, and they had told him certain things. They weren't the things he wanted to know, but still, the principle had proved out.

A faint visual memory came back to him, from that brief moment after the upstairs lights had been switched on and before the trapdoor had been shut. The memory told him there was a lightswitch on the wall that had been facing him when he'd stood there at the foot of the stairs. That was the right place for a lightswitch, the foot of the stairs; could he find it again? Would it make so much glare they'd notice it upstairs?

Dortmunder pondered. He remembered basements from earlier in his life, remembered the lighting arrangement in the back room of this very bar, even remembered another quick visual memory of one single lightbulb in the ceiling of the rectangular room in which he now stood. All in all, it seemed to him worth the risk, to light one little lightbulb rather than curse the darkness.

He was right. When he found the switch and flipped it

on, that forty-watt bulb in the middle of the ceiling created an effect very like the shadowed insubstantiality of the Kasbah at midnight, or a teenagers' party when the folks are out of town. In its fretful murk, he could see rows of kegs: beer kegs, wine kegs, even kegs handmarked in white chalk, *Amsterdam Liquor Store Burben*—hmm.

The place was also cluttered with broken barstools and tables, open tall metal lockers in which hung the remnants of waiters' uniforms from some era of O.J. history before Dortmunder's time, and many cartons of empty bottles, some of them bearing the logos of long-extinct bottlers.

And halfway down one side wall, close to that overhead light source, which was a blessing, there stood a battered old gray metal desk, with an equally battered gray metal swivel chair in front of it. The kneehole was on the left of the desk, while on the right were two tall file drawers.

Okay, that's more like it. Dortmunder settled himself into the squeaking chair with his left elbow on the desktop, opened the upper squeaking drawer, and let his fingers do the walking among the folder tags in there, stopping when he came to "SLA."

SLA. The State Liquor Authority, the god of the taverner, whose rules are the closest thing in their world to Holy Writ, because they have the ultimate power of life and death: they can shut you down.

The SLA folder was more than an inch thick. When Dortmunder opened it on the desk and bent low to read it in the uncertain light, he saw that the papers were roughly in chronological order from front (old) to back (new), and that the earliest documents were forty-seven years old. That was when Jerome Hulve and Otto Medrick, d/b/a Jerrick Associates, applied for and eventually received a liquor license for the O.J. Bar & Grill at this address. (Why the reverse of initials? Maybe the J.O. Bar & Grill didn't sound as melodic to them.)

Thirty-one years ago, Otto Medrick, now d/b/a O.J. Partners, bought out the half-interest from the bar now in the possession of the estate of Jerome Hulve and had to go through a whole lot of paperwork all over again, as though he were a brand-new guy. And six months ago, Otto Medrick, whose address was now given as 131–58 Elfin Dr., Coral Acres, FL, sold O.J. Partners to Raphael Medrick of 161–63 63rd Point, Queens, NY, for no cash down and a percentage of profit over the next twenty years.

Raphael Medrick, when taking the reins, also had to present the SLA with a bushel of paperwork, even more than Otto thirty-one years before, and some of the extra paper was interesting. Letters attesting to Raphael Medrick's rehabilitation had been proffered by his attorney, by a judge from Queens County Court, and by Raphael's former probation officer. All wrote that Raphael's previous (brief) life of crime had been nonviolent, totally repudiated by Raphael himself, and caused by association with bad companions from whom Raphael was now forsworn. A letter from Otto Medrick further assured the SLA that Otto had complete confidence in his nephew Raphael, or he would certainly not turn over to Raphael his every asset in this world.

When Dortmunder at last lifted his head from this family saga, nearly an hour had gone by since he'd first switched on the basement light, and he realized it had been quite a while since he'd heard movement from the troops upstairs. Aware of a new stiffness in his back caused by the need to bend so close over the papers in this uncertain light, he creakily straightened himself, cocked an ear, and listened.

Nothing. When he looked over toward the stairs, he could see no lines of yellow light in the ceiling.

He stood, did a couple deep knee bends, regretted them,

and walked over to look more closely up the stairs at the un-
broken ceiling. No light. He stepped to the wall, switched off
the basement light, and still no illumination from upstairs. So
he flipped the light back on and started up the stairs to see if
it would be possible to get out of here.

All by itself the trapdoor was pretty heavy, being made of
wood thick enough to walk on. When you put lengths of
duckboard on top of it, what would that do?

Nothing good. Dortmunder went up the stairs, bending
forward, until his back was against the bottom of the trapdoor
and his knees were bent. He was on the side away from the
hinges. He braced himself, pressed upward with legs and
back, and nothing happened except that little bolts of pain
shot here and there through his body.

Not good. Not at all good. In order to get on with his life,
which he very much wanted to do, he had to get out of this
basement. Come on, it can't be *that* heavy.

Going back down the stairs, he rooted among the broken
bits of furniture till he found a cracked-off wooden barstool
leg, tapered like a simplified bowling pin. Grasping this, he
went back up the stairs, leaned up to the farthest corner he
could reach, and *insisted* that it lift, just *insisted* and *insisted,*
and then it did lift, and immediately he slid the leg into the
new narrow space. A beginning.

Next it was an entire barstool he brought, carried it up the
stairs horizontally, and forced the curved back of the seat into
the narrow opening he'd made. He levered the stool down-
ward, pushing the trapdoor minimally upward, until the broken leg fell out, which he immediately wedged upright
between trapdoor and the second step from the top. Freeing
the barstool, he jammed it in, standing up, between the trapdoor and the fourth step, causing the leg to fall over.

It was slow work, and tiring, but with every move, using
different pieces of furniture, he made the trapdoor infinitesi-

mally lift, until eventually there was a wedge of space at the top of the stairs just large enough for a person to squirm through, being very sure he didn't kick any props out of the way behind himself as he went.

He was very tired. It was almost daylight. Still, if he didn't put everything back the way it was supposed to be, they would know they'd had a visitor, and that wouldn't be a good thing for them to learn.

Weary, Dortmunder dragged the duckboard out of the way, opened the trapdoor and hooked it, then went back to the basement, took documents from the SLA folder containing uncle and nephew Medrick's most recent addresses, put everything in the basement back where it had been, switched off the light down there, and went back up by the amber light over the cash register.

Weary. On the way out, he grabbed a bottle of Stoli the wedding guests had left behind. You kidding? He deserved it.

16

I T WAS CALLED the Twilight Lounge, and it was east on Forty-third Street, between a wholesale to-the-trade-only plastic flower showroom and a store that called itself "Sickroom & Party Supplies," with an unfortunate display window. Looking at that sign, Kelp said, "Shouldn't that be the other way around?"

"Shouldn't what?" Dortmunder asked. He was feeling skeptical and unobservant.

"Doesn't matter," Kelp said, and pushed through the swinging door into the Twilight Lounge, where they were at once drenched in the crooning of Dean Martin, his voice morphine-laced molasses.

It was J. C. Taylor who'd come up with this joint for their meeting ground, now that the O.J. was becoming increasingly unlikely. "Josey doesn't know the place herself," Tiny had explained to everybody, in various phone calls earlier today, Friday, after Dortmunder had dragged himself out of bed to make his own phone calls to say they needed a place to meet and discuss his discoveries of last night. "A guy down in the post office substation in her building says he goes there, it's quiet, they mind their own business, there's a back room we could use, just say Eddie told us about it."

Well, it was worth a try. Anything, they all agreed, rather than gather in Dortmunder's living room again. So, four o'clock Friday afternoon, here they were in the Twilight Lounge, a sprawling, lowlit joint half full of wage earners taking an indirect route to their suburban homes for the weekend, the whole scene suffused by the umber gurgle of Dean Martin.

There were two bartenders at work: one hardworking, blank-faced guy with his sleeves rolled up, one friendly girl with all the time in the world. Rather than break into the three conversations the girl already had under way, Kelp leaned over the bar and said to the guy en passant, "Eddie sent me."

"Right." The guy never made eye contact, but just kept watching what his busy hands were doing with various objects on the backbar as he said, "Eddie's pal is already back there."

Dortmunder wondered who that might be, but the busy barman was still talking: "Order your drinks, you can carry them back, you can run a tab until you're done."

"Thanks," Kelp said. "I'll have bourbon and ice, two glasses."

"Same," Dortmunder said, and the bartender snapped an efficient nod and went off with what looked like a trayful of piña coladas. True, it was August outside, but where were these commuters going?

As they waited for their drinks, Kelp said, "Well, it's more efficient than the O.J."

Dortmunder thought, is that what we wanted? But he knew he was just in a bad mood, irritated by change simply because it was change, so all he said was, "I wonder who Eddie's pal is."

Kelp shrugged. "We'll find out."

That was wisdom, and Dortmunder nodded to it. Take it as it comes. What the hell. More efficient than the O.J.; maybe that'd be okay.

Efficiently the barman slapped four glasses onto the gleaming wood in front of them. "Around the bar to your left," he said, not looking at them, watching instead the next job his busy hands were concerned with, "then past the rest-rooms, it's on your right."

They thanked his departing back, picked up their glasses, and followed instructions. Past the end of the bar they found themselves in a quietly lit, neat corridor with carpet on the floor and wall sconces and gay-nineties scenes in frames on the walls. The first door on the right said LADIES. The second door on the right said GENTLEMEN. The third door on the right was open, and seated in there, looking irritable, was Tiny.

This was a larger back room than the one at the O.J., and more elaborate. The wall-sconce-and-gay-nineties theme continued in here, and there were four small round tables geometrically placed on the maroon carpet, each containing a tablecloth and a stand-up triangular menu of, on one side, our specialty drinks, and on the other, our specialty snacks. Tiny had already tossed onto the floor behind him the menu from his table.

"Hey, Tiny," Kelp said as they entered. "Different here, huh?"

Tiny held up a tall glass of red liquid that looked like, but was not, cherry pop. "They wanted," he said, "to put the vodka and the wine in separate glasses. I told them, they could give me as many glasses as they want, they get one back."

As Kelp put his two glasses at the place to Tiny's right, he said, "We made a kind of a different deal."

"The customer," Tiny informed him, "is always right."

Putting his own store of glasses at the place to Tiny's left, Dortmunder said, "Is Murch's Mom coming? If so, we're five, and this is a table for four."

"I only talked to the son," Tiny said, and Stan Murch himself walked in, a glass of beer in one hand, and a little shallow bowl with wavy blue designs on it in the other. "I'm glad my Mom isn't coming," he informed them. "If she could see the traffic in Manhattan. What's this, I got to sit with my back to the door?"

"You get to close the door," Tiny suggested.

So Stan put his glass and his bowl at the remaining spot at the small table and turned about to shut the hall door. When he turned back, Kelp said, "What's the bowl?"

"They say, salt." Stan sat, sipped beer, frowned upon the bowl without affection, and said, "I asked for a saltshaker, they don't have saltshakers here, they got these little bowls."

Leaning forward to look at the grains of white salt almost completely filling the bowl, Kelp said, "That's gotta be wasteful. You won't use hardly any of that."

"They don't throw it out," Stan told him. "I saw on the tables out there, they just leave them around."

Kelp said, "You mean, everybody's fingers in the same salt?"

Stan shrugged. "What are you gonna do? I figure, the alcohol in the beer'll kill the germs. The problem with Manhattan, on the other hand, it's August, nobody's here, it's full of tourists."

Dortmunder said, "Then whadaya mean, there's nobody here?"

"There's nobody here that *belongs* here," Stan explained. "The real New Yorkers go away for the summer. Right now, there's nobody driving in the city that knows *how* to drive in the city. You got people now, they're from some other *continent,* they come here in the summer, they got a special deal, hotel and a car rental, they're so pleased with themselves. They come to New York City to drive a *car*? Drive a car at home in Yakburg, not here, you'll never figure out what you're *doing* here, a week in circles, lost, they go home, their friends say, 'So how'd you find New York?' they say, 'We didn't.' "

"We're here," Tiny said, "for Dortmunder to tell us how he found the O.J."

"I'm ready," Stan said. With thumb and forefinger, he delicately sprinkled a few grains of salt onto his beer, which enthused.

When Dortmunder finished watching Stan and his salt, he said, "Okay, I went in there last night," and he told them about the wedding party and the basement and the SLA and the Medrick family saga.

Kelp said, "A nephew."

"Not one of the better ones," Dortmunder suggested.

Tiny rumbled, "There are good nephews?"

Kelp said, "My nephew Victor isn't so bad."

"Victor," Tiny repeated. "The FBI guy."

"Ex-FBI," Kelp said.

Dortmunder said, "They threw him out. He wanted the FBI to have a secret handshake."

Stan said, "I thought they did have a secret handshake."

Tiny said, "Kelp's nephew Victor is not the point. The O.J.'s nephew Medrick is the point."

"Raphael Medrick," Dortmunder said, taking from his shirt pocket the two folded documents he'd liberated from the O.J.'s safe. "He's in Queens."

"We don't know what he was on probation for," Kelp pointed out.

"Nonviolent," Dortmunder said. "It's probably not that he's mobbed-up to begin with, he's just some schmuck, got in trouble, his family helped out, his uncle wants to retire, you can see it now. It's great for everybody, the old guy can go retire in Florida, the young guy is gonna be fine once he's got some responsibility to be responsible for, the family's gonna keep an eye on him—"

"Sure," Kelp said.

"They always do," Stan said.

Tiny said, "You know, all this is after it's over. It's over."

Dortmunder said, "The O.J.'s still open."

"If you call that open," Tiny said. "But the goods have been bought, Dortmunder, the credit line's used up. The place is a shell, it's going down. What we're *supposed* to be thinking about is that place on Fifth Avenue, full of good things that Albright is gonna pay us all this green."

"We're thinking about it," Kelp assured him. "We're working on it. Aren't we, John?"

"In a way," Dortmunder said.

"Let's think about it some more," Tiny suggested.

"Definitely," Dortmunder said.

Stan said, "Just for the heck of it, though, why don't we go and take a look at this Raphael?"

"Well, yeah," Tiny said. "Sure we're gonna go look at Raphael. Just don't think anything's gonna be done about the O.J."

Kelp said, "In that case, why bother to go see him at all?"

Tiny smiled; the others flinched. "Because," Tiny said, "I wish to attract his attention."

17

THERE WERE SO many ways in which Preston Fareweather found Beryl Leominster beautiful. Her body was beautiful, hard and trim and as bronzed as an award statuette, with only the faintest little scars here and there to record a lifetime of nips and tucks. Her face was beautiful, if a little blank, but framed by cascades of honey blond hair, penned in a snood at night so it wouldn't "get in the way," as she'd explain. Which was another thing that was beautiful about her—her thoughtfulness. She was eager and knowledgeable in bed, without being too greedy. She was probably within seven or eight years of her declared age, twenty-nine. She was happily spending an ex-husband's money, which wasn't beautiful in itself but created the potential for Preston eventually to wreak some indirect revenge, which was certainly beautiful. But the most beautiful thing about Beryl, in Preston's eyes, was that today was Friday, and tomorrow morning Beryl would go away.

The system was, most vacationers reached the resort on Saturday afternoon, coming down from mainland North

America on charter flights. Some were singles; some were couples; some were families. Among the singles, the pairing off was usually accomplished by some time Sunday and frequently involved fraternization between guests and staff, an activity on which management neither beamed nor frowned. Just as often, however, guests would find each other perfectly acceptable. And the most acceptable often was the long-term guest like Preston, who could, in his phrase, "show the ropes" to the lovely newcomer.

Over the following week, the newly minted couples would explore the wonders of the island and of one another, and then, on Saturday morning, the vacationers would leave again, so that the staff had the few midday hours to prepare the rooms for the next week's arrivals. Friday night, therefore, was the moment of truth among many of the pairs at the resort. Was this good-bye? Would phone numbers and e-mail addresses be exchanged? Would lies be told?

Not by Preston Fareweather. He lived for Friday evening and the truths he would tell the current stand-in for the despicable ex-wives. This week it was the lovely Beryl.

"I've had the most wonderful time, Pres," she murmured in his ear, on her bed on that final Friday, after an evening spent mostly with white wine on the veranda outside her room, contemplating a wonderful moon, barely one-quarter full but gleaming as white as a mime's smile for all that.

"I know you have, my darling," Preston murmured back, left arm curled around her, one eye on the bedside clock. Physically he was spent, but mentally he still had a few moves to make. "And I know," he murmured, "you haven't minded my little japeries."

"Of course not," she murmured, snuggling her button nose in close to the artery so strongly beating in his throat.

"The snake in your underwear drawer."

The chuckle against his throat was lifelike but not entirely realistic. "That *was* a bit of a surprise," she murmured. "I don't know where you even found a snake on this island."

"It wasn't easy, but it was worth it," he murmured. "Then there was the glass of icewater I 'accidentally' spilled on you sunbathing."

"You *are* a scamp," she murmured, good humor and forgiveness purring in her voice.

"But you didn't mind, did you?"

"Not really," she murmured. "Not when it's *you*."

"Not even when I removed your bathing suit top in the swimming pool?"

She reared up a bit, to give him a serious but accepting look. "That *was* going a bit far," she said. "Especially when you carried it all the way here and wouldn't bring it back. If I hadn't been able to borrow that towel, I don't know *what* I would have done."

"I hope you thanked the person who loaned you the towel."

"Of course I did." Then Beryl gave him a keen look and said, "The *woman* who loaned me the towel, Pres. I certainly wouldn't borrow a towel from a *man*."

Innocent, he said, "But why not?"

"Not when I'm with *you*."

"But you weren't with me. I was here, with your bathing suit top."

"You know what I mean."

"I'm not sure I do."

"Oh, for heaven's sake, Preston," she said, forgetting their private little nickname in her agitation. Sitting up completely, topless again, she said, "We've been together all week, you know we have. You've absolutely monopolized me."

"Monopolized?"

"You know what I mean. Ever since your friend Alan introduced us last Saturday, I've felt there was something . . . I

felt there could be something . . . I just sensed a kind of special— Oh, you *know* what I mean!"

He stretched lazily on his side of the bed, an overweight
but extremely comfortable cat. "You mean we had good fun
for a week," he suggested. "Fuck and frolic, a little time out
from the cares of everyday life."

She stared at him. "*What* did you say?"

"Frolic," he said, and beamed at her, the cat with the canary feather in the corner of his mouth.

"Well, frolic," she said, distracted, but her agenda would
not let her dwell on a passing bewilderment. "That *has* been
wonderful, Pres, of course it has. This last week—"

"Yes, I know," he murmured.

She lay down beside him again. "This last week has been
so much more than I could have hoped—"

"Yes, it has."

That his responses were just a little off forced a certain
jump-start quality to her own presentation. "Yes," she
echoed, then got back to her script: "You'll be staying here
another week, won't you?"

"Another week, mm, yes," he murmured, thinking already
of what tomorrow might bring.

"How long *have* you been here, Pres?"

"Oh, when we're in paradise," he murmured, "we never
count the days. Forever, I believe." Because he could never
tell any of them that he'd been here so far nearly three years,
with no end in sight. That might make them a little skittish.

"I've been so sad," she murmured, "at the prospect of our
parting tomorrow, I asked at the office if they could squeeze
me in for just one more week. Would you like that, if I could
stay?"

"Oh, absolutely not," he murmured. "You can't put yourself in a financial fix just for little me."

That response was *so* off-kilter it got her up to a seated

position again. "Financial fix?" She stared at him, not quite sure how she was supposed to handle this one. If he'd agreed to her staying on, he knew, she herself would have mentioned her financial woes and suggested he might help ease her burden in the days ahead, since he so much wanted her companionship, but once he'd mentioned her money troubles himself as a reason for her not to stay, what was she to do?

"We don't care about finances, Pres," she finally decided on. "We care about one another."

"Oh, darling, Beryl," he told her, "by last Monday morning at the latest you were e-mailing friends to find out everything you could about my finances."

"How can you *say* such a thing?"

"Because you bimbos always do. But you don't—"

"Bimbos?"

"But you don't realize," he went inexorably on, while discreetly moving his arms to protect his privates, just in case she turned out to be one of the physical ones, "that of course I'm doing the same thing. I know exactly how much you're into Mr. Marcus Leominster for, darling Beryl, and I know you don't otherwise have a single asset worth mentioning, other than your singular ass, of course, and I know that one week here husband-hunting is already a strain on—"

"Husband-hunting!"

"I'm afraid, Beryl," he said, chortling by now, "I've wasted an entire week of your dwindling finances, your dwindling time, and if I may say so, your dwindling looks."

"How can you— How can you—"

"Beryl," he said, smiling at her face, which now looked like a wax museum piece in the middle of a major fire, "why on earth would you put up with a fat boor like me except that you wanted to get into my pants? For my wallet, of course."

"You son—"

The phone rang. Beryl stared at it, as Preston rose for the last time from her bed and said, "Timing is everything."

"Timing?" The phone rang again, but now Beryl was staring at Preston. "You know who that is? On the telephone?"

"Of course," Preston said, reaching for his flame red bathing trunks. "It's Alan Pinkleton. He's calling to ask me to play Scrabble."

"Scrabble!"

"Tell him, would you," Preston said, as he moved toward the door, "I'm on my way?"

The phone continued to ring, fading with distance, as he strolled along the bougainvillea-scented wandering concrete path among the bungalows. Pathway lighting was dim and discreet; the air was soft and warm, the night a joy. The fading sound of the telephone made him think for some reason of the song "I Love a Parade," so that's what he whistled as he strolled back to his own little bungalow, where Alan had long since hung up the unanswered phone and where the Scrabble set was already laid out on the table on the veranda.

He was in such a good frame of mind, Preston was, that he didn't even object when Alan, who wasn't supposed to win, won handily.

18

RAPHAEL MEDRICK LISTENED to "The Star-Spangled Banner" as he'd recorded it during last winter's Super Bowl—MCXIV?—sung by a nervous girl pop singer with excessive tremolo, an unsteady grasp of key, and not much upper register; cool. His fingers moved on the control panel, adjusting the gains, and the middle range faded, taking with it much of the ambient crowd noise, leaving mainly the aggressive brass sounds, both high and low, like sturdy lines of cathedral columns, with that frightened little voice vaguely wandering among them, a little trapped bird. Nice.

Stop; set coordinates; save; set aside; move on to the Beatles' "Hey, Jude." Strip away high and low, leaving a broody midrange with tatters of a barely recognizable voice and an obsessive baritone rhythm section pulsing forward like a predator fish, eyes flicking left and right, tail flashing behind.

Reset "Jude"; sync with "Banner"; play both. "Jude" had to be speeded up just a bit to blend with the "Banner" tempo, which served to lift the notes of "Jude" just a fraction so that they became dissonant with any melodic line played

anywhere in the history of the world. The two treated
themes weaved discordantly through each other. Now the
ruined cathedral columns were underwater, the forlorn "Banner" singer clearly the dinner the predator "Jude" was hunting for.

"*Now* we're getting somewhere!" Raphael said aloud,
hearing his own voice not through his ears into his brain but
first through his skull into his earphones—an effect he was
used to by now. Too bad he couldn't mix *that* doomy sound
into the soup. But now he had one more minor adjustment
in tempo to be completed before moving on to the next
phase, and a shadow crossed the control panel.

He barely registered it at first. His task here was to complete the match of the first two elements before adding the
stutter-stop Gregorian chant he'd already assembled on another CD. But then, as "Jude" and "Banner" approached max-
imum synchronicity, like a space shuttle docking at the
station, memory and observation within Raphael's own brain
coalesced, and he thought: Shadow. *Moved* across the control
panel. In my living room.

When he lifted his head, yes, there were people in his
room, and no, he'd never seen any of them before. A lot of
people—four, in fact—all male and all looking at him, all
somehow seeming to disapprove. Why?

I'm not on probation any more, he thought.

Can these people be from Mikey, he wondered?

No, he decided, I can't take time for this, not just this second. I'm at a crucial intersection here, I can't let my concentration be disturbed.

Thus, he held up one finger, showing it to them all: wait.
Not being rude, not saying no, I won't talk to you, not saying, I don't see why you have to cluster in *my* living room,
whoever you are, but merely saying: wait.

Upon which he bent over his control panel once more, a

scrawny nerd of twenty-four with a pitiful goatee, barefoot, dressed in cutoff jeans and *Mostly Mozart* T-shirt, whose contact lenses glinted in the light to make him look blind. Over the next seven minutes—though it barely seemed like twenty seconds to him—hunched here in the living room of his tiny underfurnished house at the dead end of a poky side street in remotest Queens overlooking Jamaica Bay, he laid in the Gregorian chant. Since he listened to his work strictly through the earphones, these strangers wouldn't hear any of it, except possibly some faint cricket noises floating up from beside his head. Not that he cared; deeply involved in his collage, he barely remembered he had company until he was done.

There. Finished. At least, the first assemblage of the basic idea was finished. After that, of course, it's easy.

Earphones off, briskly massaging both ears with the palms of both hands because they tended to itch and feel all crumpled after long sessions like this, he at last dropped his hands into his lap, shook his head like a dog coming out of water, looked at his unexpected guests, and said, "Good morning."

"Good afternoon," one of them said—a carrot-haired, edgy-seeming guy, who said "afternoon" as though there were something wrong with afternoons and as though Raphael were to blame for it.

Before Raphael could ask him what was wrong with afternoon, another one, a slope-shouldered, depressed-looking fellow, said, "You *are* Raphael Medrick, aren't you?"

"After all this time," added a third, a sharp-nosed, impatient type.

"Oh, sure," Raphael said.

The depressed fellow said, "You own the O.J.? The O.J. Bar and Grill?"

Raphael lit up. "Sure," he said, and smiled in relief, because now at least he knew the subject. It wasn't every day you had four complete strangers suddenly in your living room, so it was nice to have some idea of their reason for being here. "Did Mikey send you?"

They looked at one another. The one who hadn't spoken yet, a huge man similar to several Raphael had seen during the Super Bowl—JXQVIII?—with a head like a Darth Vader lunchbox, said, not to Raphael but to the others, "He wants to know did Mikey send us."

"I heard that," the sharp-nosed one said, and nodded, and in a very pleasant way said to Raphael, "Why would Mikey send us? What would Mikey want to send us *here* for?"

"I dunno," Raphael said. "I just thought."

The one with the Darth Vader head extended his right hand. Even though his middle finger was bent, with his thumb-tip pressed against that finger's nail, Raphael had no idea what he planned to do until all at once, like somebody flicking an ant off a picnic table, he *pinged* the left side of Raphael's skull above the ear. Just, in fact, above the part that had been covered by the earphone.

"Ouch!"

Interesting reverb. How to get *that* on disc? Not by getting yourself pinged in the head a lot. As Raphael rubbed the now-burning part on the side of his head, the big man with the pinging finger remained in a loomed position above him, saying, "Pay attention to us."

"I *am* paying attention."

"You own the O.J."

"I already said so."

"So since you're the owner of the O.J.," the looming man went on, "we come to talk to you about the O.J."

"Oh, come on," Raphael said, grinning, forgetting the sting in his skull to look in surprise at the big man. "That's just a joke," he said. "Everybody knows that's just a joke."

They exchanged another enigmatic look. The big man

stepped back a pace, and the sharp-nosed one, whose manner was much more pleasant, took his place. "Just a joke, Raphael?" he asked. "Didn't your uncle sign the place over to you?" Turning his head, he said to the gloomy one, "How long ago?"

"Four months."

"But that doesn't *mean* anything," Raphael said. "I mean, Uncle Otto gets all the money. Don't you know the deal?"

"Tell us the deal, Raphael," suggested the sharp-nosed one.

"Uncle Otto is old," Raphael explained. "I mean really, really *old*. He had to get to Florida before it was too late, but nobody wanted to buy the bar because the neighborhood changed."

"Wait," said the big man, holding up his pinger hand. "You're gonna talk for a week, we need a place to sit down. You got a living room?"

"*This* is my living room," Raphael told him.

They all swiveled their heads around to study his living room, and he supposed it did look different from most living rooms. Most living rooms had chairs and sofas and things, but he had only this one chair that he was sitting in, that he could swing around to watch the television over there, if he wanted to watch television. Otherwise, the room was mostly electronic equipment on tables, and lots of open storage cabinets around the walls, so that what it mostly looked like was a recording studio. Which, in addition to being his living room, it was.

The gloomy one now said, "We don't have to sit. You say nobody wanted to buy the bar."

"It's too down-something," Raphael said. "The lawyer told me. Market!"

"So," the gloomy one prompted, "the uncle sold it to you."

"Well, I signed for it—the family made me do that—but I pay him a mortgage, which is just about everything the place makes, so I basically ignore it."

The sharp-nosed one said, "Who are those guys in there, running it? Not Rollo, the new ones. Friends of yours?"

"Maybe friends of Mikey's," Raphael said. "I don't know, I only ever saw the place just that one time."

"Maybe," the gloomy one said, "it would help if we knew who this Mikey was."

"I met him when I was on probation," Raphael explained. "He was on probation, too."

The big pinger man said, "What were *you* on probation for?" as though he couldn't believe it.

"Well, downloading," Raphael said, and gestured at his equipment.

They frowned at him. They were all very blank. Raphael saw the pinger finger twitch, and hurriedly said, "Taking music off the Web. You know, sharing files. Some big German record company came after me, me and a bunch of other people, even some kids, and said we were doing felonies."

The sharp-nosed one said, "You were on probation because you were listening to *music*? This is a *crime*?"

"They said so," Raphael said, "so I guess it is."

The gloomy one said, "Was Mikey downloading music, too?"

"No, I don't know what he did," Raphael admitted. "I think maybe he knows some real criminals."

"You mean," the edgy, carrot-haired man said, "people even more dangerous than music bandits."

"Uh huh. I know his father has a bunch of restaurants and bars in New Jersey and Long Island," Raphael explained, "so when my family made me take over the bar so Uncle Otto could go to Florida and die in the warm instead of up here in the cold, I told Mikey about it, and he said he'd take care

of everything, he could use the practice for when someday
he'd go into his father's business. So I signed a paper that says
he's running it, and now I don't have to worry about anything any more."

They all sighed, all four of them. The big man turned to
the others and said, "You know what I want to say to this
nephew?"

"You want to say good-bye," the gloomy one suggested.

"I do." The big man nodded at Raphael. "Good-bye," he
said, and they all left.

Gee, Raphael thought, I wonder what that was all about.
I hope Mikey isn't making trouble up there in the city.

Well, what did it matter? The important thing was
"Phaze," the piece he was constructing here. This was where
he made his money, not some bar, now that he understood
you could charge for music on the Net. Put it out there, avant
garde fusion, let them sample, but before they download they
have to pay, all major credit cards accepted. He had more customers in Japan and Norway than in the United States, but
all currencies are good on the Net.

The O.J. Bar & Grill. Who cared? That was so yesterday,
back when people used to leave their houses.

19

"HOW CAN YOU know nothing?" Tiny demanded, spread over much of the backseat of the Cadillac Conquistadore Kelp had borrowed for this journey to the Middle Earth section of Queens. "That guy didn't know nothing. I never seen anybody know such a total goddamn nothing."

Kelp, in the remaining portion of the seat beside Tiny, sounded a bit strangled as he said, "He was different, I'll give him that."

Stan, at the wheel of this monster machine, frowned out at the low buildings and broken sidewalks and stunted trees of this landscape he maneuvered through, which looked as though it had never received good nutrition in its formative years, and said, "What gets me about him is, he don't react. Four guys walk into his house, Tiny bings him on the head, what does he do? Does he yell, does he call the cops, does he make a run for it, does he tough it out, does he beg for mercy, does he say, 'No, you want Medrick the Meshugah next door'? No. He does nothing."

"He does nothing," Tiny agreed. "And he knows nothing."

They were all silent as they considered Raphael Medrick, who continued to recede uselessly behind them in his rickety little hovel beside the bay. It was probably the first time an automobile of this magnificence had ever driven down that dead-end street—dead-end in more ways than one—but what a waste of time.

It was a nice car, though. Kelp had picked it out, in the staff parking area of an East Side hospital—a very big vehicle to accommodate Tiny, MD plates to accord with Kelp's belief that doctors, living as they did on the cusp between pleasure and pain, could be relied on in their choice of transportation, and a green the color of money for that homey look.

"What I think it is," the diminished Kelp said after a couple of silent blocks, "I think he's one of those artists."

The others considered that idea. With a glance at the rearview mirror, Stan said, "One of *what* artists?"

"You know," Kelp said, "the artistic kind of artists, unworldly, all he knows is his art."

Stan said, "I thought they wore berets."

"Maybe not in the summer," Kelp suggested.

Tiny said, "I didn't see any pictures."

"I think," Kelp said, "he was doing music art in there. In the earphones and stuff."

"Oh, *that* crap," Stan said. "Every once in a while, I get in a car, it's tuned to a station like that, I gotta pull over, switch it around. You can't drive to that stuff, believe me."

Until this point, Dortmunder, in the front passenger seat, had been silent, brooding out at the undernourished neighborhood, but now he said, "I'm thinking about the O.J. He's gonna be no help on the O.J."

"None," Kelp agreed.

Tiny said, "Now more than ever, Dortmunder, the O.J. is history."

"Don't say that," Dortmunder asked.

"Raphael Medrick is not gonna be of any use," Tiny told him, "and Mikey and his friends are not gonna change their minds for nostalgia."

"This Mikey," Kelp said, "he's the *son* of a mob guy, which is even worse than a mob guy. He came up soft, and he thinks he's hard."

"So it's over," Tiny said.

Dortmunder, frowning mightily at the windshield, said, "I don't want it to be over."

Kelp, as he made minor adjustments in his body in a vain attempt to become comfortable back there with Tiny, said, "Then you know what you have to do, John."

Silence.

"John? You wanna give up the O.J.?"

"No."

"Then you know what you gotta do."

More silence. Finally, Dortmunder sighed and nodded at the outside world and said, "I think it looks a lot like this."

"I understand there's some nice parts," Stan said.

Dortmunder shook his head. "Otto Medrick won't be in one of them," he said. Then he cleared his throat and, as though casually, said, "Will you guys come along?"

"No, John," Kelp said.

"I'll drive you to the airport," Stan offered.

"What the heck," Dortmunder said. "Florida can't be *that* bad."

"Why not?" Tiny asked.

"In August?" Stan asked.

"It's just, you know," Dortmunder said, "it's better if I don't go alone. More intimidating."

"No, John," Kelp said, "Some things you got to do by yourself."

"If you even gotta do them," Tiny pointed out. "You

know, what we're supposed to be thinking about right now, we're supposed to be thinking about that apartment we're gonna take down."

"That can wait," Dortmunder said. "The O.J. is right now, but that apartment is empty. It'll wait for us."

20

AFTER THE CHARTER flight from Philadelphia, after the greeting in the main recreation hall with a bouncy song from the resort staff and a mimosa Roselle didn't drink, after the receipt of the beads the guests would use here in lieu of money, after a bellgirl had escorted her to her room and she'd unpacked her wheelie and taken her after-travel shower, Roselle stood in the airy if impersonal room in front of the drapes closed over the view—both hers out and others' in—and from her store of bikinis, each in its own Ziploc bag, she selected the pale beige number barely two shades from her own body color. It was a powerful marketing tool, as she well knew.

Before leaving the room, she put the wheelie on its back on the bed and opened the Velcro secret compartment to take out the manila envelope and shake from it the photos of Preston Fareweather, wanting to be certain she would close with the right man. These well-fed, self-indulgent rich men of a certain age tended to a type—round, jowly heads and round, flabby bodies, more so in bankers, a little less so in movie producers—so she wanted to be absolutely certain to dock onto nobody but her own Tweedledee among all the Tweedledums patrolling the sands here in this paradise of no consequences. There had been a number of those among the previous week's holdovers, eyeballing the new arrivals as they moved from airport van to recreation hall to reception to the meandering paths to their rooms, but she hadn't risked meeting anybody's eye, hadn't tried yet to make contact, preferring the first strike to be the finisher, like the zap the cow gets as she enters the slaughterhouse.

Yes, here he was, Preston Fareweather, with the usual deficit of hair and surplus of flesh. Even with nothing to gloat at but a camera, he still bore on his lips—virtually the only thin part of him—the hint of that sardonic smile that says, "I'm rich, and you aren't."

In the same manila folder was the thumbnail bio of Fareweather, but she already knew that cold. Venture capitalist from a wealthy family, all the right schools, all the wrong education, fingers in pies all across the economy from New York City real estate to second-wave California Web start-ups. And now here, hiding in broad sunlight.

Not from me, Roselle thought, smiling back at that smirk. Returning the photos to the envelope and the envelope to the secret compartment, off she went in her bikini, her ballet slippers, her wide-brimmed white straw hat, and her huge dark Jackie O sunglasses. On the prowl.

And there he was, eventually, after nearly an hour of strolling the paths and the beach and the resort's central square. But there he was, sprawled on a chaise longue on the little ground-floor balcony outside what must be his room. That was Preston Fareweather, all right, garbed in nothing but the briefest possible bright red swimsuit; not so much a fashion statement as a provocation.

Protected by her sunglasses, Roselle observed Fareweather sidelong as she sashayed by. She knew he was eying her; how could he not?

Unfortunately, though, Fareweather was not alone on that porch, so she couldn't permit connection just yet. Seated beside her man was a younger, thinner man, a narrow-headed ascetic sort that Roselle had never found of any use at all. He and Fareweather chatted together in desultory fashion— Fareweather, she knew, was saying something to him about her at that very second—and they seemed totally at ease in each other's company.

What was that fellow there for? Fareweather couldn't be a queen, could he? No, not with that many ex-wives. Not unless he was a demon of overcompensation.

Roselle moved on, having made, she knew, the kind of impact he would not forget. Now it was simply a matter of holding herself ready for his inevitable approach.

How would he do it, exactly? Strolling along, enjoying the sunlight, enjoying in a smallish background way the effect she had on the other males she passed, Roselle wondered what method Fareweather would choose in this odd place to attract her attention. Usually, she knew, men of his type drew notice by strewing money around themselves, the way male lions spray their urine to lure the female, but Club Med removes cash from the guests' lives, replacing it with beads for use in the gift shop and bar and so on—a fun gimmick that makes it seem as though you're not spending actual money at all.

How would Preston Fareweather lure the female in an environment without money?

The arrangement in the dining room was mix-and-match, with everyone expected to combine haphazardly among the large round tables, and with guests and staff all

sharing their meals together. Not the native maids and gar-
deners, of course—no point carrying égalité *that* far—but the
lifeguards, sports instructors, musicians, office staff, and other
socially acceptable types mingled happily with the guests,
who mingled just as happily right back.

Dining was buffet style—load your tray and take it to
any table. Roselle chose a half-full table with a mix of
younger and older, male and female, and a spot where she
could sit with an empty chair on either side, just in case
Mr. Fareweather should happen to feel the urge to intro-
duce himself.

But who joined her, in the chair at her right, within a
minute of her taking her seat, was not Preston Fareweather
himself but the thin-faced man who'd been sitting with
Fareweather earlier today. "Hi," he said. "You just got here,
didn't you?"

"This afternoon."

"I'm Alan," he said, with a smile, as he removed plates and
silverware from his tray and pushed the tray to the middle of
the table with the others already there.

"Pam," Roselle said.

"Hi, Pam. How long you staying?"

"Two weeks, I think."

"You think?"

She shrugged. "I might stay longer, if I feel like it."

Beneath the conversation, her mind was very busy. Why
wasn't Alan dining with his friend Preston? Was it *Alan* who
hoped to pick her up? On the other hand, would it be possible to use Alan's presence as a means of meeting his friend?
Remain amiable but not quite available, she told herself, and
see where it goes.

"I've been here for some time," Alan was saying, "and I
must admit, I never get tired of it."

"It's my first time."

"You're going to love it," he assured her.

The arrival of another person at the seat to her left brought that conversation to an end, at least for the moment, as the newcomer said, *"Bonsoir, madame,"* forcing Roselle to swivel her head and smile upon him, a whippet-thin Frenchman in his mid-twenties whose tray was piled high with nothing but fruit and salad and sparkling water.

"Bonsoir," she agreed.

"You are new," he said. His teeth were very white but very small. She thought he smiled like a fox.

"I am new *here,*" she said.

He chuckled; she was amusing. "I am Francois."

"Pam."

"I instruct in the dance."

"Ah."

"You perhaps," he said, with his fox smile, "already know the dance."

"Perhaps," she said, with her own carnivore's smile, and turned away to eat a dainty morsel of her own salad, during which Alan, on her right, said, as though there'd been no break in the conversation, "You know what's the most wonderful thing about the atmosphere of this place? The absolute openness. Guests and staff eating together, for instance, everybody sharing this beautiful place. It really *is* one big happy family."

"That's why I'm here," she said.

"And the best of it," he told her, "is the lack of money. Only beads. Do you realize how democratic that is?"

"Democratic?" She affected friendly bewilderment. "I just thought it was kind of cute."

"Well, it is. But besides that. Everywhere else you go in the world, you can tell in one second the rich people from the rest of us. But here, everybody blends in."

"That's true," she said. "When you point it out."

He gestured at the roomful of diners. "Look how we're all alike. And yet, would you believe it, there is a multimillionaire in this very room."

She showed a gently skeptical smile. "Oh, really?"

"I've gotten to know him here," Alan said, "and he's just like everybody else. At home, of course, he's the center of the world. *His* world." Smiling, he gestured again, encompassing all the tables, all the diners, all the grand egalitarian world. "Can you guess which one?"

"Of course not," she said. "Everybody's the same here."

"Exactly what I'm saying." With a wink, he said, "I'll give you a hint."

"All right."

Smiling at her while he nodded his head rightward in the general direction of Preston Fareweather, he said, "He's one of the people at that table over there."

"With the man in the red-and-white-striped shirt?"

Alan had to look. "Yes, that's the table."

"But that's not your millionaire."

Alan's smile broadened. "No, no," he said, "that's an operator of the glass-bottom boat. He's French."

"There are French millionaires."

"Not working at Club Med."

"No, I don't suppose so." She looked at that table over there, let her glance pass over Preston Fareweather, who was thoroughly engaged in his own conversation among his tablemates, and said, "I can't guess."

"In the dark blue shirt," Alan told her. "Now he's drinking wine. See?"

"Oh, him." Roselle smiled, as though made happy by the look of the fellow over there. "He just looks like a very nice man," she said.

"He is," Alan assured her, and then, as though the thought

had just that instant popped into his head. "Would you like to meet him?"

So that's how it's done, Roselle thought. "I'd love to," she said.

21

Turned out Coral Acres, Florida, Otto Medrick's waiting room for departure, was about as far north in Florida as you could go and still be in Florida; but on the other hand, you were still in Florida. The way to go there was to fly Continental from Newark to Jacksonville, and then Coral Acres was on an estuary off St. John's River south of the city, between the river and the ocean.

The trouble was to get there. At first, because everything about air travel is so revolting, from the food to the security to the crowding to the simple fact of being thirty thousand feet in the sky, Dortmunder thought maybe it would be more restful to take the train from Penn Station, but unfortunately that would be a little *too* restful: two and a half hours by air, seventeen hours by rail.

Still, there had to be an overnight in it. There were no flights north in the late afternoon, and he'd have to give himself time to find the town, find the guy, and tell him the story. So it looked as though he had to fly down from Newark at nine Sunday morning and then come back from Jacksonville starting at nine the next day.

Fortunately, if that word could be used for any part of this experience, once it became clear to everyone that Dortmunder really meant to go ahead and find the O.J.'s former owner way down there in Florida, he got various kinds of help. J.C. Taylor, for instance, went on the Web and got him bargain rates for the airfare and a motel out by the airport and a rental car. Murch's Mom offered to drive him to the airport and back without throwing the meter, but her son Stan said he could find a much more comfortable car than a New York City hack, so he'd do the driving.

Other help. Kelp, also a dab hand with the computer, got him printout maps showing exactly how to get from JAX, the airport, to 131–58 Elfin Drive, Coral Acres. May got him up early Sunday morning and gave him his favorite breakfast—Wheaties and milk and sugar, in a ratio of 1/1/1—and then there was nothing to do but take the damn trip.

"Otto Medrick?"

"Maybe."

"The O.J.'s going out of business."

Not a sound from the man under the black cloth. Dortmunder watched, and the black cloth seemed to tremble a little, but that was all. The guy must have heard; Dortmunder decided to wait him out.

What was he doing under that black cloth anyway, him and that wooden tripod standing under there with him? Dortmunder, having driven through mile after mile of suburban landscape among low flat-roofed houses full of glass—although what view did they have, except of each other?—had found 131–58 Elfin Drive with far less difficulty than he'd expected, thanks to the Web maps Kelp had conjured for him. He'd parked the little yellow Nissan Pixie on the shiny black driveway in front of the little avocado-and-pink house, identical except in color scheme to every other house in Coral Acres, had scrunched up the crushed-clamshell walk to the front door, and been just about to ring a doorbell when he'd realized he was looking completely through the house, through the living-dining room, through plate glass doors at the back there, and out to the parched backyard, where a bent-kneed man in gray work pants crouched next to a tall tripod under a black cloth draped over his head and upper body. So Dortmunder had walked around the house, delivered his news, and now waited for a response.

Which at last arrived: "Gimme a minute," snarled the man under the cloth.

"Sure."

Dortmunder waited some more, and something said *click* under the black cloth, and then at last it was lifted and the man beneath came out from under.

He was short; that was the first thing. He was short and gristly, with wiry gray arms extruded from an ancient gray sweatshirt—YWHA, ASTORIA—with its sleeves cut off. His head was beaked, with Brillo hair and a pointy pepper-and-salt goatee that looked sharp enough to do damage, so that all in all, he mostly resembled a pocket Lenin. Or maybe a collectible Lenin doll for your whatnot shelf, except that he also wore heavy, dark-framed eyeglasses jammed up onto his forehead.

Now he glared at Dortmunder, wriggled his brows, and those glasses dropped down to his nose, so he could see through them as he said, "And who the hell are *you?*"

"I'm a guy goes to the O.J. sometimes," Dortmunder said, "and I thought you oughta know what's happening there."

"I'm *here,*" Otto Medrick told him, "so I don't hafta know what's happening there, I got family looking after it."

"No, you don't," Dortmunder said. "Your nephew Raphael, I have to tell you the truth, I met him, and I don't think he could look after a pet rock."

"Yeah, you met him all right," Medrick agreed. "But there's the rest of the family, his mother, cousins by the dozens."

"Nobody," Dortmunder said. "Whatever they're supposed to be doing, they're busy doing something else."

"By God, that *sounds* like those useless sonsabitches," Medrick said, and peered all at once more closely into Dortmunder's face. "I bet," he said, "you're one a them back-room crooks."

Dortmunder blinked. "One a them what?"

"You know Rollo, my bartender."

"Naturally."

"For years," Medrick said, "he was my eyes and ears in that joint."

"Then," Dortmunder said, "he's gone blind and deaf."

"No, it's not him," Medrick said. "I told him, I'm outa here, let somebody else collect the tsouris. Rollo don't even have my phone number. So what's happening?"

"Raphael," Dortmunder told him, "turned control over to a guy named Mikey, whose father's a mob guy, who's busting it out."

Medrick thought hard, then said, "Remind me."

"Buy buy buy on the store's credit," Dortmunder explained, "everything from booze to cash registers. Use up the credit, then some night move everything out, sell it all someplace else, let the joint go bankrupt."

"*My* joint?"

"The O.J. Bar and Grill," Dortmunder agreed, "on Amsterdam Avenue."

"I know where it is!" Medrick squinted past Dortmunder at his house, thinking again, and then said, "What's your name?"

"John."

Now Medrick squinted at Dortmunder and slowly nod-

ded. "Could be true," he decided. "Come inside, it stinks out here."

It did. Following Medrick through the sliding glass door into the house, Dortmunder said, "What's with the tripod, anyway? If you don't mind my asking. And the black cloth."

Medrick gave him a surprised look as he slid the door closed, then nodded through its glass. "That's my camera," he said.

"It is?"

"I was doin a close-up," Medrick said, pointing at his small backyard, "that sundial back there."

"No kidding."

"I only count sunny hours," Medrick quoted, and shrugged. "Hah. Nice if you can get away with it. Come over and sit down. You want ice water?"

Not an offer you'd expect from a bar owner, but in fact, Dortmunder realized, he was thirsty, so he said, "Yeah, nice."

"Take a seat there," Medrick said, and waved a hand, and stumped away.

Dortmunder sat in a living room that was small, neat, and impersonal, as though Medrick had brought none of his possessions south with him but had started afresh, in discount stores. After a minute Medrick came back with two glasses of water, no ice, sat facing Dortmunder, said, "Use the coaster," and then said, "This isn't supposed to happen."

"You thought the family was gonna cover you."

"Years ago," Medrick said, "when the issue first come up, I told Jerry, whadawe want with a bar?"

"Jerome Hulve," Dortmunder said. "Your partner."

"Well, you do your homework," Medrick said, "What it was, for forty-two years I had a camera store on Broadway. Jerry was the dry cleaner next door. He's the one found this tavern was up for sale, got all its licenses, the bar and the fixtures all in place, the price is right, just open it up and that's it."

"I never saw you there."

"You never saw either of us there." Medrick shook his head. "I was reluctant to get into it, but I have to admit, up to now, Jerry was right. The place was never a big problem. On the other hand, it was never a big earner, either."

"It gets a lotta trade," Dortmunder suggested.

"If you call that trade." Medrick shrugged. "At the start," he said, "we thought we'd do a dinner business, it's a neighborhood, all apartments around there. We had waiters, cooks, silverware, the whole thing. Never happened. The *trade* we got, it was a bar trade."

"That's true."

"In all the years we had the place," Medrick said, "nobody has ever seen any of our customers eat."

"No, I haven't, either."

"But at least no trouble." Medrick made a disgusted face. "But now," he said, "if it all goes to hell, it doesn't just land on Raphael. That piece of paper between us, he still pays me off, I still got the responsibility. These mob guys, they're gonna what-you-say bust it, that comes to *my* doorstep. How'd you like it, a dozen New York City wholesalers, coming after you?"

"I wouldn't like it," Dortmunder said.

"These are guys," Medrick opined, "don't *want* you to return that deposit bottle, they got uses for that nickel. Florida is not far enough away, *Mars* is not far enough away, you stiff those guys, they'll eat your flesh, a little more every day."

"Then," Dortmunder said, "I think you gotta do something about it."

"I'm in Florida," Medrick pointed out. "Raphael is in cyberspace. What am I supposed to do?"

"I don't know things like that," Dortmunder said.

"I had a cat once," Medrick told him, "used to bring dead things into the house—this is after we moved out to the Island—she'd bring them to wherever I was, drop them at my feet. I'd say, 'Hey, what's this? I don't want no bloody corpse,' she'd give me a look: 'Not my problem.' Stroll back outside." Medrick lowered a dissatisfied brow in Dortmunder's direction. "Now," he said, "I wonder what made me think of Buttercup after all these years?"

Dortmunder said, "What would you do with the bodies?"

Medrick sighed, looked exasperated, looked at his watch, said, "Rollo, on a Sunday, he comes in at four. I used to have a home number for him, but I didn't bring it south. I can call him then, see what he says. You had lunch?"

Remembering the flight down, Dortmunder said, "No."

"I ate a little before twelve," Medrick said, "but I could have a soup with you."

"A little before twelve?"

"When you're very young or very old, you get to eat whenever the hell you feel like it, which, when you're very old, is just a little bit earlier every day. Six o'clock, five forty-five . . . I figure, the day you sit down to supper at four o'clock, that's God saying hello. Will that car of yours seat two?"

"Well," Dortmunder said, "you're short."

Medrick led him to a no-name eatery in a sprawling one-story half-empty mall where most of the parked cars were the largest Cadillacs made twelve years ago. Over lunch in which the only thing Dortmunder recognized was mashed potatoes, Medrick explained that he'd been a widower for six years— "Esther was a wonderful person until the end, when there was nothing good about it"—and he'd been in a relationship with a widow named Alma the last two and a half years. "We don't live together," he said, "we aren't gonna get married, but we hang out, we kanookie."

"How come you aren't gonna get married?"

"The government," Medrick said. "If you're on Social Security and you get married, it costs you actual money out of your benefits, so what you got down here, you got an entire state here of people, been upright citizens their entire lives, in their golden years they're living in sin, because the government's got these rules. The government. These are the same people talk about the sanctity of marriage." Medrick rubbed a thumb and forefinger together. "We know what sanctity they care about."

During dessert—key lime pie should sue for libel—Medrick explained about the camera in the backyard. Having spent all those years selling cameras and camera equipment, he finally got the shutterbug bug himself and started taking nature pictures around and about, figuring he'd found a hobby that would satisfy him for many years of retirement.

"Then came digital," he said, and shook a disgusted head. "What you got with digital, you got no highs and no lows. Everything's perfect, and everything's plastic. You see those Matthew Brady pictures from the Civil War? The Civil War! I'm talking a long time ago. You try to take those pictures with digital, you know what they're gonna look like?"

"No," Dortmunder admitted.

"Special effects in a Civil War movie," Medrick told him. "People look at it, they say, 'Wow, that's great, that's so life-like!' You know what is it, the difference between life and lifelike?"

"I think I do," Dortmunder said.

"Well, there's fewer and fewer of us. Digital finally drove me out of the business. I mean, I was gonna retire anyway, but digital made me go a few months early."

Which was why, in recoiling from the advances of photography, Medrick had bounced back farther and farther in time, until he had settled at last on his current choice, a 1904 8x10 Rochester Optical Peerless field camera, with the mahogany body, nickel trim, and black leather bellows.

"The negative is full-size," Medrick explained, "no enlargements, no loss of detail."

"Sounds great," said Dortmunder, who couldn't have cared less.

At the end of lunch Dortmunder somehow paid the entire tab, not entirely sure how that had happened, and then they went back to Medrick's place, where, for the next two and a half hours, Dortmunder lost at gin, at cribbage, and at Scrabble until, at five minutes past four—"Give him a chance to put on his apron," Medrick said, playing *pluckier* across the double-double—Medrick finally phoned the O.J.

"Rollo? Medrick. It's sunny, it's hot, whadaya want? Listen, I got one of your back-room guys here, he says some mob people are killing the place. Yeah . . . uh huh . . . yeah . . . uh huh . . . . yeah . . . uh huh . . . yeah . . . uh huh . . . yeah . . ."

Dortmunder was just about to stand and go out to the backyard to look at Medrick's camera for a few hours, when Medrick abruptly said, "Good-bye, Rollo," and hung up.

Dortmunder sat. He looked at Medrick, who turned a bleak gaze on him and said, "Rollo says, they're moving everything out tonight."

22

IT BEING AUGUST, when the big semi left Pittsburgh to get first up onto Interstate 79 north and then 80 east across Pennsylvania, it was still daylight, though already evening.

The cavernous trailer was empty, but the interstate was a solid road, even through the Appalachian Mountains, so the trailer did very little bouncing around. The driver, alone in the cab, a big-shouldered guy in white T-shirt and black baseball cap worn frontward, kept the cruise control at a steady eight miles an hour above the speed limit and sat there at his ease, listening to one country music radio station after another as he rolled across the state. From time to time, the setting sun gave him photographs of itself in his rearview mirror, and traffic was moderate.

By the time the semi reached the New Jersey border, darkness had long since descended, and the traffic, less than one hundred miles from New York City, was considerably heavier, but for the most part the driver could still let cruise control do all the work. A country station out of Bergen, New Jersey, announced midnight, and not long after that he took the George Washington Bridge across the Hudson River into upper Manhattan, where the easy part stopped.

Big trucks weren't allowed on the through roads in the city, so he had to steer and shift and turn and brake and angle and maneuver and in various ways work his ass off just to get off Interstate 95 and down onto Broadway at 168th Street.

From here the route was straight and simple, but not easy. The driver, who drove big trucks for a living but almost never in major cities, hated Manhattan, as all drivers of big trucks do. Every fifteen inches another traffic light, so you haven't even finished shifting up through the gears when it's time to hit the brakes again.

Also, no matter what the hour of day or night, there was always traffic everywhere in New York City, darting cabs and snarling delivery vans and even aggressive suburbanites in their Suburbanites. Unlike normal parts of the world, where other drivers showed a healthy respect tending toward fear when in the presence of the big trucks, New York City drivers practically dared him to start something. They'd cut him off; they'd crowd him; they'd even go so far as to blat their horns at him. The people operating small vehicles in New York, the driver thought, drove as though they all had a lawyer in the backseat.

Slowly, painfully, bit by bit, the driver lugged his trailer, which now did bounce around like a roulette ball on the pot-holed city streets, southwestward down the long esophagus of Manhattan, staying on Broadway all the way till Ninety-sixth Street—by then it was almost two in the morning, but there was still too much traffic on the city streets—where he took the left turn to go one long block over to Amsterdam Avenue. The right onto Amsterdam wasn't so hard, and the street was a little better, being one-way.

Down Amsterdam he went, able to keep his up-and-down shifting to a minimum because of the staggered lights. He was grateful for that, and for the fact that the streetlights were bright enough to show him the numbers of the cross streets. And there was his goal, lit up but not gaudy, just ahead on the right.

When he hit the brakes while engaged in city driving, the truck tended to emit a sound very like a hippopotamus farting, which it did this time, which alerted the people loitering on the sidewalk down there that he was the one they were waiting for.

He stopped, in the right lane, just uptown from them, to let them clear the way. During the daytime, there was no parking along here, but this evening, as soon as that restriction was lifted, these people had put three cars in place, to be sure he'd have the proper location available to him at the curb. Now three guys among the loiterers, with waves of the hand toward the driver, hopped into these cars and drove off, and he slid the truck neatly into the opening they'd provided. The three cars all went around the block to find someplace else to roost, and the driver switched off his engine, opened his door, and felt unair-conditioned air for the first time since Pittsburgh. Yuck.

Well, this shouldn't take long. He climbed down to the street, hitched his belt, worked his neck muscles a little, and walked around the front of the truck to the group of guys clustered on the sidewalk—about a dozen of them, mostly muscle to carry the goods out of the bar and into the truck, but among them was supposed to be a guy in charge.

"I need somebody named Mikey," the driver said.

"That's me," said a cocky bantamweight featuring so much lush, oiled, wavy black hair lifting over his ears to undulate back around his head that he looked as if he were wearing Mercury's winged helmet. What he was in fact wearing, though it was quite hot and humid out here tonight, was a black satin unzipped warmup jacket with

MIKEY in gold script over his heart and, for those who cared to walk around him and read it, EAT ME WORLD TOUR in various bright colors on the back. Under the jacket was a white T-shirt, while ironed designer jeans and huge white sneakers completed the ensemble.

The driver nodded at this Mikey, unsurprised, and gestured at his truck, saying, "It's all yours, I'll just open up the back and maybe go grab me a late-night snack somewheres and—"

"Say, pal," one of the other locals said, "your truck is movin'."

"What?" Thinking in-gear, brake-on, engine-off, not-my-fault, the driver turned, and by God, the truck *was* moving. In fact, it was accelerating, hustling away from the curb and on down Amsterdam Avenue.

"Hey!" the driver yelled, but the truck ignored him and just kept moving farther and farther away.

Two or three of Mikey's associates ran after the truck, trying to grab a door handle or a rearview mirror or *something,* but without success. One guy did manage to clutch the hasp lock on the truck's rear doors, but the truck was already moving faster than he could run, so he simply fell down in the street and was dragged along until he decided to let go, which was soon.

Meanwhile, Mikey was yelling at the driver, "Who *is* that?" and the driver was yelling back, "Who's *what*? I'm alone in the truck!" Then, seeing the traffic light red at the next intersection, and the truck still accelerating directly at it, he screamed, "Not through the red light!" Which the truck also ignored.

Traffic was finally light at this hour on a Sunday night, and in one of those miracles you shouldn't go through life counting on, there were no vehicles rushing out of the cross street to cream themselves against the side of the truck at that particular instant, only a panel truck delivering tomorrow morning's *New York Post,* and of course those trucks never travel at more than seven miles an hour—union rules—so its operator had plenty of time to stop, to honk, and to deliver, loudly, a monograph on the encroaching miscreant's pedigree.

The three guys who'd taken their cars away were just then returning, but as Mikey screamed at them they reversed and ran off again to get the cars back, while two other guys ran to the little red Audi 900 parked behind where the driver had placed his truck, and Mikey shrieked, "After it! Get it! Get that guy! Get that truck!"—all of which was unnecessary, because that's what they were all doing.

"For cryin out loud," the driver said. "They'll steal *anything* in New York."

One of the few guys still standing around, not running hither and yon, gave the driver a New York look. "You wanna make a comment?"

"Not me," said the driver, and a large black SUV, a Chrysler Town & Country LX, raced past, headed down Amsterdam Avenue. The driver had time to notice that the Chrysler had doctor's license plates, that it was being driven much faster than most doctor-operated vehicles, and that the traffic light was still red at that intersection down there, although *just* as the Chrysler arrived and the *New York Post* delivery truck finally cleared out of the way, the light snapped green and the Chrysler tore on through, only then hitting its brakes.

So did the truck, by now almost to the next corner. All those red brake lights flashed on down there, and now the red Audi leaped away from the curb in pursuit.

But the truck was stopping, and so was the Chrysler, right next to it. Whoever was driving the truck now jumped out of it to get into the front passenger seat in the Chrysler, while the Chrysler's right-side rear door slid back to open and a truly huge man-monster climbed out, carrying an axe.

"Holy Toledo!" the driver cried, as the huge man swung the axe twice at the nearest tires on the left rear of the truck, making two sharp reports very much like gunfire. He then turned to heave the axe at the fast-approaching Audi.

To avoid getting an axe through the windshield, the Audi veered into the rear of the truck as the man-monster climbed back into the Chrysler, which immediately hustled around the corner and out of sight, so that when the three cars that had earlier gone away came screaming back around the block, there was nothing to be seen but a disabled truck and, tucked under its tail, an Audi, starting to smoke though not yet to burn, while the two guys who had been in the Audi now kept trying to run away from it but spent most of their time falling down.

The driver and Mikey and some others walked the block and a half to the truck and the Audi, but as they neared the mess, the Audi did start to burn. Stopping, the driver said, "You know, when a car catches fire, what usually kinda happens next is the gas tank blows."

"He's right, Mikey," said one of the others.

So they all turned around and walked the other way, toward the closed but not empty O.J. Bar & Grill. As they walked, the driver said, "You know what this means, I hope."

Now it was Mikey who gave him the New York look. "Tell me, pal," he said.

"This means," the driver assured him, "a whole shitpot of overtime."

23

"I SWITCHED YOUR seat," Medrick said.

At seven-fifteen in the morning, Dortmunder wasn't ready for trick questions like that. "Into what?" he said.

"Another seat." Medrick seemed as bright-eyed and alert at this awful hour as he had while board-gaming Dortmunder into the ground all afternoon yesterday. "I was awake all night thinking about it," he explained, "and now I know what to do. So I need a seat with a phone, and I need you in the seat next to me. So now you got an aisle—"

"I like an aisle," Dortmunder said. He remembered that much, even at an hour like this.

"Well, you got one, and I got the middle, and that's where the phone is."

"Who's got the window?"

"Who knows? Who cares? For two hours and ten minutes, we can put up with it."

"If you say so."

They were on the line at that moment for security inspection, strung along with a whole lot of sleepy, grumpy, badly dressed, overweight people who were traveling even though, from the look of them, nobody would be very happy to see them at the other end. "The plane's gonna be full," Dortmunder said.

"They're all full," Medrick assured him. "Everybody wants to be somewhere he's not, and as soon as he gets there he wants to go home."

"Even when I'm home," Dortmunder told him, "I want to go home."

"When we get through security," Medrick suggested, "we'll have a cup of coffee."

"Probably," Dortmunder said, "I'll be able to find my mouth by then."

The uniformed fat woman at security immediately regretted demanding that Dortmunder remove his shoes; he could tell she did, but she was too professional—or maybe just too stunned—to let it show. With that little triumph over the Security League of the Air behind him, he joined Medrick at a too-small table in an overcrowded franchise, for a cup of rotten coffee, and Medrick said, "I blame smoke signals."

"Uh huh," Dortmunder said.

"For where we are now, I mean."

"Uh huh," Dortmunder said. At this hour, he was prepared just to let the whole shebang slide on over him.

But Medrick had a point and intended to pursue it. "It's communications technologies that did us in," he said. "Now you got your Internet, before that your television, your radio, your newspapers, your telephone, your signal flags, your telegrams, your letters in the mailbox, but it all goes back to smoke signals, the whole problem starts right there."

"Sure," Dortmunder said.

Medrick shook his head. "But," he said, "I just don't think society's ready to go back that far."

"Probably not," Dortmunder said, and yawned. Maybe he could drink the coffee.

"But that's what it would take," Medrick insisted, "to return some shred of honesty to this world."

Dortmunder put down his coffee mug. "Is that what we're trying for?" he asked.

"Right just this minute it is," Medrick told him. "You see, with smoke signals, that was the very first time in the whole history of the human race that you could tell somebody something that he couldn't see you when you told him. You get what I mean?"

"No," Dortmunder said.

"Before smoke signals," Medrick said, "I wanna tell you something, I gotta come over to where you are, and stand in front of you, and *tell* you. Like I'm doing now. And you get to look at my face, listen to how I talk, read my body language, decide for yourself, is this guy trying to pull a fast one. You get it?"

"Eye contact."

"Exactly," Medrick said. "Sure, people still lied to each other back then and got away with it, but it wasn't so easy. Once smoke signals came in, you can't see the guy telling you the story, he could be laughing behind his hand, you don't know it."

"I guess that's true," Dortmunder agreed.

"Every step up along the way," Medrick said, "every other kind of way to communicate, it's always behind the other guy's back. For thousands of years, we've been building ourselves a liar's paradise. That's why the video phones weren't the big hit they were supposed to be, nobody wants to go back to the eyeball."

"I guess not."

"So that means they'll *never* get rid of the rest of it," Medrick concluded. "All the way back to smoke signals."

"I don't think they use those so much any more," Dortmunder said.

"If they did," Medrick said darkly, "they'd lie."

"Seating rows six forty-three to six fifty-two," said the announcement, so they boarded the damn plane.

Their third seatmate, next to the window over beyond Medrick, turned out to be okay, a very neat little old lady who put her own robin's egg blue Samsonite bag in the overhead rack, tucked her worn old black leather shoulderbag under the seat in front of her, kicked off her shoes, and opened a paperback novel by Barbara Pym, which she then proceeded to read with such intensity you'd think there was going to be a test on it when the plane reached Newark.

All Dortmunder wanted was the experience over with. He strapped himself in as though this were the electric chair and he'd just received word the governor was on the golf course, closed his eyes to pretend he was unconscious, experienced the rinse cycle of the plane taking off, listened to the announcements even though he knew in his heart he would never willingly associate himself with a flotation device, and at last the stew, who'd warned them ahead of time about futzing around with electronics during takeoff and landing, said, "Electronic equipment may now be used," and Medrick said, "Good."

Dortmunder opened his eyes. The phone was a neat gray plastic hotdog inset in the back of the middle seat ahead. Medrick yanked it out, did some credit card stuff, then did some dialing stuff, and then said, "Frank? Otto. It's nine-seventeen in the morning—what, you don't have any clocks on Long Island? I'm calling you about your son. Well, Frank, I'm in an airplane and I'm headed for Newark, which is not what I had planned for today, but while you been looking

around for a clock the last four months your boy Raphael
has been robbing me blind. Of course he wouldn't do that,
and in fact— Frank, I know he's a good boy, and the reason
I know he's a good boy, same as you know he's a good boy,
is, he's too stupid to be anything else. Now, listen to me,
Frank, I'm not blaming you, and I'm not blaming Maureen,
you and me got the same genes inside us, so if there's moon-
child genes floating around inside Raphael, which you
damn well know there is, they're just as likely to come from
our side of the family as hers."

Medrick listened for a minute, nodding impatiently,
while a whole lot of nothing went by outside the window,
past the Barbara Pym fan, and the stews started serving the
beverage from the other end of the plane. Then Medrick
said, "I wouldn't be giving you tsouris, Frank, but the fact
is, the O.J. is gonna go into bankruptcy in like fifteen minutes unless we do something about it, and *I* happen to be in
this airplane, and *you* happen to be on the ground, so what
you can do— All right, I'll tell you what's going on.
Raphael hooked up with some Jersey kid that's mobbed up
or something, and he turned over running the joint to that
kid, and now the kid—"

More pause. More impatient nodding. Then Medrick
said, "I don't doubt that, Frank, Casper the Friendly Ghost
is probably a better businessman than Raphael, but there's
businessmen and businessmen, and what *this* businessman is
doing, he's bleeding the joint white. If you'll listen to me,
Frank, I'll tell you how he's doing it. He's using up the corporation's credit, he's buying stuff, not paying for it, he's
gonna strip it all out, sell it to somebody else, walk away.
Wait."

Medrick shook his head. Turning to Dortmunder, he
said, "Like what is he buying?"

"Well, I happened to notice, four cash registers."

Medrick blinked. "Four cash registers?"

"They're all in the back room."

Into the phone, Medrick said, "Four cash registers, Frank, all in the back room."

"Maybe thirty barstools."

"Maybe thirty barstools."

"Already," Dortmunder said, "they took out a lot of French champagne and Russian vodka for a wedding."

Medrick, phone pressed to the side of his head, turned that head to give Dortmunder an outraged look: "A wedding? Now I'm paying for a wedding?"

"Looks like."

Into the phone, Medrick said, "Thank you, Frank, I'm glad you asked me. So I'll tell you what I want from you. Remember the phony doctor they made Raphael go to when he was on probation? Leadass, that's right, the psychiaquack, Oh, Led*vass,* I beg your pardon, Ledvass the distinguished nut doctor. Call him, Frank, call him now, you'll get an answering service, tell them it's an emergency, when Leadass calls back you—I know, Frank—you tell him the diagnosis, and the diagnosis is delusions of grandeur, it's making him buy things he's got no use for, and for his own protection you want Leadass should commit Raphael *today,* so when I get off this plane—"

"Hurray," Dortmunder said.

"—I can go to all the vendors been unloading this stuff on the O.J., whado *they* care, I can say, take it all back, you been selling to a fellow mentally deficient, here's the commitment papers. You've got keys to the place, Frank, after you talk to Leadass go there— Frank, you want me to be your dependent? If the O.J. goes down, Frank, I've got nothing but what the government gives me, I got no choice, I'm moving in with you and Maureen."

Dortmunder noticed that several people in nearby seats

were openly staring by now, and it seemed to him at least one of them had brought out an audio recording thing, though with the usual airplane background garble it was unlikely he'd wind up with anything he could bring into court. Anyway, the Barbara Pym lady was still deep in her book, and if Medrick didn't care how the whole world knew his business, what skin was it off Dortmunder's nose?

Now Medrick was saying, "So you're going to the O.J., you'll look at all this stuff piled up in there, you'll find the paperwork, receipts, vouchers, invoices, whatever, with all of that you and Leadass can get Raphael committed, and I mean *today*, I want him inside from now until we get this whole mess straightened out. Frank, it's okay, don't apologize, I understand, we're all busy, like you say. Well, not me, in Florida we're not what you could call *busy*, but I know you are, and Maureen is, and everybody on Long Island is, and I'm glad you're taking this seriously, Frank, because it is serious, and— No, no, Frank, forget that, don't worry about it, just save me the O.J., and that's where I'm going just as soon as I get off this plane—"

"Hurray."

"—and I'm bringing with me this back-room crook that—"

"Hey."

"—told me about it, he's the one rescued the O.J., if in fact we're getting it in time, we owe him a debt of gratitude, I'll see you at the O.J. before one."

With a certain savage satisfaction, Medrick slammed the phone back into its cave. Ignoring the cry of pain from the seat in front, he said, "Oh-kay."

"Beverage?" asked the stew.

"Yes," said Dortmunder.

"I will have a frosty beer," Medrick said.

"Me, too," said Dortmunder.

"A Bloody Mary for me," said the Barbara Pym lady. Smiling sweetly at Dortmunder and Medrick, she said, "It's called a bust-out joint, and I hope you pin those cocksuckers good."

24

BIG JOSÉ AND Little José, as the most recent security hires at the Imperiatum apartment house at Fifth Avenue and Sixty-eighth Street, got all the drudgery. They were the ones who had to carry Mrs. Windbom's groceries from the lobby to her apartment, since she was afraid the supermarket's delivery boys would rape her. It was they who periodically checked the anti-pigeon electric tapes on the roof, and who carried to its separate disposal bin the hazmat materials from the two doctors' offices with their own street-level building entrances around on the Sixty-eighth street side, and who walked the two stairways once a week in search of blown lightbulbs or other anomalies. And twice a month they did a security sweep of Penthouse A.

Monday, August 16, ten a.m. Big José wrote *P-A sweep* in the security office logbook, and he and Little José rode the elevator to the top. The uniformed elevator operator this trip was a surly Serb named Marko, who saved his smiles and chitchat for the tenants, so on the way up, the two Josés continued in Spanish their lies about their sexual conquests over the weekend, ignoring Marko, who just as thoroughly but more silently ignored them right back.

Penthouse A was empty yet full, vacant yet occupied. The owner was some rich guy named Fareweather who was out of the country somewhere, and had been out of the country for so long that neither of the Josés had yet been hired for this job the last time Fareweather had been in residence. Imagine, a guy so rich he can own a huge penthouse on top of a big, rich building on Fifth Avenue in Manhattan and not even live in it. Not even sublet. Not even have a cousin in to house-sit.

Since on the top floor of the building this elevator only served Penthouse A, it opened not into a public hall but into a small reception room with white marble floor, Empire chairs, twisty-legged little occasional tables, and four Picassos on the walls. Pocket doors, always kept open by the Josés, led to the main living room beyond—a huge space with big, bright windows straight ahead and to the right, to give views of Manhattan and the park as though you were in a low-flying plane.

From the Persian carpets through the plushly antique furniture and the marble statues on pedestals and the old masters in massive dark frames all the way to the elaborate plaster moldings on the ceiling, this living room screamed money and luxury and comfort. Big José had been known, at slow moments, to come up and nap on that eight-foot-long golden sofa; Little José would beep him if a problem came up.

Anyway, the security sweep was not the time to stretch out on any sofas. For the next two hours, as they did twice every month, they went through a standard routine. They checked to be sure that the refrigerator, empty but running, was still doing its job, with trays of ice cubes waiting in the freezer. They flushed the toilets and ran water in the sinks in all four bathrooms, they made sure all the windows were still firmly shut and locked, they verified that the two alarm systems—a simple electric eye for the entrance from the elevator, a more complicated motion sensor in the long corridor down the apartment's north side, with its doors opening onto the south-facing bedrooms—were both working properly, and they saw to it that the two fireplaces, in living room and master bedroom, had not let in any dirt or rodents and that the flues were still properly shut. Also, they checked that the answering machine was still functioning, responding to any callers but also letting those callers know that no messages would be taken.

There were two bars in the apartment, one off the living room and the other at the far end of the place, next to a kitchen big enough for a hotel, with the equipment to match. There was hard liquor in both bars, though no wine or mixers. The Josés knew better than to tap into that supply, and in fact they weren't even tempted. This job was too good and too easy and too low-stress to risk.

Steadily they made their way through the apartment, which they figured they must know by now better than the actual owner did. The master bedroom was full of the missing master's clothes: a dozen expensive suits ranging from dark blue to light gray, drawers of shirts and sweaters, racks of neckties. Trying on some of the nicer pieces, they came to the conclusion that Fareweather was shorter than Big José, taller than Little José, and fatter than either of them. Also, there was not much by way of casual wear. If the guy played golf, either he did it in a suit or he'd carried his golf stuff with him when he left.

The other bedrooms were obviously all for guests, not live-ins, though the owner did treat those guests very well, if he'd ever had any. Wrapped toothbrushes in the bathrooms, white terry-cloth robes and backless slippers in the closets. All of the beds were kept made, with an extra-large sheet over each to catch dust; the cleaning crew that came in twice a month must change those from time to time.

At the very rear of the vast apartment, past the kitchen and next to the small but completely equipped bar back there, was another entrance, never used. Or at least never used when Fareweather wasn't around. This was an ordinary door that looked like a closet door, except that it had a small rectangular window in it at eye level, at Big José's eye level, that is. He'd shone his flashlight in there one time and had seen a small, dark squarish space with what looked like grimy metal walls, and thick black cables hanging down in the middle. It had taken him a minute to figure out that he was looking at an elevator shaft. At the top of the shaft, that is—angling the flashlight beam upward, he could just see the bottom of the big metal wheel up there with the cable wrapping around it.

So this was some private entrance of Fareweather's, not used by anybody else. What was clearly the button to summon the elevator was mounted discreetly in the wall near the doorknob, but when Big José experimentally gave it a push, nothing happened, so it must be shut off while the boss was gone. But he would use it, all right. That's why there were an extra two alarm keypads next to that button, matching the keypads beside the elevator up front.

The Josés had no idea where the elevator went, but occasionally would make up salacious stories about it anyway. Even though they had not yet seen doors to that elevator in any of the other apartments they'd entered in the course of their duty, which was nearly half of them by now, they liked to tell each other that Fareweather used to sneak down in his private elevator to 4-C, where that hot television newswoman lived with her rich fashion designer husband that anybody could see with half an eye wasn't straight.

Or maybe there was a Batcave in the basement, and back in the old days off he'd go, late at night, to fight crime. But if so, where were his capes? You don't take your capes along on vacation.

Anyway, among the grunge duties the Josés were handed on account of being the newbies around here, the twice-monthly sweep of Penthouse A was certainly the easiest. Finished again today, they buzzed for the regular elevator, and both of them hoped the bad-tempered Marko would be on his break by now, replaced by Teresa, fat and too black, but at least with a sense of humor. You could kid around with her.

Thinking about what they might say if it did turn out to be Teresa running the elevator, trying to remember some good dirty jokes they might have heard recently, they looked back through the open pocket doors at what had to be one of the premier living rooms in all of New York City. And to think that man stayed away from it for years at a time. Good. Let him stay away forever. Big José and Little José—*they* lived here now, as much as anybody. And no reason to change.

The elevator door opened, and they turned away from the view of their living room. "Hey, Teresa! Listen, you hear about the Russian lady and the dog?"

25

H OWIE CARBINE, CAPO of southeast Morris County, New Jersey, part-owner of several restaurant chains—Grandmamama's Fish 'n' Fillet, six outlets, New Jersey; Salty Pete's Sea-tacular, four outlets, Staten Island; Leaning Tower of Pizza and Pasta, seven outlets, Queens and Brooklyn; many more—sat at his kitchen island in his very nice if slightly gaudy McMansion, dressed in bathrobe and slippers and peach jockey shorts, and scoffed down some Cap'n Crunch with half-and-half. He looked over to watch as down the stairs from all the bedrooms above came Mikey, fourth of his five sons and, if truth be told, not the brightest apple on the tree. "So," said the father, "how'd it go last night?"

"It didn't," muttered Mikey. He'd been born sullen, he would die sullen, and he was doing a whole lot of sullen in between.

Howie paused with a spoonload of Cap'n halfway to his mouth. "It didn't go? Didn't the fuckin truck show up?"

"The fuckin truck showed up," Mikey said, as he poured Froot Loops into a bowl and came to join his father at the island. He was dressed in shiny black swimming trunks with red flames coming out of the crotch, and a gray sweatshirt that read NYPD in blue.

The father waited, but the son merely loaded up with some Froot Loops and glowered at the countertop, so at last the father said, "So? What happened?"

"The fuckin truck showed up," Mikey said, speaking through pastel pieces of grain, "but then somebody fuckin wrecked it."

"Fuckin wrecked it? What, the fuckin driver was drunk?"

"It wasn't the fuckin *driver*," Mikey complained, taking on more pastels. "He got outa the fuckin truck, some *other* fuckin guy got into it, drove it the fuck off. We never even got a look at the fuckin guy."

"Drove the fuckin truck *off*?"

"Ran it two fuckin blocks," Mikey explained. "We're racin the fuck after it, you know we are. Then this *other* fuckin guy shows up, some other fuckin car, gets out with a fuckin axe, takes the fuckin axe to the fuckin tires, cuts them all to fuck."

"And what are you fuckin guys doin?" demanded the father. "Standin around with your fuckin thumbs up your fuckin asses?"

"Nicky and Petey went after them in the Audi," Mikey said, "but then this monster fuckin guy with the axe, he *throws* the axe at Nicky and Petey in the Audi, and the Audi rams into the back of the fuckin truck and the whole thing goes up in fuckin flames."

"Anybody killed?"

"No, everybody got out."

"Too fuckin bad. And these other guys, these fucks, they got right away from there? You never got any idea who they were?"

"Not a fuckin clue," Mikey said. "Unless it was Pauly and

Ricky and Vinny and Carly, tryin some kinda fuckin mind game on me."

Howie pointed his milk-dripping spoon at his number four son: "Your brothers got fuckin orders from me: lay the fuck off. They know, Mikey, this is important to you."

"Fuck, a course it is."

"It's your own operation," Howie told him. "You conceived it and you're runnin it yourself, and nobody's gonna fuck with you. All right? You hear me? Nobody's gonna fuck with *your* operation, take it from me."

"Well, yeah, but, what the fuck," Mikey mewed, "somebody *did* fuck with my operation, they fucked with my operation last night, and now those fucks out in Pennsylvania are pissed off, they blame *me* for the fuckin truck, they say they can't get some other fuckin truck here until Wednesday, and now, because of the insurance and the cops, they gotta make up some manifests, what the fuck was this truck supposed to be anyway and how come it was in New York on Amsterdam Avenue at two o'clock in the fuckin morning. Meantime, my fuckin customers in Ohio, they're pissed off, too, and that was the best part of the whole fuckin plan, I've got my middlemen in fuckin Pittsburgh, for Christ's sake, I've got my end buyer in Akron, nobody's ever gonna find this shit or trace this shit, and I'm sittin pretty on nothin but fuckin profit."

"With a little slice over here," the father said.

"Well, sure," Mikey said, "naturally a little slice over there, I know how the world works, you didn't make yourself my old man for nothing."

"I'm glad to hear it."

"Only now," Mikey said, "we got these three extra fuckin days to wait, the fuckin bar's supposed to be padlocked by now, but I can't do it, the fuckin goods are still in there. We squeezed the fuckin customers out, but we still got the shit, stacked up all over the fuckin place in there."

"What about the owner?"

"What, Raphael?" Mikey offered a scornful laugh. "He don't know shit from green soup," he announced. "He's off there in some Dumb Fuck, Queens, with his head full of this faggy fuckin music, when it's all the fuck over, he *still* won't know what the fuck happened." Mikey shook his head. "I don't know what went on last night," he said, "I don't know who the fuck or what the fuck, and I'd like to know, but one thing for sure, Raphael Medrick I don't got to worry about."

26

RAPHAEL VERY SLIGHTLY lowered the speed of tape number two, and the Tibetan temple bells took on a fogbound aura, mournful tolling lost in a gray swirl of nothingness, and a shadow moved across the table.

Oh, not again. Were those four people back? I will not permit distraction, Raphael promised himself. This is a critical moment, a critical—

Was he going to get pinged again? The memory of the large man returned to him, that finger cocked, then fired, ricocheting off Raphael's skull. Through the clouded temple bells, he could almost hear again that painful ache in his head. Should he give it up for now and hope to get back to *Voyij* once the four had left, hope he was still at that point in the zone? What a shame.

A balloon face appeared, very close, coming in like a dirigible from the right. It was sideways; it was smiling; it was speaking; its glasses were starting to drop off its head; it was female—

It was his mother.

"Hiy!" cried Raphael, recoiling. But it wasn't as though he'd sprung back; it was as though that dirigible had abruptly receded, still smiling, still talking, becoming somewhat smaller but also regaining its body, bent sideways in a pretzel shape over his table, dressed in a high-neck white blouse and loose golden slacks, twisting down to get that balloon into Raphael's line of sight.

Raphael's bounce had taken him, on his castered chair, immediately to the limit of the cord attaching his earphones to his editing equipment, which gave him an immediate choice: reverse, or lose your ears. Meanwhile, his mother was definitely losing her glasses, and then, in an effort to grab them before they hit his control panel, her balance.

Mother and son did quick, separate dances of survival, and then stopped, she with her glasses on, he with his earphones off. "Ma!" he cried, shutting everything down with both flailing hands. "What are *you* doing here? What are you doing *here*?"

Because his mother had never set foot in this house before. No member of his family had ever set foot here, or even close to here. This was his retreat, his nest, his safety net. But now, his mother. Here?

Wildly staring around, still shutting things down, not waiting for an answer to his first two questions, he stammered, "I was about to sweep, uh, laundry, I figured tonight I'd get, uh . . ."

"Raphael."

"It isn't always like this, Ma, I've been working very—"

"Raphael."

"A lot of times the place looks just like any—"

"Raphael, I've come to get you, dear."

He blinked. "Get me?"

"You'll want to dress nicely," she said.

He gaped at her, trying to understand what she was talking about, trying to read her mind, but of course that was doomed to failure, because of the smiley face.

Raphael's mother always smiled, day and night, in sickness and in health, in warm sun or wintry blast, stuck in a traffic jam or just sailing along. Apparently, she'd started taking the medication for stress way back when she was carrying Raphael, and somehow had never quite stopped taking it, and quite obviously was still taking it today.

There had been times in Raphael's childhood when he had envied the other kids he knew whose mothers lost it, went ape, freaked out, dissolved into bitter tears, screamingly accused their children of everything from leaving the toilet lid up to attempted matricide, threw things, slammed doors, drank before lunch. There was none of that at Raphael's mother's house. In her house, everything was serene.

And now she was here, in his house, talking about "getting" him, talking about "dressing nicely." The way he dressed, in fact, was so that he wouldn't feel his clothes and wouldn't be distracted by them. He *liked* his loose T-shirt and baggy shorts. What could be nicer than that?

The question he asked, though, was slightly other: "Why do I have to dress nice?"

"Because you're going to court, dear. Come along," she said. "Your father is waiting in the car. He's afraid people will steal it. This is not a very nice neighborhood. Come along, Raphael."

"Court?" He'd said that word three or four times, while his mother had just kept calmly speaking on, and when at last she finished, he said it again: "Court? Why? What court?"

"Well, it's all to do with your uncle Otto's bar," she told him. "*You* know the one, you're taking care of it now that Uncle Otto lives in Florida."

"Everything's fine there," he said, but he did feel a moment of queasiness, thinking again about those four people.

They'd been here because of something to do with that bar, too. Oh, why couldn't the O.J. just go out of business and leave Raphael Medrick alone?

Meanwhile, his mother smiled and said, "Well, there does seem to be a little problem, dear, and Uncle Otto has flown up from Florida to do something about it. As I understand it, if this problem with the bar doesn't get fixed, your Uncle Otto will have to stay up here and not go back to Florida, and move in with your father and me."

"Why would he do that?" I'm not frightened, Raphael assured himself. There's nothing really wrong.

"Let's hope he doesn't have to," his mother said. "So, to help, *your* job is to go to this court and explain everything to the judge."

"What judge?"

Ignoring that, she said, "And remember that nice Doctor Ledvass, from when you were on probation? He'll be there, too, and he'll help you with the questions."

"Doctor Ledvass?" A droning, yawning, boring man, who'd been assigned by that other court, and couldn't have cared less about Raphael, and was only doing it for the money, and made no bones about it. He and Raphael had come to an understanding of mutual disinterest at once. Why would *he* come to help?

There was something wrong here. "I don't want to go," Raphael said.

"Oh, dear, darling," she said, but the smile never faltered. "If you won't go, they'll just send state police officers to come and take you there, and that might make the judge think you had something to hide or you didn't want to help or I don't know *what* judges like that think, but you'd better come along with your father and me."

Raphael looked mournfully at his equipment. "I'm in the middle of something here."

"Oh, it'll keep, dear, don't you worry, everything will be just fine. Now, let's not keep your father waiting, dear, go get dressed. As nicely as you can, dear. Socks, if you have them."

"Sure I've got socks," he said.

"Oh, good. Put them on. Go on, dear."

Reluctant but unable to refuse, he got to his feet and padded barefoot toward his bedroom, and his mother called after him, "And bring your toothbrush, dear."

He looked back at her. "Bring my toothbrush? To court?"

"Oh, just to be on the safe side, dear," she said, and gave him the most reassuring smile in the world.

27

AFTER A NOONER with the limber Pam, Preston and she showered together, lathering the oddest places, then dressed minimally in his cool, dim room, in preparation for lunch.

As another preparation for lunch, Preston slipped into his shorts pocket the fart buzzer he intended to place on her chair in the dining hall, the first of the jollities with which he intended to test this new one through the week. He certainly hoped that, like most of the women down here, she would condone and accept his little jokes by keeping her mind firmly fixed on his bank accounts, so that he would have a free hand to plague her at the same time that he would be taking pleasure from her in the more normal way. He did hope she'd react the way most of them did, because in fact he quite liked Pam, especially physically.

But then, as they were about to leave for the dining hall, Pam already in her big, sweeping straw hat and deep sunglasses, she said, "Honestly, Pres, I'm not the slightest bit hungry. You go ahead, I think I'll go for a sail."

Preston stared at her, not believing it. "Not hungry? How could you be not hungry? *I've* just worked up an enormous appetite."

"I'm glad," she said, with that contented-cat smile and purr. "Myself, I just feel like stretching, laaazily stretching in the sun, on one of those little sailboats. I'll see you for drinks, shall I?"

"Yes, of course," he said, keeping disappointment out of his voice. A fart buzzer was less effective in a bar setting, less disgusting somehow. Well, he had other tricks.

They stepped out to the shaded walk, the soft air, the yet-another beautiful day. "Later, my darling," she said, and smiled, and turned away, with all those wonderfully padded joints moving in all those wonderfully complex ways. They were such marvelous *machines,* women; pity about the brains.

But then she turned back: "Why not come along?"

He actually didn't understand her: "Come where?"

"For a sail. It's wonderful, Pres, you'll love it."

"Oh, I don't think so," he said. He knew there were those among the guests on this island who from time to time went offshore, in sailboats, or snorkeling expeditions, or little jaunts in the glass-bottom boat, or even scuba diving, but he was not among their number. Since his arrival on this island, he had not once so much as set foot off it. If his body insisted on a swim, there was the pool, non-salt and heated. Sailing and those other boat things held no fascination for him at all.

"I'll just wander hither and thither," he told this one, "thinking about our rendezvous this evening."

"So will I, on my little boat," she told him. "Rocking slowly up and down, on my little boat. You'd be astonished at the movements those little boats deliver, Pres, *very* different from a waterbed, *much* more erotic."

"In front of the boatman?"

Her smile turned quite lascivious. "They know when to

go for a little swim, Pres," she said. "If you ever change your mind, be sure to tell me."

"Oh, I shall."

"Ta," she said, with a little wave, and walked off, all her parts in gentle, persistent pulsation. He watched her go, admiring the look of her, but at the same time sorrowing for the poor fart buzzer, bereft in his pocket.

Alan Pinkleton shared his lunch instead. There was no point playing fart buzzer with a paid companion, so the simple humor machine remained in Preston's pocket as he collected food from the serving tables and joined Alan at a half-occupied table. Lunch was always the least-attended meal, since so many of the residents were off doing physical things here and there around the island.

Preston settled himself and his tray, settled his napkin onto his lap, and said, "A good afternoon to you, Alan. Did you have a lovely morning?"

"No," Alan said. He seemed out of sorts. "I can't find her," he said.

Polite, Preston raised an eyebrow. "Can't find whom?"

"Your new one," Alan said. "This Pamela Broussard. Not a trace."

One of Alan's jobs, as Preston's paid companion, was to do background checks on the women Preston chose to pal around with on this island. But this one he couldn't find? "Oh, well, Alan," Preston said, "all these women have so many different last names, you know. Like Indians with scalps on their belts."

"Yes, but they still have to have a background," Alan insisted. "They have to *have* those scalps. Pamela Broussard has nothing, no history, nothing."

"Alan, that's impossible," Preston pointed out. "She can't be paying *cash* for her room here."

"No, that's all right," Alan said, "I've got that much. Pam Broussard's bills are paid by I.T.L. Holdings of Evanston, Indiana, which is very near Chicago."

"And what," Preston asked, "is I.T.L. Holdings?"

"The financial investment arm," Alan said, "of Roper-Hasty Detergent, a Chicago conglomerate with a base business in home-cleaning products."

Preston considered this information. He also considered his lunch and ate some omelet. Delicious. "I wonder," he said, "if she's too rich for me."

Alan didn't understand. "Too rich? Preston?"

"I know Roper-Hasty," Preston told him. "It's no longer entirely family held, but the Roper family still maintains a commanding interest. If Pam Broussard is related to the Ropers, it's perfectly logical the company will pay her expenses, to turn them into something tax-creditable farther down the line. But that would mean that Pam would be far too rich for me to play with. The only reason these women put up with me is because they want my money. If Pam Broussard is a Roper, she's already at least as rich as me, and all my little witticisms will fall quite flat. In fact, I could be quite extensively humiliated. Before we do anything else, Alan, find out for me for sure and certain just who Pam Broussard is when she's at home."

"I signed on to this death ship as a paid companion," Alan pointed out, "but it seems to me you're converting me into a private eye."

"Let's hope," Preston said, "you're good at it."

28

WHEN DORTMUNDER AND Otto Medrick and Stan Murch walked into the O.J. Bar & Grill at ten to three that afternoon, having left Stan's most recent transportation, an eight-year-old Taurus, in a restricted area in front of a neighborhood funeral parlor, it was two hours later than the time Medrick had promised, or threatened, to meet his brother Frank. The reason for that was, once Dortmunder and Medrick were safely on the ground and out of that flying metal cigar and walking with Stan toward the transportation du jour, Dortmunder had insisted that people in physical contact with Mother Earth not only were required to eat but were required to eat solid food.

"The O.J. isn't going anywhere," Dortmunder had pointed out, "which I could only wish I could say about myself."

Stan had offered strong support for this view, adding to it that he happened to know, between Newark and Manhattan, a diner that wasn't half bad, because it was patronized by long-haul truckers who well knew there was nothing to eat in America from New York City to either New Orleans or Chicago.

Medrick, while he made it clear that what he really wanted to sink his teeth into was a relative, was at last persuaded that the good will of his new friends was worth a detour. So they'd filled up on Cajun this and Lake Shore that, and now, as they entered the O.J., Dortmunder felt he was ready for anything.

Except he wasn't. It was awful; it was like a natural disaster. No, not natural; that was why it was so awful. This wasn't a disaster; it was an atrocity. The middle of the afternoon, and the O.J. was empty. Empty stools, empty booths, empty floor, empty backbar. Not a customer, not a regular, not even Rollo. To look at this muffled, tomblike dark space, in which even the good aromas of beer and whiskey were beginning to fade, was to come directly to the concept of mortality. That this could happen to the O.J.

On second look, after one's eyes had adjusted to the dimness from the bright outdoors, the place wasn't absolutely, totally empty after all. A man was seated at the bar, over to the left, where the regulars used to hang out. He wore a green polo shirt and brown shorts and white sneakers and a Red Sox baseball cap worn frontward. There was no glass in front of him, only a pair of glasses on his face, and he was reading a magazine.

Which he tossed onto the bar when the trio walked in. Getting to his feet, walking forward, he said, "No clocks in Florida, either, huh?" Since he looked like Otto Medrick, though some years younger, and sounded like him, though some degrees less irascible, this must be the brother Frank.

Yes. "Don't blame me, Frank," Medrick said, and waved a dismissive hand at Dortmunder and Stan. "With these two, the stomach comes first."

"Well, you know, Otto," Frank Medrick said, "with a lot of people, that's true." Looking at Dortmunder and Murch, he said, "Which of you's the back-room crook?"

"Hey!"

"Both of them," Medrick said, pointing. "That's the one came down to tell me."

"Well, I guess I have to thank you," Frank Medrick said, sticking his hand out. "You saved a lot of people a lotta agita."

"Not yet, he hasn't," Medrick said. "That's why I'm here."

"I didn't catch your name," Frank Medrick said.

"John," said Dortmunder, who hadn't thrown it.

"Catch this one," Stan Murch said, sticking his own hand out. "Stan. I drove them here from Newark."

"Via today's special," Medrick said. "So what's happening on the Raphael front?"

Frank, who actually did have a watch, now looked at it and said, "At this moment, Raphael is in front of Judge Bernice Steinwoodvogel, being railroaded into the loony bin with the assistance of Dr. Leonard Ledvass."

"That's a very short railroad," Medrick commented. "What else we got?"

"Let me show you," Frank said, and went around behind the bar.

"While you're there," Stan said, "would you feel like drawing one? With a side of salt."

Frank looked very blank, like a person being addressed in Urdu, and Dortmunder said, "Let's wait a little, Stan, take care of this other stuff first."

"Oh, sure, no problem," Stan said. "Driving is a thirsty-making process, that's all."

Impatient, Medrick said, "You'll get it," as his brother came up with messy stacks of paper from under the bar and spread them out in front of them all. Bending over these, pushing papers disdainfully back and forth, Medrick muttered, "*Here's* some old friends. Oh, and can *these* fellas turn a blind eye. Look at this shit."

"You don't want," his brother advised him, "to look in the back room. Or the ladies."

"The ladies I wouldn't look," Medrick said. "The rest I don't got to look, I can see for myself. Frank, the phone is back there."

Frank brought over a black phone on a long cord, and Medrick chose one of the invoices before him, then punched out a number as though killing cockroaches with one finger. He waited, tapping that finger on the bartop as his brother and Stan and Dortmunder all watched with interest, and then he said, "Hello, sweetheart, this is Otto Medrick, lemme talk to Harry. No, you haven't, but you're hearing from me now. Thank you."

The pause that followed might very well have been diagnosed as pregnant, and then Medrick, grinning like an old timber wolf who's just seen a young lamb, said, "Harry? Yeah, it's me, yeah, I've been away. Florida, that's right. Well, you know, it's Florida. But I had to come back because there's a little problem with my joint. No, Harry, it's *my* joint, my nephew Raphael was what we call a caretaker, and he's— Who? I don't know anybody named Mikey, Harry, and if God is good I never will know anybody named Mikey. Well, there you go, that's another symptom, I didn't even know about that one. Symptom of what? Mental disease, Harry, it's terrible, the whole family's in a state of shock. Well, I can't, I can't tell you everything that happened because I don't know yet everything that happened, but I do know this much, Raphael Medrick is right at this minute in a court of law being committed to an upstate loony bin because of diminished capacities, and one of the proofs of this diminished capacities, which happened to be shown to the judge, was this purchase of his, from you, Harry, of thirty barstools. Where did you think he was gonna put thirty barstools, Harry? No, I don't suppose it is. Well, that's not exactly right, Harry, in this particular instance the customer *was* wrong, and I've got the judicial system of the State of New York to put it in writing that the customer was a fruitcake that no decent entrepreneur such as yourself, Harry, could properly— Harry, that's up to you. What I'm telling you is, you've got a choice here. You can either try to sue a nutcase in an upstate laughing academy, or you can come get your barstools back."

"Still in their plastic," Dortmunder said.

"Thank you," Medrick said, and into the phone, "Still in their plastic, Harry, make it easier for your crew. You'll send somebody today? Oh, we'll be here, Harry. No, I understand, you're right, business is business. Nice to hear your voice again, Harry," Medrick said, with his savage smile, and slammed the phone into its receiver. "Eleven more of these bastards to go," he said, and the front door opened.

They all turned to look, and here came two more of them, or maybe two from an earlier occasion. Associates of Mikey, in any case, swaggering chunks of veal in Day-Glo shirts, ironed designer jeans, handtooled boots, and hair like chocolate mousse. Entering, looking around, they said, "This place isn't open."

"You're right," Medrick told them. "Come back after six, we'll be open then."

One of them placed himself in front of Medrick. "You're not following me, Pops," he said. "This place is *closed*."

Medrick spread his hands. "So whadaya doing in here, if it's closed?"

"I don't know who you think you are, Pops—"

"I am Otto Medrick. I own this joint. If I was your pop I'd kill myself. Lucky thing I'm not. Get outa here."

"Hey, you," the other one said, and they both did that thing of the hand reaching under the shirt to the waist in back.

Mildly Dortmunder said to Frank Medrick, "There's a pistol in that drawer there. Next to the parasols."

"And a telephone in my hand here," Medrick said. "What was that number again? Nine one one?"

As Frank opened the drawer in which Dortmunder, on an earlier occasion, had found that firearm, the two visitors backed away, hands out from under their shirts but many stormclouds on their brows. "You better know what you're doing," one of them said. "We're gonna call Mikey, we're gonna see about this."

"You do that," Medrick told them, turned away, and dialed a number. As the veal left, he said, "Rollo? It's me. Yeah, I'm here, in the O.J. Well, it's a mess, you know that, but we're gonna deal with it. Could you open here at six? Good. And those pals you told me about, all belong to that ex–Merchant Marine club? You still hang out with them? Good. Spread the word, in honor of me being back and you staying on, those pals of yours, it's open bar for a week. And you could tell them, they might even get a chance to bang some heads, like the old days. Great, Rollo. I'll be here."

Medrick banged the phone down and looked at the stacks of invoices. "Which bastard next?"

In far-off darkest New Jersey, Mikey hung up the phone and turned a plaintive face toward his father. "Well, what the fuck?" he asked.

29

THE MOST INFURIATING thing about men was that they were both predictable and impossible. Their buttons were ridiculously easy to push, but unfortunately, every button came with its own self-destruct program.

As Roselle had learned long long ago, on the very first occasion that she might climb into bed with a man he would be practically purple with lust, all stumbling haste and slack-jawed avidity, high on urgency and low on technique. With each repetition, though, the balance between hunger and technique would shift, as his initial craving for the fantasy he had originally pursued became replaced by his interest in this one actual woman. The lust would never return in that original incandescent way, at least not with her, and eventually, unless some other factors entered the picture—shared fondness, shared interests, shared phobias, shared *something* other than sex—the interest, too, would begin to wane, until eventually all of that heat was reduced to yesterday's campfire.

Roselle had no interest in sharing much of herself, other than her body, with anybody, so her time of ascendancy over every man she targeted was a limited one, and with someone like Preston Fareweather, all narcissism all the time, that window of opportunity would be a very narrow opening indeed. Time to crack the whip.

Tuesday morning, therefore, she donned her teeny-weeny polka-dot bikini, red polka dots on white—so much more carnal—and went off for breakfast with every intention of making Preston suffer a little. It was, after all, supposed to be good for the soul.

Preston was already in the dining hall, with the undertaker Pinkleton. Roselle collected her yogurt and fruit bowl and coffee and joined them: "Good morning."

Preston's eyes lit up at the sight of her: "Don't *you* look good enough to eat!"

"I am. Good morning, Alan."

"Morning, Pam." Sour as ever.

Preston, talking mostly to her breasts, said, "I thought, this morning, we might just nestle in for a while, then go over and watch the volleyball. That's always pretty amusing."

"Oh, Preston," she said, "that does sound like fun, but I had such a good time sailing yesterday, I just want to do that again."

"What, out in the ocean?" His nose wrinkled with distaste. "We're *land* creatures, Pam."

"Actually," Roselle said, "we all come from Mother Sea. Well, you don't have to go if you don't want to, we're all on vacation here, we can all do whatever we want."

"And I want us," Preston said, with a meaningful little grin, "to just have some kidding-around time together this morning, just the two of us."

"Maybe later," she said, "if I'm not too tired from sailing. I wonder if I could find someone else to go with me."

"I'm sure you could," Pinkleton said, with just a trace of the snide in his voice.

Innocent as a newborn hawk, Roselle smiled upon Pinkleton and said, "How about you, Alan? Sailing's really fun."

The look Preston gave Pinkleton at that point would have wrinkled aluminum. Affecting not to notice, the nasty little sycophant said, "Oh, I think I'm just another landlubber, thanks just the same."

It wasn't hard to find a single man—no husbands, please—who would be pleased to go sailing with her. Robert, his name was, and he claimed to be a stockbroker from Chicago, though that bushy mustache did read *firefighter* to her. Not that it mattered; Robert was only for show. And a perfect show, given that Preston was the primary audience—fortyish, tanned, well built, with a smile full of gleaming teeth.

The resort offered several small sailboats that the guests could either operate themselves within the adjacent cove or simply ride in while an accomplished sailor did the work if they wanted to venture out to sea. These professional seamen were all locals, and Roselle happened to know that the operator of the boat she chose was named Tonio. As they boarded, Tonio looked at Robert and then at Roselle, but she infinitesimally shook her head—not this one.

As they set off from the dock, gently bobbing, the sky huge and blue, the sun a fierce high gold, the sea a gently heaving gray-green as though it were the breast of the sleeping Earth, Roselle said to Tonio, "Oh, let's go along close to the shore for a while. It would be fun to see the resort from out here, wouldn't it, Robert?"

"Sure," he said.

So they sailed along past the curving row of little bungalows, and there were Preston and Pinkleton, on Preston's little porch, and Roselle gave him a big wave and a jolly, "Yoo hoo! We're off to have a *wonderful* time!"

Preston's answering wave could not have been more surly.

30

THE REGULARS, THE few of them who'd shown up this first night of the O.J.'s rebirth, were discussing homecomings. "Who was it said," one of them wanted to know, " 'There's no place like home alone'?"

"Greta Garbo."

"No, she said, 'I want to be home alone.' "

"Switzerland, she meant."

"Switzerland? Greta Garbo came from Switzerland?"

"This place was closed for a couple days."

Wait a minute; that wasn't a regular. That was a little droopy-nosed guy sitting in front of his beer a little off to the right of the regulars who, being so thinned out in number, hardly took up any bar frontage at all.

It was the first regular who answered: "It's been a hairy couple days. Nobody knew what the future was gonna hold. It was like that time Amelia Earhart got lost."

"She's still lost," pointed out the second regular.

"She is? Well, D. B. Cooper, then."

"The guy went outa the airplane with the money? He's still lost, too, but I think he wants it that way."

"Well, dammit, Judge Crater, then."

"He's also still lost."

Exasperated, the first regular said, "Doesn't anybody ever get *found*?"

The droopy-nosed guy said, "The O.J. wasn't ever *lost,* you know. It was still here. It just wasn't open."

"Gave me the whim-whams," the third regular confessed. "You leave your place, you go out on the street, you go in where you're supposed to go in, there's guys in the place make you very uncomfortable."

"Exactly," the first regular said, "but whadaya gonna do?"

"So you come back the next day," the third regular said. "You know, it's like your *route,* it's what you do. But then you come down the street, you're braced for the uncomfortable guys, you turn in at the door, *bang,* it's locked. You can't go in. Walk around the block, try again, same thing. This whole neighborhood, man, I felt like it was goin to hell."

"Yeah, I get that," the droopy-nosed guy said. "But what *happened?*"

"Well, some people," the second regular said, "think those guys were part of a reality show, where everybody has to be difficult and obnoxious, only then it got canceled."

"That's not what I heard," the first regular said. "*I* heard they were hooked up with some Arab sheikhs wanted to buy the place without anybody knowing, so they could get booze without anybody knowing, which is why all those cases of hard stuff kept coming in, but then some of their wives found out about it and made them stop."

The second regular frowned like an olive tree. "Arabs? Those guys were Arab sheikhs?"

"No, the repre*sen*tatives. The sheikhs couldn't do it theirselves because they're not supposed to be around booze."

"That's not what *I* heard," the first regular announced. "What *I* heard, they were working for some real estate guy, wanted to buy the whole block, force people out, put up one of those middle-finger towers."

The third regular smirked a little. "Force people out," he asked, "by bringing in all that liquor?"

The first regular was still marshaling his forces for the rebuttal when the door opened and half a dozen guys tromped in. They were older guys but big and meaty, with close-cropped gray hair and lots of tattoos showing below their white T-shirts. They had a kind of rolling gait in their walk, and they headed for the opposite end of the bar from the regulars, hallooing, "Hey, Rollo! Whadaya say, Rollo? Land ho, Rollo! Permission to board, Rollo!"

"Pipe yourselves aboard, boys," Rollo replied, and immediately began dealing out glasses onto the bar, followed by a big bowl of ice, followed by *two* bottles of nationally-known-brand whiskey.

The regulars, once again stunned into silence, watched this largesse with unbelieving eyes, until the droopy-nosed guy said, "But what *happened*? I heard the old owner all of a sudden came up from somewhere—"

"Mexico."

"Puerto Rico, I heard."

"Whada you guys know? It was Padre Island, Texas."

"But," the droopy-nosed guy persisted, "what made him come *up* all of a sudden?"

"Oh, some crook told him what was goin on," the first regular said.

The droopy-nosed guy looked confused. "Some crook?"

The second regular explained, "There's these guys, they come in here sometimes, use the back room to do their plotting, their planning."

"You mean like robberies, burglaries, like that?"

"Something like that," the first regular agreed. "None of our business."

"We buttoutski," explained the second regular.

"See no hear no speak no," expanded the third regular.

"But it was one of those crooks, crook-types," the droopy-nosed guy said, "that talked to the old owner down south somewhere?"

"Yeah," said the first regular, and asked himself, "Now, what's that guy's name?"

"It's the same as some beer," the second regular told him. "I know that much."

"Ballantine?" hazarded the third regular.

"No," said the second regular, as the new arrivals at the other end of the bar started in on some sea chanteys.

The first regular had to raise his voice but managed: "Budweiser?"

"No, it's something foreign."

"Molson," tried the first regular.

"Molson?" The second regular couldn't believe it. "That's not foreign!"

"It's Canadian."

"Canadian isn't foreign!" The second regular pointed perhaps north. "It's right *there*! They're part of us, they're with us, except for 'oot' and 'aboot' they talk the same language as us."

"They're their own country," the first regular insisted. "Like Hawaii."

"It's not Molson," the second regular told him, to put an end to that.

The droopy-nosed guy said, "Heineken?"

"No."

Everybody took shots at it now: "Beck?"

"No."

"Tsingtau?"

"What? He's not *Chinese,* he's like one of us, he's not even Canadian, it's just his name is—"

"Amstel?"

"No!"

"Dos Equis."

"*Nobody's* named Dos Equis! Wait a minute, wait a minute."

When the second regular put on his thinking cap, it made his entire forehead form grooves, as though somewhere there might be a socket to screw his head into. "Dortmund!" he suddenly cried.

They all looked at him. "Yeah?"

"Yeah! That's his name! Dortmund."

"That's pretty funny," said the droopy-nosed guy, and took the name with him back to Jersey, where he gave it to Mikey, who didn't think it was very funny at all.

31

"I DON'T LIKE to look a gift headquarters in the mouth," Tiny said, gazing around without love at the back room of the Twilight Lounge, where they were meeting for the second time in a week, "but I'm not warming up to this place."

"It's better than John's living room anyway," Stan said.

"Hey."

There having been general agreement that the O.J. should be left alone until it had completely recovered from its bout with organized crime—and until they were sure there would be no further activity from those people—the only alternative appeared to be Twilight again, so here they were, a little after ten in the evening, Dortmunder and Kelp and Stan and Tiny, hunkered around a table from which Tiny had removed the menu with prejudice, seated on chairs with dust ruffles.

Tiny called the meeting to order: "Could we get on with it here?"

"Sure," everybody said.

"Too many distractions," Tiny said. "So let's just do it."

"Exactly," everybody said.

Tiny looked around. "So what's the first step?"

"Open the garage," Kelp said. "Take out the BMW, put in the truck."

Stan said, "What truck?"

Surprised, Kelp said, "The truck we're gonna use to take stuff outa there."

"Yeah, fine," Stan said, "but where is this truck? What truck are we talking about?"

"*I* dunno," Kelp said. "I figure, we take one off the street."

Both Stan and Dortmunder shook their heads at that. "No," Stan said, while Dortmunder said, "Not a good idea."

Kelp nodded at them both. "Why not?"

With a graceful gesture to Dortmunder, Stan said, "You go first."

"Okay. We don't know," Dortmunder told Kelp, "is it empty, this truck. You can't go around back, figure out the locks, open it up, see is it empty, takes too much time, people looking at you. So whadaya do, just jump in and drive it outa there? Then we get where we're going, it's full of lawn furniture."

"That's another reason," Stan allowed. "My own reason," he said, "is that this is a truck we can't buy, because we can't afford it, but it's a truck we don't want the cops looking for, because first thing you know they'll find it, and I don't wanna be driving in it when that happens, so I got a suggestion."

"Tell it to us," Tiny said.

"I will." Stan spread his hands. "My automotive contact," he said, "where I will bring this BMW, and let's hope it's a little too old to have Global Positioning System, is Maximilian of Maximilian's Used Cars out in Queens."

Kelp said, "I know you've had a satisfactory relationship with him for some time."

"I have," Stan agreed. "So here's my suggestion. I drive out to see Max, I offer him a swap. We'll *give* him the BMW, straight up, flat out, and he gives me a truck clean enough we could drive it to the St. Patrick's Day parade. But what this means, first I go out to Max, we discuss, we agree, then I come back, you guys work your magic on the garage door, I take the BMW to Max, pick up the truck, bring it back."

Kelp said, "John and I had this idea, one of us—"

"One of us," Dortmunder said.

"—was gonna be on top of the truck to get at the alarm out there. But what you're saying, we don't get the truck until *after* we get at the alarm."

"That's right," Stan said.

Tiny said, "I like Stan's idea. It introduces a note of caution into the thing, and it's a good use of resources, the BMW for the truck."

"Elegance," Stan suggested.

"Like that," Tiny said. "Only the problem is, this means we're not doing this tonight."

"Well, I don't think we're ever doing it tonight," Stan said. "We don't wanna have to light up that penthouse all night, run that elevator up and down all night, when people got nothing else to see and hear."

Dortmunder said, "So how do you see the timing?"

"Tomorrow," Stan told him, "I go see Max, make sure we can get a deal. If we *can* get a deal, I bring back the truck, then late tomorrow night, because this first part we really gotta do at night, when there's less likely to be pedestrians all over the place, we do the alarm—"

"So we can do it with the truck," Kelp said.

"Yes, we can," Stan agreed. "We go in, and I take out the BMW and stash it down out of sight at my place in Canarsie, and then the next day—"

"Already we're at Thursday here," Tiny pointed out.

"Rome wasn't built in a day, Tiny," Stan told him.

"It was *robbed* in a day," Tiny said, "but I see the problem here, so okay. We're at Thursday."

"I take the BMW to Max, I make my way back, I meet you at the place, we go in, spend the day moving goods, then wait for night, drive away from there, turn it all over to Arnie."

Dortmunder said, "I think I see two more things we need."

Tiny lowered a brow at him. "Delay-type things?"

"I don't think so," Dortmunder said, "But one of them is, we need a long-term stash for that truck afterward. Arnie can't take delivery on everything the minute we show up."

"A garage, you mean," Stan suggested. "Another garage."

"Someplace we can keep the truck," Dortmunder said. "I don't know where, we have to think about that. And I think the other thing we need is Arnie."

Nobody liked that idea. Kelp said, "John? Now you wanna hang out with *Arnie*?"

"No, I don't," Dortmunder said. "But from what he says, this penthouse is full of valuable whatnots, a lot more than we can put in one truck down one elevator in one day. So if he comes along, he can point, and we take what he wants, and it's more profit for everybody."

"He won't do it," Tiny said. "Fences do not set foot on properties where the burglary is going on. It's like a rule they got."

"That's true," Kelp said. "I've known other fences, and it's always the same. *We* go, they stay home, wait for our call."

"Well," Dortmunder said, "I think it would be better if we brought Arnie with us, so if it's okay with you guys, I'll at least propose it to him."

"I've met Arnie," Stan said, and drank more than his usual amount of beer.

Kelp said, "Stan, the funny thing is, I think maybe the

Club Med intervention did work after all. When John and I met him, he was less obnoxious than of old. I don't mean you want him for a roommate, but there was less of an urge to maneuver him toward an open window."

Tiny said, "Dortmunder, if you want to lay this on the guy, and he wants to go along with it, fine by me, I can see where it would help. But I still don't think he'll do it."

"I can only ask," Dortmunder said.

Tiny looked around the gay-nineties room and lifted his glass of vodka and red wine. "Next year," he said, "in the O.J."

32

THE GUMSHOEING THAT was a part of Alan's role as Preston's—flunky? majordomo? somewhere between the two—was conducted mainly on the net. His iBook was set up in a corner of his room where window glare would not be a problem on the screen, and there, each week, once Preston had settled on this week's—predator? prey? somewhere between the two—Alan would Google them and otherwise root around in their lives for their marital histories and financial circumstances and whatever other factoid Preston might enjoy knowing or making use of. Evidences of emotional or mental unbalance were always welcome.

This backgrounding never took more than an hour or two, usually on Sunday morning, and then there was nothing left for Alan to do the rest of the week but amuse Preston whenever the man wasn't off amusing himself. Alan found his employer detestable, but quite liked him for that. Preston was so smug, so sure of himself, that it would never occur to him that anyone, and certainly not some mere hireling, could twit *him*.

Preston, for Alan, was like some great, overstuffed piñata that could be bashed to one's heart's content, because the piñata would never even notice. Alan had been private secretary to much worse egotists over the years—though none, admittedly, quite so snide—and so he found this vacation with Preston a true vacation. Hardly any duties at all, except the once-a-week hawkshawing around the World Wide Web, and that was always simple and sort of fun. Except this week.

Wednesday, and he still hadn't found a trace of Pamela Broussard anywhere in the ether. How could she not exist, when she so palpably *did* exist?

After breakfast Wednesday morning, Alan settled himself yet again at the iBook, but this time he decided to go about the question a different way. The one undeniable fact he knew about Ms. Broussard was that her bill here was being paid by I.T.L. Holdings, a subsidiary of Roper-Hasty Detergent. What if he were to tackle the problem the other way around—study Roper-Hasty to see if he could find any link from the company to our Pam?

So that was where he spent nearly two hours Wednesday morning, oblivious of the outside sun and sail and balmy breezes, trolling the Net instead, rowboating down the organizational charts of Roper-Hasty Detergent.

It wasn't until the third time he came across one particular name that it finally rang a faint, distant bell. A warning bell?

The name was Hubert Stoneworthy, and his title in the Leather Goods sector of Roper-Hasty was executive vice president, Sales. Hubert Stoneworthy. Why did that name seem to reach up to Alan from the screen? Could it be . . .

He wrote the name on a scratch pad before closing out the search engine and bringing up a different file, the one that contained all the pertinent—and some of the impertinent—information about all of the former Mrs. Preston

Fareweathers. And all at once there she was, number two on the hit parade, Helene once Fareweather now Stott, nee . . . Stoneworthy.

Her brother! It had to be. Helene Stott was using her brother to conceal the true identity of Pam Broussard from Preston. But to what end?

Pam was up to something—that was certainly true—but what? She couldn't serve legal papers on Preston, not here. She could certainly make incriminating photos or such things if she wanted, but Alan knew perfectly well that Preston would merely laugh off anything in that line and ask if he could have a set in wallet size. So what was the woman up to?

If nothing else, this link would have to be shared with Preston right away. Taking the piece of paper with Hubert Stoneworthy's name on it with him, he went out through his sliding glass door and down off his porch, then over to Preston's porch next door, which he stepped up on, and knocked on Preston's glass door, behind which the drapes were firmly drawn.

No answer. Was Preston off with *her*? Probably.

Well, never mind. He would catch up with Preston at lunch, if not before. Returning to his own porch, he settled down there and went back to reading Dostoyevsky.

33

THIS BUICK BROADSWORD in glittering goldeny green was not new, nor was it ever likely to be considered a classic, but nevertheless this was what Stan Murch drove, early on that hot sunny Wednesday morning in August, for his visit to Maximilian's Used Cars, so far out in Brooklyn, or possibly Queens, that the city buses run on firewood.

And there it was at last, in all its tattered glory. A small pink stucco office structure stood modestly at the back of a black-topped expanse lined with such melancholy, timeworn, mistreated, unloved jalopies, it looked as though a demolition derby were about to start up. Or had just finished. The triangular many-colored plastic pennants strung above these heaps, and the sentiments chalked on their several windshields—!!!Creampuff!!! !!!Ultraspecial!!! and such—did little to lift the aura of hopelessness that was all these vehicles had left.

Stan turned in at the narrow lane leading past this anthology of automotive misadventure to the pink stucco office building, where there was already a car parked, of a very different kidney. First, it had been manufactured in this millenium. Second, it had no dents or scratches in it at all, but was a clean and gleaming black Olds Finali. And third, it wore license plates—New Jersey, but still.

Stan parked the Buick behind this aristocrat, noticed that there were no personal items visible inside the Olds, nor a key in the ignition, and went on into the office.

The interior was simple to the point of anonymity. The walls were gray panels, the two desks utilitarian gray metal. At the larger of the two sat Maximilian's entire office staff, a skinny, severe, hatchet-faced woman named Harriet, who at the moment was doing a lot of rapid-fire typing on state motor vehicle department forms, using an old Underwood office machine so big and black and ancient it looked as though it should come with a foreign correspondent attached.

Harriet did not stop typing. She looked over at Stan as he entered, nodded, and finished a staccato of jabs at the form in the machine, then flipped it out and onto a pile of such forms in a mesh metal in-basket, and said, "Hi, Stan."

"Max in his office?"

"Where else would he be?" She glanced at the pile of untyped forms by her left hand, but did not reach for them. "He's in there," she said, "with a lawyer."

"From Jersey? Is that a good thing?"

"Nobody's done any shouting in there," she said, "which I count a plus, but let me buzz him."

Which she did. "Stan's out here. The one we like."

"That's nice," Stan said.

Hanging up, Harriet said, "There are Stans and Stans. He's coming right out." She reached for the next form.

"With the lawyer?"

Yes. The inner office door opened, and out first came Max himself, a bulky older man with heavy jowls and thin white hair, his white shirt smudged across the front from leaning

against too many used cars. Behind him came another person
of jowls and heft and thinning white hair, but here the re-
semblance ended. This one was decked out in a pearl gray
summerweight suit (of which there is no such thing), pearl
gray loafers, pale blue shirt with white collar, rose-and-ivory-
striped necktie, and a neckpin, yellowish, shaped like a dollar
sign. The man wearing all this finery, plus a number of rings
with stones in them, could have been any age from a hundred
to a hundred and nine.

"Stanley," Max said, "listen to this."

"Sure," said Stan.

Max looked at the lawyer and gestured at Stan: "Tell it to
him," he said. "I want to hear how it sounds when I kibitz."

"Certainly."

The lawyer gave Stan the smile that had charmed a thousand juries, and said, "Our friend Maximilian, as you know,
provides a truly worthwhile public service."

Stan had not known that. He wondered what this public
service was, but didn't interrupt.

"By providing affordable transportation to those of modest means," the lawyer explained, gesturing at the heaps outside with the graceful wave of the arm that had enchanted a
thousand juries when he had employed it to indicate the evidence, the defendant, or occasionally the jury itself, "Maximilian enables those unfortunates to seek—and at times
obtain and possibly even hold onto—employment."

Stan gazed at the array of crates out there. "Thinka that."

"However," the lawyer continued, raising the stern finger
that had alerted a thousand juries, "we must be realists here."

"Sure."

"Those at the bottom of the economic ladder, who would
be most likely to take advantage of the service Maximilian
supplies, tend to come equipped with minimal education and
marginal skills. Also the automobiles, those out there, have for

the most part already provided many years of faithful service. Given those vehicles, and given the caliber of most of their operators, there will be accidents."

"This," Max said, "is where I don't track it no more."

"No," Stan said, "I'm with him. Go ahead," he told the lawyer.

"Thank you. Now, we can assume, I believe, that when one of these accidents does occur, it will certainly not be the fault of the automobile, nor of its operator."

"Natch," Stan said.

"But *some* entity will be at fault," the lawyer went on, "and justice requires that responsibility be fixed, and that damage, both physical and emotional, be compensated."

"Sue them," Stan suggested.

"That is the way our system works," the lawyer agreed. "But sue whom?" With the two-hands-outspread gesture that had calmed a thousand juries, he said, "There are some, either misguided or led astray by false counselors, who might consider suing their benefactor."

"Max here, you mean."

"Oh, they consider it," Max grumbled. "Believe me, they consider it."

"It is my suggestion to Maximilian," the lawyer explained, "that in furthering his good works, and in protecting himself from the onslaughts of the ungrateful, that at the conclusion of every sale of one of his vehicles to one of his customers, he place in the hand of the customer, in addition to the bank contract and the ignition key, a copy of my card, which looks, in fact, like this."

So saying, the lawyer whipped out the advertised card with the sudden snapping motion that had startled a thousand juries. Stan accepted it and looked at it, while Max said, "Mostly what they do, they come around with baseball bats. I'm a great contributor to all the charities at the precinct."

Stan looked from the lawyer's name and phone number to the lawyer. "So the deal is," he said, "they get your card when they get the car, and that way, when they get the accident they'll probably call you, and you'll find somebody they can sue instead of Max."

"Precisely," the lawyer said, with a beatific smile, and folded his hands at his waist in the comfortable pose that had put a thousand juries to sleep.

Stan, staying awake, looked at Max. "What's the downside?"

"It sounded better this time," Max admitted, "but I don't know. You got somebody wants to buy one a them heaps out there, I don't like to use the word 'accident.'"

"So don't use it," Stan said. "Look. You give them the card," and he gave the card to Max. "You say, 'You ever got a legal problem with the car, this is a guy that knows laws about cars. Keep it in the glove compartment."

Max beamed all over his face—a sight so rare that Harriet actually stopped typing for three seconds. "Fantastic!" he said. "Stanley, I knew you were the one to ask. Okay," he told the lawyer, "I'll be your tout. Cuts out the ambulance chase."

"We'll both be happy," the lawyer assured him, and from within his suit he brought a little stack of his cards, wrapped in a rubber band. "A starter set," he said, handing them to Max. "I'll mail you more." Then, with his own broad, beaming smile, he shook Stan's hand, saying, "An honor to meet you, sir, you have an agile mind. If ever the occasion arises, I will be happy to assist you in any way possible."

"Sounds good," Stan said, and waited until the lawyer, with more effusions hither and yon, took his leave.

"Thank you, Stanley," Max said, "I just couldn't get my head around the proposition."

"And if any of them ever *does* sue you," Stan said, "you can make that bird take the case, on the arm, or you'll have Harriet write an innocent inquiry letter to the Bar Association."

"That much I know," Max assured him. "What's this you got out here?" He stood at the window to frown out at the Buick as the snazzy Olds took itself off. "You usually pick with a little more discrimination, Stanley," he commented.

"It has one great advantage," Stan told him. "No Global Positioning System. But that out there, that's just a little taste, something you can give me cabfare for. What I mainly want to do is bring you, tomorrow, a beautiful BMW, which I will give you straight up, in trade for one midsize truck for which the only requirement is, it can't be hot."

"A new complication?" Max squinted, as though a fog had formed between Stan and himself. "You wanna *give* me a BMW, no charge—"

"A free gift."

"—and I should give you a truck?"

"You got it."

"No, I don't." Max waved at his lot. "You see what I got here, I got cars. No trucks."

"You're in the business, Max," Stan pointed out. "You can find a truck."

"It's a little work you're asking."

"With a beautiful BMW at the end of it," Stan said, "that the owner's out of the country for years, it won't even be reported stolen for who knows how long. And it's a gift, for you."

"Well, the BMW is or it isn't," Max said, "and I'm not saying I'll kick it outa bed, but I'll tell you the truth, Stanley, if I'm gonna put myself out to find you a truck it's mostly because you made me see the legal issue a little better. You know, when a lawyer talks to you, the natural thing to do is not listen."

"I know."

"Certainly, not believe. But you listened, Stanley, and you heard the kernel of good in there, and so for that reason, plus the BMW, I'll see what I can do, get a truck. Call me day after tomorrow."

Stan said, "Not today?"

"Today is when you asked the question. Give me a little break here, Stanley, call me day after tomorrow."

In his mind, Stan could hear the low rumble of Tiny saying, "Another delay." But what could be done? "It's a deal, Max," he said. "I'll call you day after tomorrow. And now, if it's okay with you, we'll exchange a little cash and I'll call for myself a cab."

Max said, "You wouldn't want to buy a little runabout for yourself?"

Stan and Harriet both laughed politely, and then Stan called himself a cab.

34

PRESTON SAID, "WHO is he calling?"

"Who? Oh, Tonio," Pam said, because the pilot of this small sailboat, the bronzed Tonio, was murmuring into a cell phone as he sat hunched over the tiller at the rear of the boat, steering them out of the cove, toward the open sea. "Oh, he always does that," she said. "He has to phone the marina whenever we set sail, it's a safety thing."

"Oh," Preston said, and faced forward again, as the open sea grew increasingly open. The little sailboat did bob around an awful lot, did it more and more the faster they went and the farther from the protection of the cove. Preston tried to think of the movements as sensual, but it was difficult.

This was the first time he'd been off the island since he'd flown down from New York, almost three years ago. He'd never felt the need to frisk about on the briny, and in fact he still didn't, but Pam was so difficult to pin down, a phrase he meant quite literally. She was always either off sailing with some lout or too tired from her outer-sea exertions to be of much use.

Well, if you can't fight them, join them. Last night, when once again Pam had been too tired to drop by his place for a little kidding around, he'd brought up the sailboat idea himself: "Tomorrow, what do you say, if you want to go sailing again, I'll came along with you."

She was delighted: "Oh, would you, Pres? You'll love it, I know you will."

So here they were, and so far he wasn't loving it. Not that he was going to be seasick—that sort of thing had never been a problem—but maintaining one's balance was definitely a problem, perched here on this padded seat at the prow of the sailboat. Also noise; he would have expected sailpower to be silent, but the rush of the little boat through the sea created two kinds of white noise that made conversation difficult, they being wind and wave. The wind of their passage rushed past his ears, and the surface of the ocean hissed as the boat sliced through it.

So Preston merely sat silently, clasped his knees, frowned mightily at all that empty water, and waited for the good part. Are we having fun yet?

Once he looked back, and Tonio was off the phone now, and the island was really surprisingly far away. The sailboat traveled faster than one would have supposed. Preston looked at Tonio, and the man just sat there, one hand on the tiller, no expression at all on his face. Preston faced forward again.

He let another minute whish by, then leaned very close to Pam's lovely left ear and murmured, "When does Tonio take his little swim?"

"Oh, Preston, not till we're out of sight of land."

"Out of *sight*?" Twisting again to look back past the stolid Tonio, Preston said, "By God, we almost *are*." Facing Pam, he called, into the roar of wind and wave, "Should we be out this far?"

"Oh, these boats are completely safe," Pam assured him. "They wouldn't let us go out if they weren't."

"Presumably." Preston gazed out at the illimitable ocean, and on it there moved a speck. "What's that?"

"What?"

"That," Preston repeated, and pointed at the black-looking speck with the tiny white line of wake behind it.

"Why, it's another boat," Pam said, sounding pleased.

"Why don't they find their own ocean?"

Pam caressed his near knee. "They'll be gone in a minute, darling."

Preston frowned toward that other boat, which, instead of going, was definitely coming nearer. "It doesn't have a sail."

"No, it's a motorboat." She shielded her eyes with a hand, gazing at the interloper. "I think it's one of those they call the cigarette boats."

"Noisy and fast," Preston said, disgusted with the idea. "Drug dealers and the like."

"Oh, some very decent people, too," Pam assured him.

"Is that boat going to crash into us?"

"Of course not, darling."

"They're coming right at us."

"Maybe they want to say hello."

Preston looked back past Tonio, and there was no island back there at all any more, no land anywhere in sight, nothing and no one except themselves and that other boat. "I don't like this," he said.

Scoffing, Pam said, "Oh, there's no bad people in this part of the ocean."

Preston shielded his own eyes with his hand. That other boat was surging powerfully through the sea, thundering on like a seagoing locomotive, nose up. It could now be seen to be mostly white, with blue trim, and with names and numbers in blue on its side. Sunlight glinted from its windscreen, so that whoever was driving the boat couldn't be seen.

Preston made a sudden decision. Twisting around again, he called, "Tonio, take us back! Now!"

Tonio didn't even bother to look at him. They continued to sail as before. Wide-eyed, Preston stared at Pam, but she was smiling at the approaching boat, apparently mightily amused by something or other.

And now Tonio did do something with the sail, so that they definitely slowed. Instead of rushing, all at once they were wallowing. And the cigarette boat was just *there,* also slowing, turning in a large, carnivorous circle as it approached.

Pam turned her beautiful head to meet Preston's stare, and her smile now was savage with triumph. "It's been fun, darling," she said.

"You're taking me off the island!"

"You *are* off the island, darling."

The cigarette boat eased in close, and Preston made a belated and bitter discovery. "You *look* like my wives."

She laughed, lightly. At him. "Of course," she said, and Tonio held out a hand to catch the cigarette boat's rope.

35

OF THE SEVERAL guarded telephone conversations that took place on that Wednesday, Kelp was involved in most if not all of them. The first was midmorning, when Kelp's cell vibrated against his leg, and the caller turned out to be Stan Murch, who, based on the balalaika music in the background, was calling from a cab: "I seen our friend."

"Uh huh."

"About the swap."

"Gotcha."

"Says he can."

"Good."

"Day after tomorrow."

"Not today?"

"No. Looks like we'll move the smaller one first, take it out there."

"But," Kelp objected, hunkering over the phone, "what we said, we'd use the big one to pick up the small one."

"Not the way it's gonna work."

"Too bad," Kelp said, wondering how they'd get at that alarm without a nice, tall truck to help.

"So what we've got here," Stan said, "is what Tiny would call another delay."

"Yes, he would. In fact, he will."

"I was wondering, could you call him."

Kelp made a regretful face, which, of course, Stan could not see. "Gee, I don't think I could," he said. "I think of it as your news."

"Well, it's everybody's news."

"It was yours first."

"Well, then, there's the other issue."

"Other issue?"

"The location you were gonna find, for the trade."

"I'm working on that."

In fact, Kelp was at that moment sharing muffins and eggs with Anne Marie at a neighborhood beanery, but he had actually turned his thoughts once or twice so far to the question of where to stash the truck once it was full of product for Arnie Albright. "But now, turns out," he said, "I got an extra forty-eight hours."

"Use them well," Stan advised.

"Thank you."

Kelp broke the connection, pocketed the cell, kissed Anne Marie on the cheek, the nose, and the lips, and went off to look for a little cranny somewhere. It was such a nice sunny August day, without that humidity that sometimes happens, that he decided to leave the medical profession alone for once and start his search on foot. If I were a truck, he asked himself, where would I want to stash myself?

The problem is, Manhattan is not only an island, it's crowded. Other places, where people and their civilizations spread out like kudzu, you've got your front lawns, back yards, side driveways, alleys, mewses, cul-de-sacs, empty lots. In Manhattan you've got three things: street, sidewalk, building. Bang bang bang, that's it. (Forget parks; they're *watched*.)

There was a cubbyhole in Manhattan once, way down-town, about the size of the original Volkswagen Beetle, and one day an immigrant from Pakistan found it, moved in, and sold CDs and sunglasses from there for years until he retired to Boca Raton. Sent a son through NYU, a daughter through Bard. Is this a wonderful country or what?

Or what, if you're trying to stash a truck. The upside to this crowded-island thing was that always, somewhere, here and there around town, something that wasn't wanted any more was coming down to make way for something new that would be much more useful, at least for a while. The city is forever pockmarked with construction sites, some of them quite extensive, up to a full city block rectangle (city blocks aren't square; would you expect them to be?).

It was Kelp's initial idea that he would ankle this way and that around town in the pleasant sunlight and see did he come across a construction site large enough for its workers not necessarily to notice the addition of one extra truck parked in a corner, particularly if it was in with matériel not yet in use or a section they were temporarily finished with. After all, how long would it be before Arnie found some other location for the goods? Just a few days, probably, espe-cially if they insisted. Especially if they sent Tiny to insist.

It's true the extra two days was a bit of an irritation, but on the other hand, it took the pressure off Kelp in his search. So he ambled along, and when next his cell vibrated against his leg, he took a couple of extra steps to get in the shade of a very nice plane tree before he uncorked the thing, and said, "Yup."

"Another delay."

Tiny—so the news had spread. "I've been thinking about that," Kelp told him, "walking around here remembering the three most important things about real estate—"

"You got your location yet?"

"I'm not gonna need it till day after tomorrow, you know."

"Where you looking?"

"Around and about."

"I don't like these delays."

"We just roll with the punches, us guys."

"Not *my* punches," Tiny said, and broke the connection.

Over to the west by the river was where a lot of construction was taking place these days. For many years, New York City ignored its riverfronts, got along somehow without all those esplanades, boardwalks, colonnades, market piers, and waterside restaurants that lesser cities tried to console themselves with, but now the real estate devil-princes, in their aeries on top of the taller buildings, have noticed that gleam of water far below and have devised just the perfect way to deal with it. Put up a Great Wall of separate huge buildings, jammed together, marching for miles up the West Side, with windows. That way, the office workers and residents in those buildings can have terrific river views and then come out and describe them to everybody else.

Moving up along this serial construction site, Kelp had made it into the upper Fifties when he thought he saw something that might serve. So he swerved that way, but then the cell started vibrating, so he swerved the other way, unleashed the cell, and it was Dortmunder:

"I understand you're out lookin for the place."

"I am."

"Even though we got the delay and all."

"Well, the weather's nice, so why not take advantage."

"You want company?"

"What, to walk?"

"Well, yeah, to look around, see what's happening."

What is he up to? Kelp asked himself. "I don't know," he said, deliberately not using any of Dortmunder's names, not out in public like this, "I seem to be doing pretty good as a solo here. You're at kinda loose ends, I guess."

"Well, kinda. Except, naturally, I gotta go have a word with our friend."

Kelp immediately saw what was what. "Our friend" was Arnie Albright, and *Dortmunder* had volunteered to have a word with him, Dortmunder and nobody else. Hence, "Ah hah!" said Kelp.

"Whadaya mean, 'ah hah'? I just said."

"You want you should come with me so then I should go with you."

"Well, it seems kinda the thing, you know, we went there together last time, worked out okay."

"I don't think so."

"He'd probly expect us to show up together."

"He'd be wrong."

"You said yourself how much he improved."

"Not that much."

"Well, anyway."

"Get it over with," Kelp advised. "It's one of those things better looked back on than forward to."

"Sure," Dortmunder said, and grumpily hung up.

By that point, walking and talking, Kelp had almost circled the construction site that had caught his eye, and was being stopped by a tall chain-link fence where there used to be, more than likely, all three of the city's basic elements: street, sidewalk, building. There was quite a dropoff beyond a low metal barrier to his right, with the West Side Highway rushing back and forth below, and the Hudson sparkling all the way from there over to the squat towers of New Jersey.

The Hudson is a tidal river for up to a hundred miles inland, and the tide at the moment was coming in, which was slightly disorienting. It was a little weird to know that upriver was to your right, and yet the strong flow of water was headed up that way. He knew it didn't actually slop over the sides when it reached the top up in the Adirondacks, but it felt that way.

Anyway, this chain-link fence. Kelp turned and ambled back alongside it, and here was a broad gate kept open during work hours because cement mixers and other large workhorses were pretty steadily passing in and out. Inside, a temporary dirt road led down to a cellar level, where the work was going on. Far over to the left, down there, half a dozen trailers were set up as site offices. Guys and vehicles moved in constant random motion, like a disturbed anthill.

Kelp waited while an empty flatbed truck groaned up and out of there; then he entered and walked down the slope, because it seemed to him some unused vehicles were parked behind the office trailers. Would they like a playmate?

"Where's your hard hat?"

A guy called that from over to the right, just as Kelp reached the foot of the slope. With a big smile and wave, Kelp pointed leftward at the trailers. *"Just going to get it!"* And he moved on, striding pretty fast.

Yes, as he approached the trailers he could better see the other things parked back there, and they were tow trucks, a couple of pickups, and some other things, including a dump truck with its forward-tilting hood standing up like a parrot's nose.

"Where's your hard hat?"

This safety expert was a guy coming out of one of the trailers. *"Just going to get it!"* Kelp assured him, with a big smile, and pointed the direction he was going.

Definitely this was the place. The parked vehicles were not all jammed in together like a parking lot, but just left here and there in the empty space behind the trailers as the drivers had no more immediate use for them. The truck Stan would bring here after the visit to the penthouse would fit in per-

fectly right *there,* between the hook-nosed dump truck and a
red pickup with a see-through Confederate flag covering its
entire rear window.

Having seen enough, Kelp turned about and headed back
for the ramp.

"Where's your hard hat?"

"Just going to get it!"

Kelp kept moving, kept smiling, kept looking around at
everything there was to be seen. They wouldn't be able to
move their truck in or out at night, because that big gate
would be locked and there would be night watchmen in
here, but that was okay. The penthouse was a day job, and
they could finish it up and get the truck over here long before the end of the workday. Then, once again, when Arnie
was ready, they could move the thing out during the day. No
problem.

The only thing was, before he came back here, he'd really
have to get a hard hat.

36

PRESTON DIDN'T APPEAR for lunch. That *never* happened; Preston was not a man to miss a meal. Alan looked around the half-full dining hall, and Pam, this week's tootsie, was also not present. Had they chosen to lunch together, in his room or hers? Not entirely like him, but not impossible, either. Still, Alan didn't like this nonappearance, so after lunch he went looking.

Nobody home at Preston's place. Door locked, shades drawn, nobody home. Alan called through the glass door just to be certain, calling Preston's name and his own, but no response.

At Pam Broussard's place, though, the situation was quite different. Alan knocked on her door, and when almost immediately she opened it, he reacted first to her clothing—she was wearing clothing, all over, even shoes—and then to what she said: "They're on— Oh." Surprised, but not awkwardly or guiltily so. "I thought you were the bellboy," she explained.

In the dimness of her room, he could see two rather large suitcases on the bed, closed and ready to go. The less a woman wears, the more luggage she needs to carry it in. Feeling a sudden apprehension, he said, "You're leaving us?"

"The office here got an e-mail for me," she said. "My mother just died, very unexpectedly." Said with no more emotion than if she were saying, "I'll have the fish."

She doesn't care if I believe her or not, he thought. "That's terrible," he said, matching her emotional level. "I was wondering if you knew where Preston was." She does know, he thought, she does know, and something has gone dreadfully wrong.

But she said, "I have no idea, I haven't seen Pres since breakfast. I went sailing, and you know how he *never* wants to go sailing. Then I came back from my sail, and there was the message about my poor mother."

"Of course." There would actually be such an e-mail message—he had no doubt of that—but if this ice statue had ever possessed a mother, that mother had not unexpectedly fallen down dead today. What has she done? Alan thought. Where is Preston? What on earth can I do about it?

"Oh, good, here's the bellboy now. Very nice to have met you, Alan," she said, and extended a steady hand.

What else could he do? He shook her hand, a cold hard thing like a falconer's glove. "We'll miss you," he said, and gave her back her hand.

The bellboy, young, thin, French, and leering, stripped the clothing from Pam with his eyes, then went on inside to get the luggage, while Alan's brain spun madly, searching for something to grasp onto, something to make sense. They wouldn't kill him; no one would kill him; everybody wanted Preston Fareweather alive. He was the goose that lays the golden eggs, safe here on this remote island in the Caribbean, so *where was he?*

"I'm so sorry not to say good-bye to Pres," Pam said, already turning away. "Would you say it for me?"

What has she done? "The next time I see him."

She smiled; something about that amused her. "Yes, that's when I meant," she said. "Good-bye, Alan." And she followed the bellboy away, down the curving path.

37

"Y AR?"
   "Arnie, you know who this is. You don't have to shout out my name."
   "Well, naturally, I know who this is! And is this also the best news in the world?"
   "Well, no."
   "So soon? The whole thing done, every—"
   "No, Arnie, it isn't done."
   "It isn't done. Is this *bad* news you're calling me with?"
   "No, Arnie, no bad news. In fact, no news, nothing."
   "That's why you're calling? To tell me no news?"
   "The *reason* I'm calling, I want to come over, have a conversation. On the same subject, you know what I mean."
   "You wanna come *here*? You *wanna* come here?"
   "I thought I'd come over now, if that's okay."
   "This never happened to me, you know, back when I was obnoxious. This is a whole new world opening up before me here."
   "I'll come right over."
   "Yeah!"

★   ★   ★

Dortmunder rang the bell, and a voice trying very hard to be musical rasped from the speaker: "Is that you-oo?"

"Yeah, Arnie, it's me."

Buzz, slam, smell of wet newspapers, Arnie at the head of the stairs. Dortmunder plodded up, and Arnie said, "Wait'll you see. I made a change like you wouldn't believe."

Dortmunder looked at what appeared to be the same actual Arnie, and said, "A change in the apartment, you mean."

"It's the new me, John Dortmunder," Arnie said, ushering him over the threshold. "I dunno, I just gotta pat myself on the back. What a terrific guy I'm turning out to be!"

"Uh huh."

Arnie closed the door, Dortmunder started across the room, and all at once he was struck by any number of sensations. Sound, for instance—a rather loud, continuing *whoosh,* as though your neighbor were warming up his jet plane. Smell, for a second instance—there was none, not a whiff, not as much as you'd smell in a museum at midnight. Touch— there's another one, a feeling of coldness all over his body. And finally, sight—a big black, hulking box now filled the airshaft window, vibrating all over and giving off both the sound and the cold.

Dortmunder said, "Arnie? Is that an air conditioner?"

"It's August out there, John Dortmunder," Arnie said, "and yes, to answer your question, that is an air conditioner. All these years I didn't have an air conditioner, because I didn't have *nothing,* because I didn't think I *deserved* nothing, I was such a hopeless scumbag, the clerks at Gristede's would pay me to shop at Sloan's."

"I heard that."

"But this is the *new* me, John Dortmunder, and I deserve, I deserve, I deserve . . . the *best!* Of everything! So it happened, this air conditioner moved into my life along with a few other odds and ends, I looked at it, I said to myself, why don't I break a link in the chain of commerce just for once and *keep* the goddamn thing? And the extra reward is, the smell is gone! Even from the bedroom!"

"That's great, Arnie."

"I am a changed man," Arnie explained. "I tell you, John Dortmunder, the next toaster comes into this place, it's *mine.*"

"I think you're right about that," Dortmunder said. "But the reason I wanted to come over, and this is even before I know about the air conditioner—"

"It's brand-new. I mean, to me."

"So maybe we could sit and talk?"

"Absolutely," Arnie said, but then he frowned and looked around, betraying a little uncertainty. "The one little problem I got to admit to you," he said, "is, it's a little tough to sit at that table now. I mean, the air conditioner's great, but it does give you a little Mount Everest feeling if you get too close to it. I almost got frostbite at breakfast before I figured out what was going on."

Dortmunder looked around. "There's space on that wall if you move that other chair over," he said. "You and me, we could drag the table and chairs over there. You wouldn't have your view, but you don't have it any more anyway."

"It wasn't that much of a view to begin with. Let's do it."

So they did some furniture rearranging, and Dortmunder got just a glancing shot of the arctic blast up close, just enough to let him know there are worse things in life than heat and smells, and then they sat down in the new location, and Arnie looked around to say, "I never seen the room from this angle before."

"Yeah, I guess not."

"Maybe somebody'll move me some paint."

"Probably not Preston Fareweather," Dortmunder said, hoping to segue into the real topic.

Arnie laughed. "No, all *his* paint's on canvas, signed 'Picasso,' signed 'Monet.' You want to be sure you get some of those."

"That's what I wanted to talk to you about," Dortmunder allowed.

Arnie looked alert. "Yeah?"

"We figure we're going in Friday."

"Friday's good."

"It's when we'll get the truck, that morning. We figure to do it all day, as long as it takes, get out of there long before dark."

"That sounds like a good plan."

"But from what you said about the place, it's got to be just jam-packed with goodies."

"It is, John Dortmunder, you'll have a ball."

"It's gonna be too much stuff for one truck, and we can only make the one trip."

"So choose the best," Arnie said, and grinned from ear to ear. "I can hardly wait."

"But that's what we're afraid of," Dortmunder told him. "What if we leave some really good stuff behind, and take same other stuff that's maybe okay, but not so good as the stuff we didn't take? We'd all feel bad about that. *You'd* feel bad about that."

"Come on," Arnie said, pooh-poohing the idea. "Don't sell yourself short. You know value, and I bet those other guys do, too."

"We're just uncertain," Dortmunder said, "and that's why we decided, we want to ask you to help."

Arnie looked pained. "I don't see how," he said. "I can't make a *list,* you know. I never seen the place."

"Exactly," Dortmunder said. "That's the problem."

Arnie looked at him, waiting for him to go on, but Dortmunder didn't go on; he just sat there, expectant, so finally Arnie had to say, "*What's* the problem?"

"You never seen the place."

"That's right." Arnie shrugged. "Even if I knew the guy back when he was in New York, I don't think he'd of invited me over."

"So you need to see the place," Dortmunder said.

Annie shook his head. "I don't get how I could do that."

Dortmunder shrugged as though it were nothing: "You come with us."

Annie frowned. "Come where?"

"The penthouse. You can point and say, 'Take this, take—'"

"The *penthouse*? While you're *robbing* it?"

"You wouldn't even have to carry anything, just point and—"

"John Dortmunder! I don't even leave the apartment! Especially not now, when I'm— Look at me," he demanded, poking a finger of his right hand onto his left forearm, "I'm still olive drab."

He was. "I noticed," Dortmunder said, "and it's very becoming—"

"It isn't *becoming* anything! It *is*! Even if I was a person went out on the street, I couldn't do it *now*. And to participate? I don't participate!"

"This is a special case, Arnie. Just remember Preston Fareweather. Just remember the kinds of things he'd say to you."

"Those are the things I'm trying *not* to remember."

"Well, remember anyway. This isn't just another job, Arnie, not for you. This is a matter of pride. This is self-respect."

"Well . . ."

"You've got those things, now, Arnie, the new you is worth standing up for."

Arnie looked thoughtful. "I didn't even feel bad keeping

the air conditioner," he said. "I felt it was okay to do something nice for me."

"And you were right. The new you wants comfort, dignity, the best of everything, you said so yourself."

"It's true, I did," Arnie said, and looked solemn as he contemplated his new self.

"So," Dortmunder said, "when the new you wants revenge, he wants the *best* revenge."

Arnie cocked his head. "He does?"

"He doesn't want to read in the paper," Dortmunder said, " 'Preston Fareweather says thank God they didn't get the Beethoven.' "

"He's a songwriter."

"Whatever. You get the idea. The new Arnie *wants* revenge. He wants to be part of it, he wants to watch it going down, he wants to read in the paper Preston Fareweather says, 'They were so brilliant, those guys, they even got the Le Corbusier.' "

Arnie squinted. "The what?"

"Whatever." Dortmunder brushed that away. "The point is, this is a special case. *You* are gonna show *that* guy what your pride looks like. He can't talk to you that way."

"No, he can't," Arnie agreed. A bit of rosy flush had appeared on his cheeks, beneath the dun.

"You're gonna step right up to that son of a bitch," Dortmunder said, "and you're gonna rob him blind!"

The sudden smile on Arnie's face was like nothing ever seen on earth before. "John Dortmunder," he said, "what time you gonna pick me up?"

38

PRESTON NEVER DID get used to the ride. When the cigarette boat crashed across the sea, if you were down in
the forward cabin, you felt it.

And the forward cabin is where he'd been put. The two
hard men running this boat, Australians or New Zealanders
or some such from their accent, had reached out strong,
tough hands and taken him off the sailboat with Pam's mock-
ing laugh loud in his ears. They'd hustled him down the steps
beside the wheel—"Watch yer ead"—and into this front
cabin, which in motion reminded him mostly of the machine
at the hardware store that mixes the paint. They'd made it
clear this is where he would remain. "Ye'll stay ere," one of
them told him, "an make no trouble, an that way we don't
have to bop ye."

"Where are you taking me?"

That made the fellow laugh. "Where do ye think, mate?"

Florida. No question in his mind. That was the scheme,
damn their eyes. They'd inveigled him off the island—Pam
had been just the perfect Judas ewe, hadn't she?—so they

could grab him and deliver him somewhere on the south Florida coast, directly into the arms of the process server. Years of thumbing his nose at them all, and now how they'd laugh.

No. He had to stop it, keep it from happening, somehow turn the laugh back at them. But how?

The two men who'd kidnapped him—were they bribable? He had no money with him, no wallet, not even clothing. He had nothing on his person but flip-flops, a bathing suit, a Rolex, and a floppy brimmed white hat with a chinstrap. But they had to know who he was, or at least something about him, enough to know he was wealthy, that if they took him to a bank instead of to the process server—

No ID. No ATM card, no driver's license, nothing.

Well, let's say. Let's say it's possible somehow to get one's hands on cash; would these fellows accept cash? Or would they bop him if he made the offer?

From the bunk where he sat braced against the sidewall in a vain effort to resist the endless pounding of their passage through the sea, he could look up diagonally and see the lower half of the one seated at the wheel. Occasionally, the other one moved in and out of view, sure-footed on the bucking deck.

Hard, methodical men in their forties, they were, with deep tans and leathery skin. They both wore battered old deck shoes, cutoff jeans, pale T-shirts that said nothing but had the sleeves torn off, and baseball caps without logos. Anonymous to a fault. Blond hair was visible around the edges of their caps, shaggy and unwashed, and their blue eyes contained no more warmth than the ocean.

They would bop him. He had to acknowledge that, that his money wasn't any good on this boat, even if he had his money on this boat. Those two were tough, methodical professionals with long careers behind them and in front of them, and he was one day's delivery.

What would they do on their other days? Smuggle people, smuggle drugs without taking any, smuggle whatever would pay. Today they were smuggling him, and they would concern themselves with his affairs no more than if he were a plastic bag of heroin.

How could he get around them, get away from them, spoil the delivery? He knew how to swim, and God knew he was dressed for swimming, but even if he could get past those two to the ocean, which he knew damn well he could not, where was land? Not to be seen outside the round window next to which he jounced.

When we get there, he thought. Somewhere in Florida. When we get there, we'll see what we can do.

Six fifty-seven p.m. in this time zone by the Rolex, when the quality of their thumping progress across the sea abruptly shifted. The August sun, God's blood blister, hung midway down the sky, and all at once the cigarette boat wasn't lunging any more. It had come to a canter, a trot; its nose was lowering as though to graze. They had arrived.

Where? Preston looked out the round window beside him and saw nothing but sea, the same old sea, if perhaps a trifle less serrated than before. So he leaned forward, no longer having to hold himself tense against the pounding motion of the boat, and there it was: land. Very low land, pale tan, with what looked like mangrove here and there against the water.

Where was this? Not Miami, certainly. Somewhere very low and undeveloped, with shallow water now beneath the boat, though they were still some way from shore, which was probably why they'd slowed so soon.

Florida is almost nothing but coastline, but most of it is very heavily patrolled, because of drug smugglers and potential terrorists and illegals from Cuba and Haiti. The two men operating this boat would know the safe places to land, where there would be no one around to ask the awkward questions, and this would be one of them.

The Keys—that's where they must be, the hundred-mile line of islands dangling south of Florida like a Fu Manchu beard. Much of it was developed and overdeveloped, but some was deserted, like this section here.

Well, no, not completely deserted. As they rolled closer, he could see, off to the left, that the low land curved outward toward the sea, and in the elbow thus created, half a dozen small boats idly bobbed, one or two people standing in each, fishing.

Bonefish. That's what people tried for down here. Those would be bonefishermen, standing in the bright, hot August Florida sun, its heat and glare and cancer-enhancing qualities redoubled by the bounce from the water all around them, the air very nearly as wet as the sea, and they were here to prove they were smarter than some skinny, inedible fish.

A thumping sounded on the cabin roof. One of his captors had climbed up to toss a rope to whoever was waiting on shore. The other had to concentrate now on maneuvering the big boat in as close as possible to land.

Could he reach the fishermen? He could only try, and this was surely his last chance. It was now or never.

His heart was pounding. What would they do if they caught him? Surely something more than just bop him, if only to relieve their feelings.

As he sat there, wanting to, afraid to, the image of his ex-wives rose unbidden into his mind. The four of them, laughing, and goddamn Pam with them, and by *God,* they all looked alike! Laughing at him for how easy he was to lead around, and not even by the hand.

A sudden embarrassed rage overtook fear, and Preston was on his feet, up the steps, *watching* his head, stomp, stomp, *over* the side like a hippopotamus into a swamp, but away, down, stroking, kicking, away, up, bright day, roar of motor far too near, bonefishermen over *there.*

It was the crawl he'd learned in college, and it was the crawl he did now, arms pinwheeling, legs kicking, trying not to hear that goddamn boat. Thrusting, thrusting, then realizing the roar of the motor had not gotten louder, it was less, it was fading.

He was swimming faster than the boat? Impossible. He dared a quick look back, a break in the rhythm of the crawl, and the cigarette boat had stopped back there, was glaring at him like an attack dog on a leash, while both men in the boat were pointing at him and yelling toward shore.

Shore. He couldn't stay floating in place out here; he had to keep swimming and somehow try to see the shore at the same time. He did it, panting, straining, and yes, there it was over there, a white limousine moving leftward beside the water, someone in the backseat yelling at the men in the boat.

Well, at least they'd sent a limo for him.

It was too shallow here for the cigarette boat—that's what had happened—so he no longer had them to worry about. Now all he had to concern him was whoever was in that white limousine.

The fishermen had realized something was up, and one of them now put down his pole, sat, and started his little outboard. Putt-putt, it came toward him as the limo stopped, unable to continue along the deep sand and wet mangrove swamp along the shore. Three men clambered from the limo, all in shorts and light shirts and sunglasses, and began fighting their way through the vegetation, waving their arms around as though mosquitoes were happy to welcome them to their island.

The little boat came to a bobbing stop beside Preston, and the man in it called, "Come on up here!"

"Right! Thank you! Right you are!"

Preston flung his arms over the gunwale but could do no more. His legs kept drifting, under the boat, and he couldn't lever his body up out of the water.

Finally, his rescuer grabbed Preston under both armpits from behind, pulled, and scraped his chest up and over the splintery wooden edge of the boat, until he could reach the top of Preston's bathing suit and yank on *that,* at which point Preston found it was possible to help, thrashing and lunging and kicking and beating until he landed himself on the wet, dirty bottom of the boat.

The man gazed down at him with a grin. He said, "I like that watch."

Gasping, Preston cried, "Get me out of here!"

"Oh, maybe you wanna see your friends, man," the fisherman said, with a snotty little grin. He was Hispanic, heroically mustached, unshaven, dressed in a hopeless straw hat, a Budweiser T-shirt, and ratty green work pants. He was barefoot, and his toenails did not bear thinking about. Still grinning at Preston, he said, "Maybe we wait for them. That's some nice limo."

Preston sat up. No time for nonsense. "If those people capture me again," he said, "they'll kill you. You're a witness."

Abruptly the smile went away, and the fisherman gave a worried look toward the running men. He would know the stories about what sometimes happened in this part of the world. He said, "I don't want none a this shit, man."

"You're already in it," Preston told him. "Get me away from here, and this watch is yours."

"Oh, it's mine, man, I know that," the fisherman said. "Okay, get down now." And at last he turned back to his outboard motor.

Get down? Preston was already seated on the bottom of the boat. "What are you doing?" he wanted to know, and twisted around to look forward.

The fisherman was steering them directly toward the shore. The trio from the limo had found some sort of path and were running much more strongly than before, their arms pumping. The boat and the three, it seemed to Preston, were all going to meet at the same spot, on the shoreline.

"What are you *doing?*"

"Get *down,* man!"

Then he saw it. A tiny inlet curved away into the mangroves, and just visible way back in there, a footbridge stood barely above the water.

"We can't go under *that!*"

"Not with you sitting up that way, fool!"

Preston flopped down onto his face as the three men ran on, almost to the bridge, which slapped Preston on the backside as he zoomed by.

39

WEDNESDAY WAS THE most jam-packed day of Judson Blint's life, beginning when he got to the office in the morning and J. C. paid him for his first week's work, and ending when he rode in the rented Ford Econoline van full of his earthly possessions through the Midtown Tunnel into Manhattan just before midnight. And in between, he'd joined a gang and learned a skill.

The start was nine in the morning, when he entered suite 712. He started toward his desk, and J. C. stuck her head out from the inner office to say, "Come on in. It's time you got paid."

He'd wondered about that. He'd been working here a week now, taking care of all the businesses J. C. didn't need any more, Intertherapeutic and Super Star and Allied Commissioners, and apart from a few cash advances he still hadn't seen any money. Yes, this was essentially a criminal operation going on here, or a whole bunch of criminal operations, but he still needed to get some kind of salary.

However, he hadn't yet figured out how to raise the subject, so it was a relief that J. C. had brought it up herself. "Good!" he said, and followed her back into her office, still a neater place than his own.

She gestured to him to sit in the other chair, herself sat behind the desk, and opened a drawer to take out a ledger book and a gray canvas sack with a zipper on it and a bank logo across the side. Setting the sack apart, she opened the ledger and said, "You started here last Wednesday, so I guess it's just easiest to put you on a Wednesday to Tuesday week."

"Okay."

"I gave you a couple advances—a hundred fifty—so that comes out of it."

"Uh huh."

She took a wad of cash out of the sack and started counting it on the desktop as she said, "Your take this week comes to seven hundred twenty-two, but I don't do singles, so we round it down to seven-twenty, subtract the yard and a half, five-seventy, and here you are."

Five hundred and seventy dollars, a thick wad of cash, was thrust toward him. He took it, gaped at it, gaped at her. "J. C., uh," he said, "can I ask?"

"What, you don't think that's enough?"

"No, it's fine! It's more than I— But you said, my take for this week. I don't understand. How did you get to that number?"

She looked surprised for a second, then laughed and said, "That's right, I negotiated your deal for you, and then I never got around to telling you the agreement you made. You get twenty percent of the scams you're covering. The rest goes to me for office upkeep and thinking them up in the first place."

"Twenty— twenty percent of all those checks?"

"Judson, I just don't think I can get you a better piece. Believe me, I—"

"No no," he said. "I'm not complaining. Twenty percent,

that's fine. Fine. I didn't, I didn't realize it was going to work that way."

"What'd you think I was gonna do, pay you by the hour? Do you want wages? Or do you want a piece?"

"I want a piece," he said. Some answers he knew right away.

Later that morning, when he brought into her office today's mail for Maylohda, he said, "I want to come back late from lunch. I'm pretty much caught up out there."

"Got a nooner?"

Peeved with himself for blushing, but feeling the damn blood in his cheeks anyway, he said, "No, I just thought—I need my own place in the city, I thought I'd go look for an apartment."

She nodded. "Furnished or unfurnished?"

"Furnished for now, I mean, I don't—"

"Studio?" At his blank look, she said, "An L-shaped room, sofa over here, bed over there, separate kitchen, separate john."

"Oh. Yeah, that'd be good." Did she also rent apartments?

Reaching for her phone, she said, "Lemme make a call. There's a woman in this building, down on four, she's got a pretty good agency. Muriel, please. Muriel, it's J. C. Making a living. Listen, I got a jailbait boy here needs a furnished studio. Well, he *can* go two, but he'd rather not." She looked at Judson. "East Side or West Side?"

"I don't know, really."

"West Side," she told the phone. "Maybe downtown, one of the Spanish parts of Chelsea. He doesn't wanna pay MBA rates. He works for me, if that's a vouch. His name is Judson Blint." Hanging up, she said to Judson, "Go down to four oh six. They'll give you the address. Go now, come back after lunch."

"Thanks."

"Welcome to Big Town," she said.

He never did see Muriel. Four oh six said *Top-Boro Properties* on the door, and inside was a very high-class reception area with a very high-class receptionist. He gave her his name and she said, "Oh, yes, here you are," and gave him a card.

It was Top-Boro's business card, with *Muriel Spelvin* on the lower right. On the back was an address on West Twenty-seventh Street, and the name *Eduardo*.

"That's the super," she said. "Ask for him, he'll show you the place, if you want it, come back here."

"Thank you."

Not knowing any better, he walked the two miles, and found the block to be half very old tenement-type buildings in brick, with high stoops, and half tallish old apartment buildings in stone. The address he wanted was one of the original tenements, and at the top of the stoop was a vertical line of doorbells, half with names attached. The bottom one said SUPER, so he pushed it, waited, and a short, heavy guy in undershirt and work pants and black boots came out from under the stairs to look up and shout, "Hoy?"

"Eduardo?"

"Sí."

"I'm Judson Blint, I'm here to see the apartment."

"Hokay."

Eduardo trotted up the stoop. He had shaved this week, but not today. He was friendly but distracted, as though in some other corner of his life he were busy cooking an elaborate lunch. He said, "Come wit me."

Judson went with him into the building, up two narrow, dim flights of stairs, and to the leftward of the two doors at the rear of the hall there. Elaborately he undid three locks, then opened the door, walked in first, and said, "Empty three weeks. I keep it clean."

It was clean—shabby, but clean. All the furniture looked gnawed somehow, as though some previous tenant had kept small, nervous wild animals in here. The layout was exactly as J. C. had described, though she hadn't mentioned how small the kitchen and bathroom would be—no tub, just shower— or how old the appliances. The refrigerator door was propped open.

"Is the electricity off?"

"You call Con Ed, they turn it on," Eduardo said. "Switch your account from your old place."

"I don't have an old place."

Eduardo shrugged. "You call Con Ed."

The bathroom and the bedroom end of the L-shaped room each had a window, old, large, double-hung, guarded by expanding metal gates. Judson peered through the metal strips at half a dozen plane tree branches and the back of a building similar to this one.

"S'okay?"

"I like it," Judson said.

"See you around."

Back at Top-Boro he signed a lease that the receptionist assured him was full of loopholes, so he could always walk away if he found something better. The rent was seventeen forty-two fifty-three a month, which meant he immediately owed three thousand, four hundred eighty-five dollars and six cents, none of which he had, but which the receptionist assured him his employer was taking care of. He left with a dizzy head, a copy of the porous lease, and a lot of keys, all to the same apartment.

Upstairs, he went into J. C.'s office and said, "You're paying the rent?"

"Because you don't have it," she said. "I'll take it back from your piece, ten percent a month, one percent vig."

He thought he understood what that was. "Thank you," he said.

She nodded. "You got more stuff to do?"

"Con Ed."

"Right. And open a checking account—people don't trust you if you give them cash."

"I will."

"And no matter how late it is, come back here and finish up today's stuff. You don't wanna let things pile up."

"No, I won't."

It was quarter to five before he got back, but he now had an apartment, electricity, and a checking account. He was becoming, he realized, an actual person.

J. C.'s door was open, and she was coming out, ready to go home, looking terrific in white dress and white heels. "Call Andy Kelp," she said. "I put his number on your desk."

"Okay. Thanks." Proudly he said, "I have an apartment and a checking account."

"Today you are a man," she said, but she seemed to be grinning to herself as she left.

Casting that from his mind, Judson phoned Andy Kelp, who answered right away, saying, "Hello, Judson, I understand you're moving to town."

"In a couple days, yes," Judson said, because he planned to start setting the place up tomorrow and make the move over the weekend.

But Kelp said, "No, Judson, you've got the place now, why not move in? You've got your electric?"

"I just came back from Con Ed."

"Good. Here's what I'm gonna do for you, my kinda welcome wagon. When you get done your work, call me, then go to your place, I'll meet you there. I have a little training session for you, then we're gonna rent a van, you and me, and while I drive you'll practice some more, and when we come back to town with your goods you'll do a little something for me, then give the van back and go to your new home and sleep like a baby."

It was after seven before Judson could phone Andy Kelp and say he was ready. "I'll walk down now, I'll be there in half an hour."

"Take a cab," Kelp said.

"Oh. Okay."

So he took a cab—more grownupness—and Kelp was waiting for him on the sidewalk, a big cardboard box standing next to him. "Give me a hand with this," he said.

The box was about the size of a wheeled suitcase and pretty heavy. They lugged it up the stoop and then had to wait while Judson figured out which key opened the front door. The two flights up from there were tricky, with a number of banged elbows, but then they got to the door of Judson's apartment, he figured out those keys, too, and they carried the box in and set it down.

The only change from this morning was that the electricity was on. The refrigerator door was still open, spreading light and coolth into the kitchen, so the first thing Judson did was shut it, while Kelp was figuring out how to open the gate over the main room's window so he could open the window. Turning from that, he said, "My recommendation, get an A/C. Either that, or rent the apartment in front, too. What you want is your cross-ventilation."

"I don't know this place yet," Judson said.

"No, I know that," Kelp agreed, and turned back to the box. "Let's have a little training session, then grab a bite, then rent that truck."

Judson watched as Kelp opened the carton and pulled out
of it a dark gray metal box, laying it on the thin dark rug on
the floor. It was an alarm box. It looked exactly like the alarm
box on that building Tiny had been studying. "That's the
alarm box," he said.

"The one you wanted to be boosted up to, yeah," Kelp
agreed. He was now pulling out of the carton a packet of soft
black leather, which he unrolled to show a toolkit. "We got a
better idea," he said. "Also, it turns out, the manufacturer did
some modifications on these things since the last time I met
one."

"How'd you find that out?"

Kelp shrugged. "I went on their Web site. People will tell
you anything if they think they can make a sale. So I lifted
this one from their warehouse so we could study it. And also
use it." He rooted around in the box, came out with a little
pamphlet. "Okay, here's the instruction manual. It'd be better
if it was attached to a wall, but we don't wanna mess up your
place, so we'll do it on the floor. I'll read from the manual,
and you do like it says. Here, take the tools."

Judson took the toolkit, admiring the softness of the
leather, and sat cross-legged on the floor in front of the alarm.
Kelp sat on the sofa, bounced experimentally, and said, "My
advice, get a sheet a plywood, put under the cushions. Your
springs here are but a memory."

"Okay."

"Okay. Now, the first thing we do, we're gonna learn how
to remove the cover." Kelp bent over the instruction manual.
"You will notice four Phillips-head screws in the corners of
the cover."

"Uh huh."

"You will remove them in the following sequence. Any
other sequence, the alarm turns on."

"Pretty sneaky," Judson commented.

"All's fair in love and theft. The sequence is, top right, bottom left, top left, bottom right. What'd I say?"

Judson repeated it to him, and Kelp said, "Good. Do it."

Judson chose a screwdriver from the toolkit, then hesitated over the alarm. "If I do something wrong, will it make a lot of noise?"

"What, that one? No, it can't, it isn't plugged into anything. Go ahead."

So Judson removed the screws, then followed further directions to remove the cover, revealing a very complicated interior apparently operated by many tiny computer chips.

At this point, Kelp handed him a six-inch length of fairly thick wire with alligator clips on each end. "Your electric feed is from that black box on the upper left. Follow the green wire."

"Uh huh."

"Clip it at the other end."

"Okay."

"Your phone connection is the sheathed black wire comes up from the bottom, fastens to the works with a nut over bolt. Undo the nut."

Judson found pliers in the toolkit and undid the nut.

"Bend the phone wire back, put the other alligator clip on the bolt."

"Got it."

"Now, there should be a red button in there, it's the manual override."

"It must be that one."

"When you push that, you just unlocked the garage door. Go ahead, push it."

Feeling a little silly, because this alarm wasn't attached to a garage door or anything else, Judson pushed the red button. "Done."

"Fine. Now, when we do it, you would put the cover back

on, and you wouldn't have to worry about the sequence because at this point the alarm is out of the loop. But this time, don't put the cover on yet. Instead, put everything back the way it was. Exactly like it was."

Judson did that, and then Kelp said, "So, do you wanna run through it one more time before we go?"

"Well, it seems pretty simple," Judson said. "I don't see a problem with it."

"What you gotta remember," Kelp told him, "if you get one thing wrong with the real alarm, you're gonna suddenly be reenacting New Year's Eve on Times Square."

"I know how to be careful," Judson assured him.

"That's good," Kelp said. "Because, the thing is, you're gonna be doing the real one in the dark."

With the rented Ford Econoline van from a place on Eleventh Avenue in the Forties, and with the alarm back in its cardboard box on the floor in the back of the van, out they headed for Long Island. Once through the Midtown Tunnel, Kelp pulled over to the side of the toll plaza and said, "Get in back and practice some more."

So Judson unalarmed and alarmed the alarm all across the Long Island Expressway as evening turned into night, so that he gradually did learn to do it in the dark. They drove like that all the way out to his former home, just into Suffolk County, where he introduced Kelp to his bewildered parents, who had been briefed in advance by Judson but still didn't get it. So they simply stood and watched as their third child of seven—not that big a deal, then—and his shifty-looking companion—Kelp was never at his best on Long Island—carted out of the house everything of Judson's he thought he'd need in his new life, including, at Kelp's suggestion, his bed linen. "There's furnished and there's furnished," Kelp pointed out.

On the return, with the back of the van pretty full, Judson got to sit up front. Also, "The later the better," as Kelp phrased it, so on driving back to the city, coming through the Midtown Tunnel just before midnight, they went first to his new residence to cart everything upstairs, where many hands— four, anyway—did make light work.

Then, not long after one in the morning, they drove uptown and through Central Park, then stopped at the curb on the park side of Fifth Avenue in the Seventies, so they could get Judson and the alarm both up on the roof, which was more curving and slippery than it looked. However, Judson held on tight and Kelp drove carefully, and in no time at all they were making the turn—slowly—onto Sixty-eighth Street, where Kelp stopped, then backed around into the driveway indentation and stopped with the rear doors of the van snug up against the garage door.

Kelp stayed in the van, in case it should be necessary to leave earlier than expected, while Judson knelt in front of the alarm and reached for the toolkit. Windows loomed all around him, but every one of them was dark. He noticed that he had, in fact, more illumination from streetlights out here than he'd had inside the van.

Proper preparation is all. When he at last did get to the job, it was a snap.

40

THE KEY LARGO Holiday Inn, where the original steam-boat the *African Queen* used in the movie is kept on display in the parking lot, is such a nexus of popular American culture that it practically shimmers all over with irony—an effect less noticeable at just after midnight, when the rattle-trap old Chevy pickup truck turned in from U.S. Route 1, Preston Fareweather in the passenger seat, his rescuer at the wheel. Along the way, Preston had lost his white hat with the chinstrap and his flip-flops, but still retained his bright red bikini bathing suit and his Rolex. And his sense of entitle-ment.

"I wonder if that's for sale," the bonefisherman said, look-ing at the *African Queen.*

"I doubt it."

"Why not? Why other would you put it out there?"

"You can ask inside," Preston said. "Come along with me."

"You bet," said the bonefisherman, whose name was Por-firio.

Their hours together had not been entirely happy ones.

Initially, they were being chased, by people, boats, limos, and who knew what all. When Preston had last looked back, after that bridge had spanked him, the three pursuers had stood on the bridge, two of them pointing at him and one talking on a cell phone. Then they were out of sight.

The ribbon of water Preston and Porfirio moved on snaked this way and that through alternate areas of lush subtropical flora and dank, salty sand. Steering through it, Porfirio said, "You gimme the watch, man, I'll drop you where you want."

"No, I don't think so," Preston said. He well knew that he was old and fat and out of shape while Porfirio was none of these, but he also knew he was of the class born to lead and Porfirio was emphatically not that, either. The sheer weight of superiority was, it seemed to Preston, all the armament he would need in this situation. "If I give you my watch at this point," he explained, "you'll drop me where *you* want."

"Maybe I do that anyway," Porfirio suggested, with that sneaky grin he occasionally flashed.

"I think not, my man," Preston told him.

"Your whu?"

"We will come to an accommodation," Preston promised him, "but not yet. I take it you have a land vehicle somewhere around here."

"A wha?"

"An automobile. A car. A thing with wheels and an engine."

"I know what a car is." The smirk had been wiped from Porfirio's face.

"And you must have one."

"I got a pickup," Porfirio said, being sulky.

"Shall we go to it?"

The smirk was back, Porfirio having recovered his self-confidence. "Oh, sure," he said. "It's back there with that limo and those guys. You want we should turn around and go back there? We could do that. We got a little wide spot up here, we could turn around. That what you want?"

"You know better than that." Exasperated, Preston snapped his fingers at the fellow and said, "What's your name?"

Suspicious, Porfirio said, "What for you want to know my name?"

"So that I can call you something other than 'my man.' I myself am Preston Fareweather."

"No shit."

"None. And you are . . . ?"

Shrug. "Porfirio."

"Porfirio," Preston said, "those people back there are in the employ of my ex-wives. They mean me nothing but ill."

"Ex-wives, huh?" Full smirk now. "You got a lot of them?"

"The way this swamp has mosquitoes," Preston said, slapping at one on his forearm. "The result of their depradations—"

"Their wha?"

"Their attacks upon me, Porfirio. The result of those is that I am here with nothing but my bathing suit and my watch and your welcome person."

"Oh, yeah?"

"You are not a murderer, Porfirio," Preston told him, "nor are you a violent person."

"Oh, you think so, huh?"

"I do," Preston said. "I think you might consider assaulting me to take this watch, but then you would consider the fact that you are not a murderer and that after the theft I would still be alive and could identify you."

"You gotta find me first."

"How difficult would that be, Porfirio? If I put out a reward, how many of your fellow fishermen back there know you and could find you for the police and would be happy to do so?"

"You talk pretty big," Porfirio said, blustering now, "for somebody sitting there naked in a little teeny bathing suit."

"I *am* big, Porfirio," Preston said, using the man's name constantly both to belittle him and to remind him that Preston did know his name. "And I am big enough," he went on, "to wish to thank you for your aid back there and to offer the reward to *you*."

"That watch."

"I think not. But something very nice just the same. Substantial."

They had reached Porfirio's wide spot, a sort of inland salt pond. It reeked a bit, and salt didn't seem to deter mosquitoes, but Porfirio stopped anyway and said, "You makin me an offer?"

"I am."

"Then go ahead and make it."

"You will help me," Preston said. "I need to be gotten out of this swamp before I am eaten alive. I need to be hidden until after dark. And then I need to be transported to a place of safety where I may regroup."

"You got a lotta needs for a naked fat man in a little teeny bathing suit."

"I shall not be asking you to clothe me, Porfirio," Preston said, "though it is possible, eventually, I may ask you to feed me. But at the moment, my need is merely to remove myself from this swamp."

"It ain't bad here," Porfirio said. "I seen worse."

"I am sorry to hear that. Porfirio, why are we just sitting here in this brackish water?"

"I'm tryin to decide what to do about you."

"If you wish me to leave you now," Preston said, "I can

only accede to your decision. I take it I should swim in that direction until I find a road or habitations or some such."

Snorting, Porfirio said, "You ain't gonna swim nowhere."

"Why not? I swam to you, if you recall."

Porfirio said, "Just wait a damn minute, Preskill, Presley—wha'd you say your damn name was?"

"Preston."

"Where'd you get a name like that?"

"From my mother. It's a family name, the Prestons go back to the *Mayflower*." That last detail was a lie, but he felt it important to establish the gulf of class between them, the better to keep Porfirio under control.

It seemed to work, which is to say, Porfirio tried very hard not to look impressed. "*Mayflower*. What's that supposed to be?"

"Just a boat. A bit larger than this one. Porfirio, are you going to assist me or shall I swim?"

"Let me think a minute," Porfirio said. "My pickup's back where we come from. So what I think, we go back partway, there's a trail back there, I'll tie the boat up, walk back the rest of the way, see is those fellas still there, figure out how to get you and the pickup together. Is that okay with you?"

"It sounds like a fine plan," Preston told him.

So Porfirio ran the boat in a little half circle and took them back most of the way to the cove where they'd started. Then he steered the boat leftward and ran it up onto the sandy ground and said, "I'll be back as quick as I can."

Preston was sorry to see the man take the outboard motor's ignition key. He scrinched over to the side so Porfirio could climb past him to the prow and over onto the land, where he tied the boat's rope to a root and said, "Just keep low," and walked away.

Preston knew what was going on in Porfirio's mind, of course. The fellow would look for the trio from the limo to find out if he could make a better deal by turning Preston over to them. If only he'd left the key, Preston would steal the boat and get himself well away from here.

As it was, with the combination of treachery in the air and many mosquitoes also in the air, what he did was go over the side and swim away upstream, away from the bridge and the cove. The water was barely chest-deep, but he could make better progress swimming than walking.

When he'd made it around a curve and out of sight of the boat, he found a spot where greenery hung down low over the bank, and the bottom fell away gradually, so that he could lie mainly in water, with only his head out, resting back on what he preferred to think of as mulch. When too many mosquitoes found his head worth a detour, he covered it with mud, and that was better. And so, completely unexpectedly, he fell asleep.

"Prescott! Damn it, Prescott! Where the hell you at?"

Preston awoke, startled, floundering, swallowing salt water. Dried mud itched his head, and many branches scratched him as he jolted upward, crying, "Ow! Ow! Oof!"

"Prescott? That you?"

It was pitch black. He was seated on mud, up to his armpits in tepid water. Memory returned, and the voice became identifiable.

"Porfirio! I'm here!"

"And where the hell is that?"

"Don't you have a light? Can't you follow my voice?"

And then, preceded by the putt-putt of the outboard motor, here came a darker darkness out of the dark, and Porfirio's voice much closer, saying, "Prescott, that you down there?"

"It's Preston. Yes. Wait, let me stand. No, I need to hold on to the boat. Yes, all right, where is it? Can't you hold this boat *still?*"

"Get in the damn boat, Prescott."

Preston did manage to get into the boat, not gracefully, and Porfirio drove them away from there. Preston tried to see but couldn't. He itched all over. He said, "Where are we going?"

"To my vee-hicle. We'll talk when we get there. You shut up now. And get *down.*"

Once again the bridge gave him a welcoming slap, and then they were back out in the cove, where there was nobody any more—no fishermen, no limo, and no cigarette boat. Porfirio sped them across the cove and around the point of land, and down the other side were a few dim lights, red and green and white, where they came upon a teetering old wooden pier with many boats like Porfirio's chained along its length.

Porfirio seemed to have his own slot, which he headed straight for, then eased in, the prow bumping the pier as he said, "Hold on to that there. Can you climb up on it? You see the rope, down there by your foot? Take the end of the rope up with you."

Preston did all that, and thought for one second of legging it away down the pier, illuminated enough by these dim lights so he probably wouldn't kill himself. But why? If he had a Sancho Panza, why not hold on to him?

So Preston held on to the rope, and Porfirio shut off his motor, climbed out, chained his boat like the others, and said, "My vee-hicle's down this way." Apparently, that was going to be his joke from now on.

As they walked, Preston looked at the Rolex he had no intention of giving up. In this time zone, 10:13. Good God, he must have slept two hours! In salt water, surrounded by mosquitoes. No wonder his body felt like a loofah.

It also felt hungry. What with one thing and another, events had conspired to keep him from thinking much of his need for sustenance for some little time, but now all at once he remembered he hadn't eaten a thing since breakfast, and he was starving.

"Porfirio," he said as they walked along toward the end of the pier, "the first thing I am going to need is food. I can't go into a restaurant, I know that, not like this, but surely we can find a hamburger somewhere."

"How you figure to pay for it?"

"You will pay for it, of course, and I will reimburse you."

"We gotta talk about that reimburse," Porfirio said, trying to sound tough. "It's down this way."

The ground was stony and not kind to bare feet. Hopping along, Preston said, "Why were you gone so long? You were gone two hours, Porfirio."

"They had me out on that boat." He sounded bitter, as though his memories were more than usually unpleasant. "They wanted to know all about *you*."

"The cigarette boat?"

"Yeah, that drug boat. Here it is, get in. I don't lock the damn thing."

Neither would Preston. The passenger door squeaked loudly when he opened it, and again when he closed it.

"Food, Porfirio," he reminded him.

"You know," Porfirio said, as he started the asthmatic engine, "for a man ain't got shit on him, you bossy as hell."

"I'm just very hungry. Why did they have you on their boat?"

This was a parking lot of some sort. Driving out of it, the headlights sweeping over the unlovely scrub flora of southern Florida, Porfirio said, "They want to know where I let you off, what you say to me, all kinds a shit. When you're not in the boat, they got real pissed off."

So the rotten man *had* tried to sell Preston out, as antici-
pated. "So you took them to the boat, did you?"

"I had to, man, they were leanin on me. You heard me
talking loud, didn't you? That's why you got outa the boat."

"No, Porfirio, I did not hear you talking loud."

"Well, I did," Porfirio said, sounding sulky again. "To warn
you. Shit, man, it was *me* they was givin kidney punches."

Good, Preston thought, but didn't say. In fact, for the moment he decided to say nothing. They had come out onto a
serious road and turned right, which would be south. Traffic
was thin. They passed stores, marinas, gas stations, all closed,
even the gas stations. Then up ahead on the other side, a
Burger King appeared, brightly lit and sparsely patronized.

"Burger King! There!"

"I see the damn thing, that's where I'm headed for."

They pulled in and Preston said, "I'll have to wait here. I'll
want a hamburger."

"You already said that."

"And a Coke."

"Is that right? You want dessert, too?"

"No, just a hamburger and french fries and a Coke."

"Fries. Son of a bitch."

Porfirio slammed the pickup door on his way out, but he
did come back with the burger, the Coke, and the fries, with
a similar assortment for himself.

It was the first time in his life Preston had ingested a fast-
food hamburger—something else his ex-wives would pay
for, someday. Talking around a mouthful of food, he said,
"What I need now is a Holiday Inn."

"A Holiday Inn? How come a Holiday Inn? There's places
around here."

"I need a chain," Preston explained. "I need an organiza-
tion with a computer system large enough to verify me.
Where can we find a Holiday Inn?"

"I dunno, man, maybe there's something like that down in Key West."

Preston bit off more burger and talked around it. "I better not go to Key West," he said. "They'll probably be looking for me down there, looking in cars going by, with streetlights. It's too small and too brightly lit. Porfirio, there's got to be a Holiday Inn around here somewhere."

"I know there's one up at Key Largo," Porfirio said, "but that's gotta be eighty miles from here, way up at the top of the Keys."

"Perfect," Preston said, and some time later he and Porfirio stepped into the Key Largo Holiday Inn, where the temperature was fifty degrees Fahrenheit and the jacketed young man behind the desk was not at all startled to see a fat man in a bikini bottom walk in with a bonefisherman.

"Gentlemen?"

"I don't have any identification on me," Preston began, "nor money, but I need a room."

The young man's smile was pitying. "Sir—"

"Just a moment. Paper and pen, please."

As usual, the lower orders did Preston's bidding whether they wanted to or not. Preston took paper and pen, wrote his name in large block letters, and said to the young man, "Image Google me."

"I'm sorry?"

"Your computer," Preston said, and pointed to it in case it had slipped the young man's mind. "Go to the Google search engine. Go to their image collection. Type in my name. You will find many news and social page photos of me over the years, all more presentably dressed, but all clearly me. Please do that."

The young man shrugged. "Okay."

He turned to his computer, and Porfirio gave Preston a

grudgingly admiring look. "You're something else, man," he said.

"Of course."

"Okay," the young man said. "That's you, all right. But I don't see—"

"Hush," Preston said. Surprised, the young man stiffened into silence and Preston said, "The reason I am here, process servers attempted to waylay me. This gentleman Porfirio assisted me, for which I very much thank him—"

"And that ain't all," Porfirio said.

"Of course not." Preston turned back to the young man. "I need a room. I need to phone an associate of mine in the Caribbean and tell him to fly up here in the morning. I will phone collect, of course. He will bring my wallet and clothing and all the rest of it. In the meantime, I have to hide. Those people are still searching for me."

"They are, man," Porfirio told the young man. "And they are mean sons a bitches, let me tell you."

"Check me in," Preston said, "under my associate's name. Here, I'll write it down." And he wrote *Alan Pinkleton* beneath his own name, then said, "When he gets here tomorrow, all this will be made right."

"Sir, I don't think I can—"

"Son," Preston said, "I happen to know several of the directors on the board of the corporation you are employed by. If you wish to say good-bye to any hope of working for corporate America ever again, just turn me out into the night. I'll find help elsewhere, but, trust me, you will not."

"He's," Porfirio told the young man, "as tough as those other guys."

Sounding pained, the young man said, "Sir, you don't have to threaten me."

"I'm glad of that."

"I can see you are who you say you are, and you've had

some trouble, I guess, so I think I can take a chance on helping you out here. Will you both be staying?"

Preston and Porfirio gave a loud *"No!"* together, and then Preston said, "But before Porfirio goes, we must do something to reward him for his assistance."

"I been wondering," Porfirio said, "when we'd get to that part."

"Including," Preston said, with a nasty smile into Porfirio's face, "his *talking loud* while leading those people back to the boat."

"Saved your bacon, man."

Directing the smile at the young man, Preston said, "Please give Porfirio one hundred dollars in cash, and put it on my bill."

Outraged Porfirio cried, "A hundred dollars? I *saved* you from them people, man! I drove you all the way up here! I bought you a burger and french fries *and* a Coke! I pulled you outa the *ocean,* man!"

The young man said to Preston, "Did he do all that?"

"In fact, yes," Preston said.

Opening his cash drawer, the young man said, "I will add *five* hundred dollars to your bill, sir," and started counting it on the desk in front of Porfirio.

Who grinned broadly at the money and said, "That's better. That's more like it." Scooping up the cash, he gave Preston back his nasty smile in spades and said, "And thank *you,* my man."

41

Stan Murch was not above traveling in the actual subway, if circumstances called for that. Thus, at two-fifteen on Thursday morning, Stan, dressed in casual but dark clothing, went upstairs to leave his house.

This was an entire block of row houses, all attached, all alike, two-family, two-story, brick, with an exterior staircase to the second-floor apartment next to a concrete driveway to the one-car garage downstairs. In most of these houses, as in the one owned by Murch's Mom—he was just a boarder here—the four-and-a-half-room upstairs apartment was rented out for the income, while the owner's family lived in the three and a half rooms downstairs, plus a basement room that opened onto the backyard. Most owners turned this basement room into what they called a family room or entertainment center, but which Murch called his bedroom. Leaving this, he went upstairs where one night-light glowed in the kitchen, because his Mom, tired from a day of outrage at the wheel of a medallion New York City taxicab, had long since gone to bed.

Quietly, he left the house. This house was on East Ninety-ninth Street, a little off Rockaway Parkway, and very close to the Rockaway Parkway station, the last stop on the Canarsie Line, known to officialdom as the L, which would travel from here to Eighth Avenue and West Fourteenth Street in Manhattan.

Since this was the end of the line, there was usually a train in the station, doors open, waiting for the moment to depart, and there was one such this time. Stan became the fourth person to board that particular car, all seated far from one another. Finding a *Daily News* on a seat, he settled beside it, started to read, and an hour and forty minutes later stepped off another subway car under Lexington Avenue and Sixty-eighth Street.

His only objection to the subway, really, was that you couldn't choose your own route. On the other hand, when you got where you were going, you didn't have any parking headaches.

It was a quiet walk over to Fifth Avenue. A few empty cabs looked at him hopefully, and a couple of lone walkers looked at him warily, but otherwise he had the city to himself.

The story was, this garage door was supposed to be unlocked and unarmed at this point; just turn the handle and lift. So he did, and it lifted, but heavily, so that he had to use both hands on it. This was a door meant for the electric motor and remote control, so there wasn't much thought given to its weight, which was considerable.

However, starting to lift the door meant that a light immediately switched on inside the garage, so he only raised it to waist height and then slid through under it and eased it back down again.

And here it was, a recent BMW 1 Series in banker black, furred all over with pale gray dust. Starting at the rear, which was closest to the door, Stan made a slow eyes-only inspection of the vehicle, approving of its pearl gray leather seats and the key stuck in the ignition and especially approving of its lack of GPS.

And what else did he have in here? On the right side of the garage, facing the front passenger seat, was a metal door with a small rectangular window in it, and beyond that a set of metal shelves, and beyond that, in the corner, a closed upright metal locker.

Stan looked at the door first, and could see nothing but blackness through the little window. Would this be the elevator? Experimentally, he pulled on the door handle, and it opened, and yes, that was the elevator. It was down here, at this level, and as soon as the door opened, a light in there switched on.

A small elevator, but luxurious, with a red cushioned armless wooden chair at the back, soft indirect lighting from above, and flocked wallpaper on the walls. Pretty good.

The shelves were next. They contained cleaning and maintenance supplies for the car, including a chamois cloth, which was good; he'd use that on the car before he took it out. There was also on one shelf a remote control for the garage door, an extra one; Stan tossed it into the BMW, on the front passenger seat.

The locker was unlocked and contained only a chauffeur's uniform. It had the tired look that every suit gets when it's been hanging in one place too long.

Stan shut the locker, reached for the chamois, and the light went out.

Oh, on a timer. Fortunately, the elevator light was still on, and gleaming through the window, so by that shine Stan made his way back to the garage door and lifted it just enough to cause the light to come on again.

Okay, enough inspections; let's get on with it. He took the chamois and briskly rubbed the car down, removing the gray dust, letting it sparkle in the light the way it wanted to. While he was doing that, the elevator light switched off, but that was okay.

He was just finishing with the chamois, at the rear bumper, when the garage light went off again. This time, he pushed the door up all the way, then got behind the wheel of the BMW, twisted the key, and the engine coughed, but then started. The sound was ragged, the car not having been driven for so long, but it was ready to roll.

Stan backed the BMW out to the sidewalk, stopped, got out of the car, and pushed the garage door closed by hand, because the electric motor would be too loud at this quiet time of night.

Also, at this time of night, he figured, the long way home would be quickest—over to the FDR, down to the Brooklyn Battery Tunnel, through to the Belt, and all around the hem of Brooklyn to Canarsie. No traffic, no delays, home much quicker than doing the Manhattan Bridge and Flatbush Avenue and all that. Too bad that wasn't true in the daytime.

But it was certainly true now. At the end, getting out of the BMW in front of his house, he unlocked his way in, stepped through the side interior door into the garage, and backed his Mom's cab out to the street. Then the BMW went in, the garage door was closed, and the cab was placed on the driveway, nose against the garage.

Stan went into his house again, left the cab key on the kitchen table, had a beer, and went to bed. Nice car. Better than Max deserved.

42

FROM THE MOMENT Preston phoned him, a little after midnight, waking him from what he had to admit was in any case a troubled sleep, Alan found that Thursday, the nineteenth of August, was the most hellish day of his entire life, as well as the longest, and only partly because so much of the day consisted of travel, which, in addition to the normal irritations implicit in the very word "travel," was chockablock with extra aggravations, due both to the unforeseen nature of the travel involved and to its abnormalities—leaving a Club Med on a weekday, for instance, just to begin with.

Alan had gone to bed early Wednesday evening, having no one to talk with after Preston's mysterious disappearance, and in fact no one to talk with *about* Preston's mysterious disappearance except himself, which he could do just as well in bed in the dark, brooding on the dark person of Pamela Broussard and what sirenic thing she might have done with poor Preston, until fitful sleep had taken him, only to be shattered by that firecracker phone call:

"You know who this is."

"What? What?"

"For God's sake, Alan, you fell *asleep*? With me God knows where? What kind of paid companion do you call yourself?"

"It's not that easy to be a paid companion, you know," Alan said, having come to full consciousness by now, "to someone who isn't present. In any event, I take it you yourself know where you are."

"I am at the Holiday Inn on Key Largo."

Was that a joke? Would Preston make a joke like that? "I suppose there is one," Alan said doubtfully.

"I need everything," Preston went on. "I am standing here in nothing but my swim trunks."

"In Florida? Preston, you didn't swim— Oh, my God, she got you sailing!"

"Yes, she did, damn her eyes. If there are any policemen on that island, Alan, I want you to have her arrested, at once, for kidnapping, and—"

"She's gone."

"What do you mean, gone? How could she be gone?"

"The resort office here got an e-mail saying her mother had died. Quite unexpectedly."

"And long ago, I should think," Preston said grimly, "from the shock of having given birth to Pam."

"Who works for your ex-wife Helene's brother Hubert."

"Aaaarrrghh!"

"Exactly. Did you get away from your kidnappers? Is that what this is all about?"

"What this is all *about*, Alan, is that I am here with nothing. No identification, no credit cards, no clothing—I'm like a Dickens orphan."

"Well, not quite."

"Very like. I want you, Alan, to pack up everything of mine, everything."

"You're not coming back?"

"They're looking for me, Alan, they want to press papers on me. They'll be watching every possible route for me to take back out of the country. No, I have a better idea. *Don't* check out of there, but do come here, by the fastest, soonest means of transportation known to man."

"I think I know what that is."

"Bring everything of mine, bring everything of yours, but do not check out."

"I understand that."

"I'll be here waiting for you. I'm checked in under your name. What name do you want to use here?"

"Preston, I would rather use my own."

"I told you, I've taken it. This young man here, this desk clerk, I've taken him into my confidence—"

"Mm hm."

Away from the phone, Preston was heard to say, "What is *your* name, by the by? Duane? Very good. You will be recompensed for this good deed, Duane. Not as lavishly as Porfirio, you understand, but well."

Alan, feeling left out, said, "Preston?"

Returning to the phone, Preston said, "Duane needed a name to check me in under, which could not be my own. So I gave him yours."

"I see."

"So now *you* have to have a nom de guerre as well. Come on, Alan, it's late. I want to get to my new room in this place and have a long warm shower and a long warm sleep. Come along, Alan, whom do you wish to be?"

"Duane," Alan said. "Smith."

"Ever the comedian. You will find me when you get here, Alan, in my room, next to naked."

Not an appetizing image, but Alan was used to it. "I'll get there when I can," he promised, and hung up.

*   *   *

Which was not going to be as soon as one might like. Alan, dressed, teeth brushed, presented himself at the office, where the young woman on duty found it hard to believe she was expected to have a conversation with a guest at this hour. Being alone here on the graveyard shift meant, to her, being alone, surrounded by bright paperback examples of chick-lit, each with its cover featuring a perky, smirky girl whose face needed to be slapped.

As did this one's. Trying to be patient at nearly one in the morning after not only troubled sleep but rudely disturbed sleep, Alan said, yet again, "I am not checking out, but I do have to leave for a few days. On an airplane. To Miami."

"Okay," she said, her eyes drifting toward the scatter of books on the table behind her.

"Arrange it," he said.

She blinked at him, slowly. "You want to check out? At this hour?"

"I do not want to check out. I will continue to pay for the room, but I just have to leave for a few days. On that airplane we were discussing. To Miami."

"Okay," she said.

Having that circular feeling, Alan said, "When is the next flight to Miami?"

"There's one on Saturday."

"No, dear," he said. "Today. This morning. As early as possible."

"I only know about the one on Saturday."

"A woman left here yesterday," Alan pointed out, "due to family tragedy. She didn't wave her arms all the way to America, so there must be a plane."

"Not to Miami," she said.

"Where to, then?"

"I dunno." Wrinkling her face up like a washcloth, she said, "You want to know where Ms. Broussard went?"

"I do not. There's an airport on this island. There are planes leaving it every day. Where do they go?"

"Other islands, I think."

"Do you have flight schedules in the desk there? Anything like that?"

"Sure," she said. "You want to look at one? Which airline?"

"All airlines. Every creature that flies, that's what I want."

Eventually, she did come up with schedules for four airlines, none of them companies he'd ever heard of, and all of them, as she'd suggested, merely hopping around the islands like hummingbirds. But here was one, at 7:30 a.m. on Wednesday, Thursday, Friday, and Saturday, that flew to San Juan in Puerto Rico. From Puerto Rico, wouldn't it be possible to reach Miami?

"Let's," Alan suggested to the lit-chick, "call this eight-hundred number."

"You want to use the phone? Go ahead."

So he did, and got a person, from the sound of her accent, either in Kentucky or Bangladesh. He explained where he was and where he wanted to go, and she agreed to make the necessary reservations. All he had to do was present himself at the local airport with his credit card sixty minutes before flight time, and his ticket, all the way through to Miami, would be awaiting him.

"Thank you," he told the phone, and left a 5:45 wake-up call with the reader.

The difficulties of getting oneself on the road at the same time the sun is getting up are many and complex. In the first place, Alan didn't have a key to Preston's room, and it wasn't easy to convince a bellboy to open the place so he could pack up Preston's stuff. It was only when the lad verified Alan's contention that he not only knew Preston but that Preston had been, for several years now, paying Alan's bills in this place, that he was permitted entry.

Then there was the luggage. Alan didn't travel light, but next to him Preston was a pasha. The taxi that was called became so full of bags that Alan could barely squeeze himself in among them, and at the small local airport he was the cause of much merriment among the layabouts to be found at every tropical air terminal around the entire waist of the world.

Then they wouldn't check the bags all the way through to his final destination. He was outside the United States at the moment, which meant that he, plus all that kit and all that caboodle, would meet again in San Juan to go through Customs and Immigration.

"See you soon," he regretfully told the scout troop of bags as they bounced away on the conveyor belt, and then, while waiting to board plane number one, he went off to have a cup of rotten coffee and a worse donut.

The first airplane was quite small but quite full, entirely of island people, many of whom had brought baskets of food along in order to picnic in the sky. The food smelled, variously and mostly not pleasantly. Also, the plane, although flying through the air, gave a very realistic impersonation of being driven across a washboard-rutted back road somewhere. Crash, stink, crash, stink; he was happy to see Puerto Rico.

Whatever passenger profiles the Feds maintain on smugglers and terrorists and other unwelcome persons must have included warnings about people with ridiculous amounts of expensive luggage, because Alan was put through so many searches and interrogations that he nearly missed his next flight, and it was only by raising his voice and acting like exactly the sort of overbearing rich bastard he most loathed that he managed to effect his release.

The 10:45 a.m. plane from Puerto Rico to Miami was an improvement, mostly because it had a first-class section up front, into which Alan firmly inserted himself. He was traveling on Preston's nickel, after all, so there was no point stinting.

Also, although he did not believe in drinking before lunch, particularly when sleep-deprived, he somehow couldn't deny himself a complimentary Bloody Mary once the plane was airborne. His seatmate was a stout elderly fellow in suit and tie, of all things, who spent the entire flight nodding over a hardcover Tom Clancy novel—nodding in agreement, that is, not in sleepiness.

Alan sipped his Bloody Mary and smiled for the first time since the midnight phone call. Back in coach, they could be roasting goats over an open flame for all he knew, and probably were, but up here among the readers of hardcover thrillers, life was good.

The combination of comfort and vodka soon made Alan contemplative, and what he mostly contemplated was his future. This job with Preston Fareweather, which barely could be called a job at all, had been very pleasant and remunerative, but was that now coming to a close? Had Pamela Broussard, in her nastiness, disrupted not only Preston's life but Alan's as well? He hardly thought of himself as indispensable, so if Preston had plans that did not include a return to Club Med, it was entirely possible they would no longer include Alan, either. He'd certainly be able to find another rich bully to play courtier to—he wasn't worried about that part of it— but would the next one be anywhere near as much fun as silly, fat, teasing Preston Fareweather?

The flight was due to arrive in Miami at 1:20 and very nearly did. And it was here that Alan found out precisely how much baggage he carried on this trip: three carts full. His transit, therefore, from baggage claim to the line of auto rental

counters was tedious in the extreme. He would push a cart down a hall to a turn or a doorway, leave it, return to point A, push a second cart down the hall, leave it next to the first, return to point A, push the third cart down the hall; repeat. When he was finished, his goods stacked up like rush hour at the rent-a-car counter of his choice, he had become exhausted, short-tempered, and too harried to fight.

The auto rental clerk gave him a look. "You want a full-size car," she said.

"What I really want," he told her, "is a bed."

"We don't have those, unfortunately. That's a different industry entirely. I can give you a car with reclining seats."

"I'll do my own reclining, someday, please, God."

One had to ride a bus to get to the car, which meant he probably did more baggage handling out here today than did most of the people employed for the purpose. Finally, though, he and his goods and chattels were deposited in front of a bright red Lexus Enorma, and the bus, much lighter now, went on its way. (Chattels, when they are not slaves, are movable pieces of property, which every one of these damn things was.)

The Enorma had a capacious trunk and a pretty roomy back seat, so Alan eventually got everything stowed. Then, constantly checking the map the car-rental woman had given him, he found his way out of Miami International Airport and, after one misstep on state Route 41, which wanted to take him through the Everglades to Naples over on Florida's west coast, he managed to turn south, drop down to Route 1, and, by barely four in the afternoon, two and a half hours after landing, there, by God, was the Key Largo Holiday Inn, where—or nearly where—Humphrey Bogart and Lauren Bacall had been treated so badly by Edward G. Robinson. None of them seemed to be around at the moment, but wasn't that—? No! The *African Queen?*

The person at the desk, being female, was unlikely to be Duane. In fact, the name tag on her left breast announced that at least that much of her was named DeeDee. "DeeDee," Alan said, approaching the desk, "is that the real *African Queen* out there? From the movie?"

"Yes, sir," she said, with a happy smile, glad to be part of an operation that would have the *African Queen* in its parking lot.

"It looks smaller than in the movie," Alan said.

She nodded. "Everybody says that. May I help you, sir?"

"Oh, they do, huh? I have a reservation, I'm—" But then he drew a blank for just a second, remembering that the person he was *not* was Alan Pinkleton. "Duane Smith," he remembered.

"Oh, yes, sir," she said, "I think we have a message for you. Yes, here it is, sir."

The message was from Preston: "Call me before you check in, room 211."

"Where's the house phone?"

"Just over there, sir. Are you checking in now, sir?"

"Not yet."

"Shall we get your luggage from your car, sir?"

You don't know what you're asking, he thought, and said, as he headed for the house phone, "Let's wait on that, too."

Preston answered so promptly, it was clear he'd been sitting right next to the phone, or possibly on top of it. "Yes!"

"Preston?"

"Bring me some clothing. Not all the luggage, just one piece, with clothing."

Alan might have pointed out that he had packed this morning in semidarkness and a mad rush and wasn't certain which of those many bags contained the clothing Preston might most prize at this moment, but Preston had already hung up. So Alan swung by the desk to assure DeeDee he'd

be back, and then went out to the hot, bright sun to open the Enorma's trunk and root through suitcases until he found one that seemed to have the variety Preston might have in mind. He carried this into the building, found 211, knocked, and Preston yanked open the door.

"Where have you been?"

"Traveling. Here."

Preston really was wearing nothing but that skimpy bathing suit. Grabbing the suitcase Alan offered him, he waved a hand at the room service table over by the window and said as he receded toward the bathroom, "Have some leftover lunch if you want. Wait here, we have to talk." And into the bathroom he went, slamming the door.

Preston had done well for himself with his room service lunch. Salmon, asparagus, some sort of white pudding. Most of it was no longer in a state Alan found appetizing, but the coffee in the thermos was still at least warm, and the untouched roll was fresh, with sesame seeds. All much better than the little cardboard box of semi-edibles he'd rejected on the flight to Miami, featuring, as it had, a suspiciously blemish-free apple, as large and red and round and perfect as the one the witch had carted about in *Snow White*.

Alan had consumed half a roll and half a cup of coffee when Preston returned, arrayed in bright green polo shirt, mauve slacks, and tasseled gray loafers. "I have thrown those swim trunks away," he announced.

"You didn't tell me about the *African Queen*."

"Some things are best as surprises," Preston assured him. "Speaking of which, we've had a change of plan."

"We have?"

"My initial concept was," Preston said, "we could secrete ourselves within the bland vastness of Florida a while. Off-season, easy to move about, you could be the official presence with your credit cards and driver's license and all that. But

shortly before our young friend Duane went off duty this
morning, he phoned me to say a man had just come through,
showing a photo of *me* and asking if I had been sighted by
anyone. He didn't claim to be a policeman, but he tried to
leave that impression."

"Private detective, I suppose," Alan said.

"One of who knows how many, fanned across the state,"
Preston said, with a gesture like someone dealing out a lot of
fans. "I can't stay here," he said. "But to go back to that island
would be folly. So I've decided on the only thing I can possibly do."

"Yes?"

"Go home," Preston said.

Surprised, Alan said, "New York? Are you sure?"

"Where else is there for me? Anywhere else, I'm a hunted
man. I've been safe till now, but they smell blood, Alan, they
know they've got me on the run. The safest place for me
right now is my own apartment in New York City. Nobody
can get me there."

"Preston, I'm not sure how you hope to make it from here
to there."

Preston paused to study his reflection in the mirror over
the dresser. Pleased, he smiled as he patted his shirt over his
paunch. "That's where I've been brilliant," he said. "I know I
can't fly to New York. One has to show identification to
board an airplane, and they'll be watching for my name on
flights to New York. But they can't watch all flights everywhere, Alan."

"No, I suppose not."

"There's a flight this evening at eight-thirteen," Preston
said, "that arrives in Philadelphia at ten fifty-nine. We rent a
car *there*, Alan. An hour and a half on the Jersey Turnpike,
through the Lincoln Tunnel, and we're home. At one or two

in the morning, surely I can slip into that building unde-
tected."

"We have a lot of luggage, Preston. Maybe we should put
the rental car in that garage of yours, run everything up in the
elevator."

Preston looked scornful. "A dreadful idea, Alan," he said.
"I think you'd best leave the generaling to me."

"If you say so."

"I do say so. A lot of activity around that garage, Alan, and
my personal automobile suddenly parked on the street,
would be a *dead* giveaway. I want to be home, Alan, but I do
not want every private detective in the employ of my ex-
wives to *know* I am home."

"Then that's what we'll do, then," Alan agreed.

Easier said than done. Alan checked Preston out, using his
own name and credit card, while Preston prepared an envelope for DeeDee to pass on to Duane, containing, Alan had
no doubt, less than Duane would be pleased by, and then
Alan, having just driven all the way down here from Miami
International, turned around and drove all the way back
again.

Next, at the airport, having just checked out all this luggage, he proceeded, with minimal help from Preston, to
check it all back in again. Having rid themselves of baggage
and rental car, they did have time for a rather awful dinner
with a Spanish overcast before boarding their flight, where,
once they were safely seated in first class, Alan was happy to
forget dinner with another complimentary Bloody Mary.

And then, for quite some time, nothing happened. The
pilot did occasionally come onto the sound system with that
sedated-frog pilot voice to explain the delay—something
about traffic backed up at Chicago O'Hare, though what that
had to do with a flight between Miami and Philadelphia,

Alan did not feel competent to say—but the effect was, they left the ground not at 8:13 but at 9:45, more or less, which put them in the sky over Philadelphia not at 10:59 but at nearly one in the morning. Since they had arrived at Phila- delphia at the wrong time, throwing everybody's schedule off, they had to spend an additional fifteen minutes circling in the sky above that city until at last a niche was found for them among all those millions and millions of summer trav- elers, and the plane *finally* landed.

Luggage. More luggage. Wait, still more luggage. It was quarter to two when the last of the three carts of luggage reached the car rental desk, where, astonishingly enough, the reservation Preston had made this morning in Alan's name was still good. Not only that, they had another Lexus Enorma, this one in bright yellow.

Alan had to fight to stay awake on the long drive up through New Jersey, which meant he had to have the radio on loud. Preston also had to stay awake, because of the loud radio but also to monitor Alan's wakefulness, so by a quarter to four, when they at last drove through the Lincoln Tunnel into Manhattan, both were feeling rather shredded. The only good part of it was that neither had the strength to start a fight, even though both of them wanted with all their hearts to start a fight.

But a fight very nearly did break out anyway, when Pres- ton insisted, as they were driving through Central Park, that Alan turn the Enorma back in to its owners *tonight*. "We have to have this trip behind us," he announced, "as though it had never existed. We cannot have this vehicle, in *your* name, in front of *my* home until God knows what time tomorrow. It won't be difficult for you at all, Alan."

Of course it would be difficult, as they both knew, but Preston didn't care. However, they did finally get to the apart- ment building, where they put most of the on-duty staff to work emptying the car and transporting everything up the regular elevator to the penthouse, once they'd convinced the staff that Preston was really Preston. No one employed here now had been here in that prehistory when Preston had been an actual presence in the building.

Once everything was in and up, it was established that the doorman would recognize Alan whenever he returned from his Enorma unloading, and would deliver him to the penthouse. So all that was left for Alan to do was get back in the car, drive to the rental agency's office on Eleventh Avenue, turn the car in, roam the streets a while in search of a taxi, find one, ride it back to Fifth Avenue, ride, wilting, up in the elevator to the penthouse, and walk into a place of a million lights, where Preston paced back and forth on the living room floor.

"Where have you *been?*"

"Everywhere," Alan said. "I would like to sleep now, if I may."

"It's always about you, Alan," Preston said. "I've noticed that. Come along, I'll show you your guest room. That's why I've been waiting up for you, Alan, to be your host. There's the guest room there, it has its own bath, I've had your bags put in there higgledy-piggledy, I shall now turn out every light and go straight to bed and I do not want to know the world again for hours and hours and *hours.*"

"I'll second that," Alan said around a yawn.

When, a few minutes later, too tired to do anything but wash his face and brush his teeth, Alan turned off his own last light and declined gratefully onto Preston's extremely comfortable guest-room bed, the red LED of the bedside alarm read *04:47.*

43

THE TRUCK WAS a three-year-old Ford E-450 sixteen-foot diesel cube van, painted white some time ago, without company markings or other writing on its sides, doors, or back. The cab was comfortable, the rear door rolled up easily, and the flat floor interior was broom clean and without the odors of yesteryear. The truck's green license plates were from Vermont, a state about which there has never been a shred of suspicion, unlike some we could mention, and the CD left behind in the deck was Schubert's Trout Quintet.

Seeing this, Stan said, "The previous owner give up the ministry?"

"Something like that," Max said.

Already at eight in the morning, Max's shirtfront was streaked with gray from leaning on cars, talking over their tops at potential customers, of whom a few straggled around the lot at the moment, hoping to find something that could take them to work today. Harriet had a perky nephew who played salesman sometimes, when the customer load backed up, and he was out there now, fetching thrown sticks and talking up the merchandise and otherwise making himself useful, while Max and Stan discussed the trade at issue.

So Stan took one wary step back from the Ford and said, "Something like what, Max? Does this vehicle blow up?"

"Nothing like that at all," Max assured him. "I'll tell you the story in the office. For now, I understand you got a free gift for me."

"Stockbroker's special," Stan said, pointing at the BMW. "It's all yours except the plates."

"The plates?"

"I'll switch with the truck. I wouldn't want to drive around New York with Vermont plates. Somebody might stop and ask to borrow a ski."

"Mm hm." Max walked around the BMW to the other side, leaned on it, looked over its top, and said, "You got any papers with this thing?"

"Nothing you'd want to hold in your hands."

"We're talking virgin birth here."

"It's a miracle, Max. And it's all yours, if the truck's story doesn't scare me too much."

"I'll wanna hear the BMW story, too," Max said. "Come on in."

As they stepped into the office building, Harriet was typing and the phone was ringing—nothing new. "We get more privacy inside," Max said, as Harriet at last paused in her typing and grabbed the phone:

"Maximilian's Used Cars, Miss Caroline speaking. I'm sorry, you want to do *what* with it? Yes, I remember that vehicle, I typed up the paperwork on it. You're the rubber man in the carnival, aren't you? *So* amusing, we all— Oh, I'm sorry, Mr. Flexo, was it? All sales are final."

Max and Stan should have been in the other room by now, but both had stopped to listen to how the phone conversation would come out. Harriet listened, smiled pityingly, and said, "Well, 'final' means we don't take them back. There's a forwardness to the story of life, Mr. Flexo. That vehicle came to us, we passed it on to you, if you are finished with it, you pass— Well, it drove off the lot, if you recall. Mr. Flexo, there are strange sounds in the background, just where are you? Setting up the county fair? Where, Mr. Flexo?"

Harriet's light trilling laughter filled the little office like bouquets of roses. "In Kentucky, Mr. Flexo? I tell you what. You *get* that car here, then we'll talk." Hanging up, she shook her head, turned her smile toward Stan and Max, and said, "They *know* they're scrap iron, and still they rely on them."

"If buyer's remorse ever accomplished anything in this world," Max said, "we'd all still be living in caves. Come in before Harriet makes any more friends."

Max's inner office was mostly tall fireproof metal filing cabinets, variously locked with keys and hasps and iron bars, because what they contained was more precious than gold, or anyway on an equal par of preciousness with gold; in those filing cabinets were the customers' signatures. With them in existence, Maximilian's Used Cars could go on forever.

There was also space in this room grudgingly allowed for furniture other than filing cabinets, in the corner farthest from the door and near a barred window with views of weeds and anonymous vinyl buildings. Here crouched Max's desk, smaller than Harriet's and much messier, with everything on it from empty soda bottles to various newspapers folded open to partly done crossword puzzles, to a V-shaped metal spring-operated object meant to improve the operator's grip. As though Max needed his grip improved.

"Siddown," Max said, involving the last of the room's furniture, being his own wooden swivel desk chair and the small, sagging brown mohair sofa facing it.

Stan sat on the sofa arm, that being as much of that sofa as he cared to know, and said, "The truck had a life in Vermont."

"It did. It was an undercover for the feds."

This was a surprise. "The feds had that truck."

"And here's a fact you may not have considered before this, Stan," Max said, raising a pedagogical finger. "At all levels of law enforcement, they take very good care of their vehicles. I've had undercover narc cars come through here, look on the outside like they been run off cliffs, but the insides and the wheels are better than when they came out of the factory."

"When they need to drive, I guess," Stan said, "they really need to drive."

"You've got it."

"But why do the feds need to drive in Vermont?"

"Smuggling."

"Oh. Canada. What, whiskey?"

"Chinamen," Max told him. "And also Chinawomen. And I believe sometimes Chinachildren, too."

Stan said, "Chinese? From Canada?"

"Asians, anyway," Max said. "And yes, from Canada. The same like you got all these Hispanics coming up to the border down south, you got these other people coming down from Canada. A Chinaman can go to Toronto and you'll never notice him, they already got a Chinatown. That same Chinaman in Guadalajara? Not your best idea."

"So they used this truck," Stan said, "to infiltrate the smugglers."

"Worked like a charm," Max told him. "From what I understand, they used this truck to send a whole lot of people back where they didn't wanna go, and even put some of the coyotes, you know, the smugglers, in the can in Canada."

"So now the truck is retired. Why?"

"Well, it got burned. The word got around up there, you do business with this truck, all of a sudden you meet a lotta people that don't smile."

"Not good," Stan suggested.

"You're okay if you stay away from that border," Max assured him. "But the thing is, the way it got outed, the feds can't do the normal way to get it back into civilian life. It still has some of its previous life on it."

"Meaning what?"

"The truth is," Max said, "it has very strange papers. The fella had it, he deals in big trucks mostly, sends em overseas so nobody *ever* tries to bring them back, I envy that guy, he tells me, you get a cop, he runs a check on the registration on this truck, he gets like an asterisk, says, don't worry, keep your nose clean, good-bye."

"Pretty good."

"For you, Stan," Max said, "it couldn't be better. For a furniture dealer, maybe, somebody in the legit world, a little freaky. So my friend and I worked out a deal, and now, depending on this BMW, you and me are gonna work out a deal, and what I think, Stan, whatever you want that truck for, afterward you might as well keep it. You'll never find a better mace. Now, about your offering."

Stan told him about the owner of the BMW, off for years now in a Club Med, hiding out from process servers, nobody checking the garage where the BMW's stored. Just give it a new christening, it's gold.

"This sounds good," Max admitted.

"It is good."

"I would say, Stan, you and me, we've done a good morning's work."

"No, you have," Stan said, getting up from the sofa arm. "My work starts now. I gotta meet my guys at nine-thirty in the city."

A small amount of paperwork adjustment, and Stan was on his way, the nephew waving bye-bye. The truck felt fine. And keep it around after the job, eh? Hmmm.

And who knew the feds listened to Schubert?

44

"COME ON UP," Arnie said.

Dortmunder, at the foot of the stairs, having just been buzzed into the building by Arnie, looked up at him and said, "Arnie, the idea is, you're coming down, I'm taking you to the place."

"I've been having second thoughts about that," Arnie said. "Come on up."

Not going on up, Dortmunder said, "Don't do that, Arnie. Never have second thoughts, they just ball you up. Come on, we don't wanna be late, Stan's gonna be there with the truck nine-thirty, got the remote opener and everything, he zaps the opener, zip, zip, everybody's in."

"This is where I'm having second thoughts," Arnie said. "What am *I* doing in? Come to that, what am I doing *out*? Look at me, I'm still the color of a roll of burlap."

This was true, but Dortmunder said, "Arnie, don't even think like that, it's fading away to nothing."

"And we got more sun *today*, I heard the warning on the radio."

"You'll be indoors, in an entire penthouse. Come on, Arnie, we can't stand here in the stairwell forever, some neighbor's gonna call the cops."

"So come up, we'll discuss it."

Dortmunder well knew, if he were to go up these stairs, he would never get Arnie down them, so, without moving, he said, "Arnie, come down, we'll talk it over while we walk through the park, you'll see where—"

"Walk?" Astonished, Arnie said, "I don't walk, Dortmunder! I don't even walk anyway, and you're talking through the *park*? It's all sun out there."

"Okay," Dortmunder said, "I'll meet you halfway. No walking, we'll take a cab. I'll buy."

"A cab. Over to the place, you mean, with the thing and the thing and everybody zips in."

"Sure. Come on."

"How's this meeting me halfway? You want the cab to go halfway there and come back?"

"Arnie," Dortmunder said, "I'm not coming up."

"I just don't see—"

"Preston Fareweather, Arnie."

Arnie shook all over and looked agonized. His hand clutched to the banister in front of him.

Dortmunder pressed his advantage. "Those guys were so brilliant, they even got the Seersucker."

"The what?"

Dortmunder said, "Didn't you say he had one of those?"

"I don't even know what the hell it is!"

"Well, we'll go look for it. Come on, Arnie, Preston Fareweather. Broadway's out there, Arnie, it's full of taxicabs, and every one of them has a roof. Don't let Preston Fareweather think we're bozos, Arnie."

"Preston Fareweather thinks everybody's bozos," Arnie said with disgust.

"Including you," Dortmunder reminded him. "And that's the mistake he made, that he's gonna find out what a mistake it is. That's the whole point here, isn't it? We're not gonna let Preston Fareweather forget what happens when he messes around with *you*."

Alarmed, Arnie said, "Wait a minute, I don't want him to know *I* had anything to do with it."

"Of course not, Arnie. Just some unnamed, unknowable genius he mistreated in the past. Can you see his face, Arnie? Picture it in your mind, Preston Fareweather's face, the next time he walks into that penthouse."

Arnie thought. "Let me get my hat," he said.

45

WHERE KELP GOT the hard hats was a theatrical cos-
tumer in the west Forties, a place he'd patronized before, always very late at night, when the prices were better but
you had to serve yourself, mostly in the dark.

It was a deep, broad shop full of crannies and nooks and
little rooms, two stories of costumes and props, anything you
might want in a stage show or on a movie set or shooting a
commercial or running another day of a soap opera—all
things that happen in that neighborhood just about every day.
Kelp was always careful not to harm any locks here or otherwise be intrusive, and since they had so much and he took so
little, he doubted they were even aware of his visits. Which
was nice—he liked the opportunity to be a loyal customer,
and wouldn't like them to feel the need to increase their security.

Ordinary yellow hard hats without logos were harder to
find than cowboy hats and Nazi officer hats and football helmets and graduation caps, but eventually, on a low shelf upstairs near the rear, he came across a cluster of them, looking

like the world's largest canary eggs. He put two in the plastic bag he'd brought for the purpose, let himself gently out of the place, took a cab home, had a brief pleasant chat with Anne Marie, slept peacefully, and at nine-thirty in the morning was crossing Fifth Avenue at Sixty-eighth Street when Tiny called to him, "Kelp!"

Kelp looked, and Tiny was waving from a limo waiting for the light to change so it could make the left turn onto Sixty-eighth Street. Kelp waved back, and Tiny called, "Come wait in the limo."

"Will do."

Kelp finished crossing Fifth and turned left to cross Sixty-eighth, because the driver of the limo was stopping it at the fire hydrant across the street from the garage entrance they'd be aiming at, but before he could step off the curb, a cab stopped at his feet, and out of it, astonishingly, stepped Arnie Albright, wearing the kind of cloth cap with a soft brim all around it that really terrible golfers wear, except without the comical pins.

Kelp said, "Arnie? You sprang for a cab?"

"Not on your life," Arnie said, and from behind him, putting his wallet away, out crawled Dortmunder, looking nettled and saying, "*I* paid for the cab. It was the only way to get him here."

"Though I still got my doubts," Arnie said as the cab hurtled away.

"Well," Kelp said, "let's go over there and wait in the limo with Tiny."

Arnie said, "Limo?" but then a white truck, sneaking around the corner just as the light turned red, made the left, then a right toward the garage door, which began to lift. Stan could be seen in the truck cab, putting the remote back down on the seat.

So instead of everybody getting into the limo, Tiny got

out of it, and it drove away. Now that all the traffic had stopped, Tiny crossed the street to join them, and everybody followed the truck into the garage, where Stan thumbed the door shut again.

Stan was the only one who'd been in this place before, so everybody else had to look it over for a minute. They also had to study the truck. Kelp put the bag of hard hats on the passenger seat, and Tiny said, "Very clean. Better than I figured. What did it used to carry?"

"People," Stan said, and when they all looked at him, he said, "It's a long story, I'll tell you later, over a beer. The elevator's over there."

"We'll have to do a little alarm stuff first," Kelp said, "before we ride it anywhere."

Turned out, the alarm system for the elevator was a simpler problem than switching on the motor to run the elevator, which wanted a key they didn't have, which would fit in a slot to the right of the two buttons lined up vertically on the control panel and marked *Top* and *Bot*. Looking at those buttons, Stan said, "Did the manufacturer think the customer was gonna get confused?"

"Their lawyer made them add that," Kelp explained.

The problem with the key meant that both Dortmunder and Kelp produced leather toolkit bags and took the metal cover off the control panel, then found the way to bypass the ignition. When they checked it, it worked fine, but Dortmunder and Kelp were the only ones aboard, and the elevator just went up to the top without waiting for anybody else.

"We'll send it back down," Dortmunder said as they rose.

"And have the alarms taken care of by the time they get here," Kelp agreed.

Which they did. The second time the elevator opened at the top level, it was very full, mostly with Tiny, who seemed to be wearing Stan and Arnie as earmuffs.

(The three long rumbles of the elevator motor had not reached Preston in the master bedroom but had made a faint drone in the guest room, causing Alan to frown and shift position and have a brief, pointless dream about being in a submarine.)

"We'll just walk it through the first time," Dortmunder said, "and, Arnie, then you can tell us which things to take."

"I brung red dots," Arnie said. When everybody gave him blank looks, he said, "I got the idea from art galleries. When they have a show, if somebody buys a painting they don't get to take it home until the show is over, so the gallery has these little red dot stickers that they put on, to say, 'this one already sold.'" Taking a sheet of such stickers from his pants pocket, he said, "That's what I figured I'd do here. When I see something good, I slap a red dot on it, you guys take it away."

"I like that," Stan said. "Clear, simple and classy."

"So let's take a look around," Dortmunder said.

All the floors of the penthouse were carpeted, in Persian and other antique rugs that were themselves worthy of red dots, though Arnie wouldn't be thinking primarily in terms of furnishings. But the rugs made their progress through the penthouse silent until they entered the big living room with its airplane views of Manhattan and its array of art and antiques.

Everybody stopped, impressed, staring around at the room and the view, and Arnie said, "Forget the dots. Just take the living room."

Stan said, "Arnie, the living room is bigger than the truck."

Dortmunder said, "We like the red-dot thing, Arnie, stick with it."

"Okay, then," Arnie said, and stepped over to the nearest Picasso and whacked its frame with a red dot. Sold.

46

When Judson carried the Maylohda mail in to J. C. a little after ten that morning, she was seated at attention at her desk, speaking on the phone, using what he thought of as her High Teutonic voice—not quite an accent but definitely not native-born: "Ai do not see," she was saying, "how Ai can be of help to you. Unless we have the manifest from the port at Lacuna in Maylohda, payment is simply impossible. Ai hope you can understand. Than kyew, please do that. Good-bye."

She hung up, shifted to a more relaxed at-ease position, and looked over at Judson, who had remained standing beside her desk, waiting to attract her attention. "Something?"

"I wondered," he said, feeling he had to tiptoe around this topic because he didn't want to push himself forward too aggressively but, on the other hand, didn't want to be left out, either, "if Mr. Tiny said when they were going to do that thing on Sixty-eighth Street."

J. C. didn't seem bothered by the question. In fact, she seemed, if anything, indifferent. "They're doing it now," she said.

Surprised, hurt, Judson said, "But— Nobody told me."

The look she gave him was not warm. "Why should they?"

"Well— I was helping, Mr. Kelp taught me about that burglar alarm, I thought . . ." He moved his hands around, no longer sure what he thought.

"Look, Judson," she said, "you aren't a part of that group."

"But I thought . . ."

"Tiny told me how you volunteered, and how he tried to let you know the volunteer isn't always necessarily right."

"Oh, he let me know that, all right. But they did let me help."

"And if they need some more help," she said, "they'll ask you again. Right now they know what they're doing, so they don't need any help. Okay?"

"Well . . ."

It was just a fantasy, then, an assumption, and he'd been wrong. For one moment he'd held their coat, that's all. His position here was "the kid" and nothing else.

But if he wanted to at least keep *that* position, he'd better be careful here. So he stood up straighter and wiped the worried look from his face. "Sure," he said, as though it were no big deal. "They know—Mr. Kelp and Mr. Tiny and all of them—they know I'm here if they ever need some help again."

"They know that," J. C. agreed. "And, when they get their profit on what they're doing today, you'll get a piece, don't worry about it."

"Oh, I'm not worried," he told her, with a big self-confident grin.

Her own smile was wry as she studied him. "Well," she said, "maybe worry a little bit."

He had all day, surrounded by the incoming and outgoing mail, to wonder what she meant by that.

47

THE MUFFLED SOUNDS in the penthouse, as load after load of valuables was carried through to the rear of the place and sent down in the elevator, snagged at the sleepers but didn't quite waken them. Yesterday had been so long and tiring, and had ended so late, that as the morning progressed and the sounds neither stopped nor got louder, both Preston and Alan merely adapted their slumber to this addition to their environment, and slept on.

Meanwhile, in the living room and the formal dining room, the red dots blossomed like a bad case of measles. Dortmunder and Tiny carried the designated goods back to the elevator, loaded it aboard, and sent it down to the garage, where Kelp and Stan unloaded everything, directed the elevator upward again, and stowed the goods in the capacious sixteen-foot-deep interior of the truck.

Arnie was in heaven. After his first rapturous flurry of red-dot dispensing, he slowed down, took his time, studied the wares on offer, and even rejected some as being, while first quality, not quite at the level he was growing used to here. He also refreshed his vision sometimes by standing at the windows to gaze down on Central Park or at the pork chop of Manhattan narrowing away to the south. All in all, he felt he was enriched by having known Preston Fareweather.

Around noon, Dortmunder and Tiny, carrying a marble athlete, lost their grip for a second, and a marble elbow thudded into the wall beside them. "Watch it," Tiny said, though he was just as much to blame.

"It's okay," Dortmunder said, and they moved on while, the other side of that wall, Preston frowned in his sleep, and his mouth moved with small moist sounds, tasting itself. Like a bubble in a soda can, he was rising toward consciousness.

As Dortmunder and Tiny set the marble man on the floor in front of the elevator, its door opened, and Kelp stepped out, saying, "Stan says the truck's about full."

"We'll make this guy the last of it, then," Dortmunder said. "Help us load him."

"I'll ride down with him," Tiny said.

Dortmunder said, "Then send it back up. I'll collect Arnie. We don't want to leave him behind."

"For once," Kelp said, and the elevator door shut on the trio.

Dortmunder went back to the living room, and Arnie was over at the window again, gazing dreamily out. Looking at Dortmunder, he said, "I run outa dots."

"And the truck's run outa space. Time to go."

"I'll take a quick look around at the other rooms," Arnie said, "see is there any must-haves."

"Fine."

Arnie went off, and Dortmunder looked around for pocket-size stuff, of which there was a bunch. A Faberge egg, for example, a couple of gold medallions, a Mont Blanc pen, a nice piece of scrimshaw. Pockets bulging, he left the living

room, and in the hall he met Arnie coming out of a side
room.

Arnie grinned at him and said, "We got the cream, but just
lemme look."

"Sure."

Dortmunder walked on, and Arnie opened the next door.

The *click* of the doorknob popped Preston's eyes open.
Bleary, somewhere between awake and asleep, he lifted his
head and looked at Arnie Albright, frozen in the open doorway.

Preston blinked, there was a slam, and when his eyelids
sluggishly lifted again, there was no Arnie Albright, only a
closed door. Preston tried to frame a question, but was too
befuddled to speak it, or even very much to think it. A
dream? His head dropped back on the pillow.

A dream about Arnie Albright—too awful to think about.
Down Preston went into oblivion once more.

Arnie raced down the hall, overtaking Dortmunder, whispering in shrill urgency, "He's here! In bed!"

"What? Who?"

"*Him!* We gotta get outa here!"

Arnie scampered on, and Dortmunder followed him,
looking over his shoulder, not seeing anyone behind them.
Preston Fareweather was here? In bed? All along?

Arnie skittered in place at the elevator door. "We gotta get
outa here! Outa here!"

"Arnie, we do have to wait for the elevator."

But then it came, and they boarded, and Arnie pushed *Bot*
so hard, it bent his thumb back, which he barely noticed.
"Outa here," he said. "This is no place for a person like me.
Outa here."

48

WHAT MIKEY BELIEVED in was patience; that's what he told his crew all the time. "Don't fuckin jump into nothin, be patient. First find out what the fuck, and then it's fuckin yours."

Another thing Mikey believed in was revenge. He probably believed in revenge more than in patience or anything else, if it came to that. If Mikey were ever to build a shrine to something other than himself, it would be to revenge.

Also, a third thing Mikey believed in, passionately and without question, was profit. Everybody earns; everybody's taken care of. If you don't have profit, what have you got? Nothing. QED.

In the O.J. Bar & Grill business, the three things Mikey believed in were finally about to come together. A sweet deal he'd set up had been queered for him by some stumblebum heister named Dortmunder, not Dortmund as originally reported, plus a few of Dortmunder's unconnected loser pals. So what was needed? What was needed was to get revenge on Dortmunder and his pals, and to make a profit out of that revenge, and for all that to happen, Mikey had to be patient, which he damn well knew how to be.

This Dortmunder was such a clown, Mikey's people had been tailing him for two days, ever since Mikey's guy had picked up that name, almost the right name, in the O.J., and not once had Dortmunder even suspected there was somebody on his trail.

Not that he did much, most of the time. Once on Wednesday, and again this morning, he'd gone to the Upper West Side to the same apartment building, and this morning he'd come out of it with some gnarled little jerk, and they'd taken a cab over to Fifth and Sixty-eighth, where they'd met up with three other guys that were definitely part of Dortmunder's crew, part of the bunch that had screwed up Mikey's deal at the O.J. This time, they had a pretty big truck with them, and they and the truck all went into a garage on Sixty-eighth.

When all this was reported to Mikey, at home in New Jersey, he said, "We'll fuckin meet right there. In the fuckin park. Pass the word. We want the fuckin crew and we want some fuckin cars."

On his way to Central Park from farthest New Jersey, Mikey saw how it was going to play out, how it had to play out. Dortmunder and his people were heisters, independent heisters—he knew that much—and the story was, the reason they'd involved themselves with his sweet deal at the O.J. and loused it up the way they did in the first place was that they wanted to make a meet in the O.J.'s back room, because that was where they always met when they were *planning a job*.

Planning a job. Was that perfect? There they were now, in that garage, loading up the truck with something or other valuable from that house—or more likely the small private museum on the next street behind it.

Mikey would be patient. He would give them all the time

they needed, all the time in the world, and whenever they finally did bring that truck back out of that garage, Mikey and his friends would be there to take it away from them. Revenge and profit, in one neat ball.

The only little potential difficulty was the fact that all this was taking place in New York City. Mikey's crew, and his father Howie's entire outfit, operated within an agreement with the families in New York: that the New York guys didn't interfere with New Jersey, and the New Jersey guys didn't interfere with New York. Pulling off anything at all on this side of the river could be looked at, by anybody who wanted to be a stickler for detail, as a violation of that agreement, which could possibly end in consequences.

On the other hand, this wasn't any New York City operation Mikey was messing in; this was a bunch of no-connection independents against whom he had a legitimate beef. So this would be like what the army guys call a surgical strike: invade, pull the job, clear out. Everything beautiful.

(The O.J. bustout, if it had gone down the way it should, would also have been a technical violation of the interstate agreement, but there it was a unique deal, with Mikey the only one who could get hold of the place to squeeze it, and at the end of the operation the appropriate New York family would have been given an explanation, an apology, and a small piece, and there would have been no trouble. This, involving hijack, maybe guns shown, violence on the streets of Manhattan, was a different matter entirely.)

By eleven Mikey had everything in position. Sixty-eighth Street was one-way east, so he had a car stopped by a hydrant down toward the other end of the block. The next intersection, Madison Avenue, was northbound, so he had a car stopped around the corner on Madison, and a third waiting beyond Madison on Sixty-eighth. He had two soldiers in each car, equipped with cell phones.

Whichever way the truck went, Mikey's people would be on it, two cars at first and the third catching up. They would tail it and wait for just the right spot to crowd it to a stop, throw those people out of there, take over the truck themselves, and drive it straight to New Jersey.

Also, unless Dortmunder's crew acted wise, which Mikey didn't expect to happen, in deference to the agreement with New York there would be minimum violence and, if possible, no shooting. Smart, you had to be smart.

Seated on a bench in the park, though it faced the wrong way, Mikey could twist halfway around and look back past the low stone wall at the park's edge and across Fifth Avenue and straight down Sixty-eighth Street. Like a general with an overview of the battlefield; nice.

Mikey sat there, on the bench in Central Park, and was patient.

49

THE TALK AROUND the security desk all morning at the Imperiatum at Fifth Avenue and Sixty-eighth Street was of the astounding return, way late last night, of the mythical Preston Fareweather. He'd showed up after four in the morning with some other guy and enough luggage for a 747, all of which the staff, including security(!), had had to wrestle up to the penthouse, using the public elevator in front and not his private elevator in the back. In fact, nobody had used the private elevator at all.

So now, Big José and Little José, all ears, at last learned the story of that elevator they'd seen at the back of Fareweather's penthouse. It didn't go to some other apartment in the building for hot sex after all, but all the way down to a garage at street level.

So whadaya thinka that? In addition to everything else he's got, Preston Fareweather's got his own elevator to his own garage, in which he keeps a really cool BMW.

Well, it was nice to know the truth about the elevator, though it was a shame to lose the fantasies about that hot TV news anchor. On the other hand, this return of the prodigal Preston Fareweather meant some distinct changes in the work lives of the Josés. As Little José pointed out, "You don't get to coop up there in his living room no more, man."

"I loved that eight-foot sofa," Big José said, because he did have trouble finding comfortable places in the world where he could stretch out his long frame.

Another change was that, with the owner's return, it would no longer be necessary to do the twice-a-month security sweep of the penthouse. But that was okay. At first, going through that place had been kind of exciting, with its great views and all the art and the furniture, but of course every time they went up there, it was the same views and art and furniture, so after a while, no matter how great it was, it did get a little boring. They could remember the place pretty well by now; they didn't need to go on seeing it every two weeks.

Besides which, the other boring, repetitive parts of the job were still active, so not that much had changed. For instance, at noon they had to go out and walk around to the two doctors' offices with separate entrances on Sixty-eighth Street and pick up whatever hazmat the doctors had assembled since yesterday. All of this material, radioactive or disease-ridden or whatever, heavily wrapped in protective plastics, the two Josés would, as usual, carry around to the special safe in the back room behind the security desk, from where it would be picked up in the afternoon by the people from the special company that had the legal permits and the facilities to dispose of the crap. Until some new hires came along, this would continue to be a part of the Josés' daily duty, and they couldn't help but think, why not drop the hazmat and keep the penthouse tour?

But no. At noon today, the two Josés left the Imperiatum, out onto Fifth Avenue, and walked around the corner onto

Sixty-eighth Street, toward the doctors' offices. They were almost to the first entrance when they heard a sudden rasping sound they didn't recognize, out ahead of them, and then saw that the garage door in the next building was lifting.

It hit them both at the same time. That wasn't their building, it was the next building, but that had to be Preston Fareweather's garage! So, the first day home, he was taking his BMW out for a spin.

Poised at the doctor's threshold, they waited, watching as the garage door very slowly lifted, waiting to see both the BMW and the fabled owner of that penthouse.

But what came out first was obviously neither. Three guys emerged, ducking under the rising garage door, and walked briskly away down Sixty-eighth Street. All three of them were guys, the Josés knew, who would never get past security in the front of the building, so what were they doing coming out of the back of the building, and coming out through territory that belonged to the richest guy in the building?

The garage door opened to the top, and there now backed out, springs sluggish as though it were very full, a white Ford truck, a pretty big one with what must be a sixteen-foot box, so it must have crammed that garage from end to end. In the cab of the truck were two guys wearing yellow hard hats, which didn't make any sense, because for once there was absolutely no construction going on in this neighborhood.

The truck backed into the street in a half-turn as the garage door began to lower. The truck headed off down Sixty-eighth Street, and Little José said, "Take a look at that license plate."

So Big José did: PF WON.

"That's no commercial plate," Little José said. "That truck's gotta have a commercial plate. José, there's something wrong."

Big José already had the cell phone in his hand. The local

50

AT EVERY TRAFFIC light where they had to stop, Kelp and
Stan did some more adjustments on the cat's cradle of
straps inside the hard hats, until they were just perfect, completely comfortable. They still looked moronic, of course, riding way up above your head as though you were hiding a
cheeseburger in there, but at least they were comfortable.

And so was the truck. Not like the hard-riding workhorses
of yore, this one came equipped with air, soft bench seating,
automatic shift, and even cruise control, though you wouldn't
use that so much in the city. But the rest was very nice.

They were southbound on Eleventh Avenue, within two
blocks of the construction site where they would stash this
very nice truck, continuing to admire its qualities, Stan saying he thought he might hold on to it for afterward since it
contained this magic kryptonite stuff that robbed police
forces of their power, when all at once a black Chrysler Con-
sigliere cut in front of them so sharply that Stan had to hit
the brakes, his horn, and the roof, all at once: *"Whatsamatter-
withyou?"*

precinct was on his speed-dial, and when the bored voice answered, he said, "This is José Carreras, security at the Imperiatum."

"How can I help you?"

"There's a white Ford truck just left this building with a New York license plate P F space W O N. I think that license plate is supposed to be on a BMW instead, and there's something funny going on."

"You want me to run the plate? Hold on."

The NYPD's hold music was the Beatles' "Lucy in the Sky with Diamonds," which didn't seem right somehow, but it was more pleasant than listening to perky female voices keep you up to date on local parking regulations. Besides which, it wasn't that long before the original cop came back:

"You're right, that tag is assigned to a four-year-old BMW Series One."

"Owned," Big José said, "by Preston Fareweather."

"That's right."

"The truck just turned off Sixty-eighth onto Madison," Big José said, "and Preston Fareweather just came home to his penthouse in the Imperiatum last night after a long absence. I think you might want to stop that truck and send some people over here."

"They're on their way."

The Chrysler in front of them now stopped entirely, and all at once a Jeep Buccaneer was on their left, also stopping, and they were crowded against the parked cars on their right, unable to move.

Kelp said, "Stan, it's a hijack!"

"I don't *need* this," Stan told the world, and something tapped the windowglass to his left. When he looked over there, what was tapping was the metal end of the sawed-off double-barreled shotgun the right front passenger in the Jeep was aiming his way. The guy had a whole lot of neck and nose, very little hair, and a smile meant for pulling wings off flies. This guy made up-up gestures with the shotgun barrel, and his meaning was perfectly clear: Get out of the vehicle.

Stan, not looking away from the shotgun and its bearer, said, "They want us out of the truck. I'd rather go out your door."

Looking past Stan at their visitors, Kelp said, "Roger," opened his door, and slid out to the sidewalk in the narrow space left by their nearness to the parked cars on their right.

As Stan followed, a guy very similar to the shotgun guy came trotting down from the Chrysler to get behind the wheel of the truck, and another one from the same litter came from somewhere behind the truck to brush Stan and Kelp aside and get up into the passenger seat. With no choice in the matter, Stan and Kelp made their way past the parked cars to the curb as the truck and its three escorting cars, all with Jersey plates, noisily rushed away from there.

Sounding more bitter than outraged, Stan said, "I never been hijacked before. Never once."

Sirens screamed. The three cars and the truck, still at the other end of this block, stood on their brakes, red lights shining against the sun. Police cars came from everywhere, slamming to a stop, plainclothesmen and uniforms boiling out, armed to the teeth.

"Well, you couldn't have picked a better time to have it happen to you," Kelp commented.

"Holy shit," Stan realized.

Two plains with their badges hanging down their shirt-fronts like yellow tongues paused to yell at Stan and Kelp: "Move along, move along, nothing to see here, get on to work, get on about your business, this is a crime scene here."

"Oh, I hate those," Kelp said. "Come along, Martha."

Under their hardhats, they walked briskly away. Kelp, getting into the part, pretended he had a metal lunchbox under his left arm, and you could almost see it.

51

Preston slept through the first round of alarums and halloos, the phone-calling, the loud footsteps and louder voices, the general hullabaloo. Having been prematurely dragged to the surface of consciousness once, he had afterward burrowed in even deeper than before, so that he could be thought of now as hibernating rather than merely sleeping.

But when Alan Pinkleton burst open his bedroom door and cried, "Preston, wake up! You've been robbed!" Preston's eyes snapped open like searchlights. He stared at Alan and, though barely conscious he was doing so, cried out, "Arnie Albright!"

This stopped Alan's momentum. "What? Preston, burglars came—"

"He was right there."

Preston struggled to a seated position, struggled to free his arms from the covers so he could point, then pointed at Alan and said, "He was right there, where you are."

"Preston," Alan said, "I'm not sure what you're talking about, but the police are here, and you have to come out and see them."

"Was it a dream?"

"Please, Preston."

Preston shook his head, clearing some of the fog from his brain. "A dream, I dreamed—"

"Get dressed, Preston," Alan said.

"Yes," Preston agreed. "I'll be right there."

And ten minutes later he was, entering his stripped living room with a stunned stare at what was missing—oh, so many things—before even acknowledging what was present, which was a dozen police officers—only the two over by the elevators in uniform, but all clearly police.

They hadn't noticed him yet, all busy together at the crime scene, Preston having entered with such astounded silence, but then Preston, in awe, said, "I've been robbed. I *have* been robbed," and they all turned toward him, everybody speaking at once and then all of them shutting up except one, a white-haired, bulky man in a short-sleeved white dress shirt, maroon tie, black pants, and badge attached to a strip of leather that dangled from the shirt pocket. This man said, "Preston Fareweather?"

"Yes, of course. How did this— It wasn't like this last night."

"I'm Detective Mark Radik," the white-haired man said, and gestured at the eight-foot long golden sofa. "Let's sit down together a minute."

"Yes, of course. I'm sorry, I'm still stunned."

"Sure you are, anybody would be. Sit down."

Preston sat, and Alan appeared, to say, "Some coffee?"

"Yes," he said. "Thank you, Alan, that would be . . ."

Alan left, and Detective Radik, sitting next to Preston on the sofa, said, "Mr. Pinkleton says you had a dream, or possibly saw one of the burglars?"

"I'm not sure," Preston said. It was so hard trying to think back into that sleep-drugged state. "I thought I woke up, and this fellow Albright was standing in my bedroom doorway. I'd met him a while back at a Club Med, he's from New York and I'd always had an impression of him as some sort of crook, I don't know exactly why. I mean, I just thought of him that way."

Alan appeared again to put a cup of coffee silently on the table beside Preston, who said, "Thank you, Alan."

"It would be nice," Detective Radik said, "to know which it was: a dream or the real thing. It's possible, in your sleep, you heard the burglars and put the face of this fellow you think of as a crook on it, but it's just as possible you really did see him. He might have been in that Club Med particularly to help background you for this eventual burglary. I take it he wouldn't have known you were coming back yesterday."

"No one knew it. Until yesterday, I didn't know it myself." Preston looked around the room. The astonishment didn't let up. "They took everything."

"Well," Detective Radik said, "give me this fellow's name, and we'll see if we can track him down. It could be a lead, Mr. Fareweather, so we'll certainly follow through on it."

"His name is Arnie Albright," Preston said. "One 'L,' I think. I know he lives somewhere in Manhattan, the west side, I think."

Through all this, the other police in the room had been moving around, talking together, taking still pictures and videos, taking measurements, talking into telephones and radios, and now one of them came over to say, "Sir, they got them."

Detective Radik smiled. "That was quick."

"Two members of the security staff here," the other cop said, "saw their truck leaving, and recognized Mr. Fareweather's car's license plate on the truck."

Preston cried, "What! My license plate? My car? Is my *car* gone?"

"We'll soon find out, sir," Detective Radik said, and to the cop he said, "Have you ID'd any of the perps? Is there an Arnie Albright among them?"

"No, sir," the cop said. "They were apprehended on Eleventh Avenue, with three escort cars. There were six guys, it turns out, they're all New Jersey mobsters."

"New Jersey?"

"All members of the Howie Carbine crew. They're not supposed to operate in New York."

Detective Radik offered a humorless brief laugh. "So they're not only in trouble with us," he said, "they're in trouble with the New York families. Good."

"The truck is being taken to the Fifty-seventh Street police garage."

"Sir," Detective Radik said to Preston, "after you've had some breakfast, I'd like you to come along and identify the contents of the truck. There'll have to be an inventory, and you can help us there, if you would."

"Of course," Preston said. "Just think, mobsters from New Jersey. Not Arnie Albright after all." Chuckling, Preston said, "I might have made some trouble for that poor man. I feel I owe him an apology."

52

I'LL BE BACK a little late from lunch," Judson said, "I've got some stuff to get for my new apartment."

"Fine," J. C. said. "See you then."

That's the way to lie, Judson told himself as he left the office. Casual, straightforward, confident.

He walked up Fifth Avenue as far as Sixty-seventh Street, but then, not wanting to go past the building up at Sixty-eighth, because he couldn't be sure what was going on there, he turned right, went over to Madison and up a block, then came to the building along the Sixty-eighth Street side.

Yes, there was the garage door, and there was the alarm he'd fixed. From what little they'd told him, and from what more he'd guessed, their object was the penthouse atop the corner building, and this garage would lead to a special elevator up to it.

Were they in there now? Or maybe they hadn't gotten here yet. Of course, if they'd already come and gone, then there was no point in his being here. But if it was such a big thing they were doing, it wouldn't be over by lunchtime, would it? In any case, he couldn't get here before now, because he didn't have a cover story to give J. C.

The point of what he'd done to the alarm system was to make it possible for them to unlock the garage door and then open it whenever they wanted to. Was it still unlocked? Had they been here? Were they here now? Had they not yet arrived? Judson took a quick look left and right, saw no one paying him any particular attention, tugged on the door, and it lifted.

Oh. Should he do this?

Too late; he was doing it. He pulled the bottom of the door up to waist height, slipped in underneath, and pushed it down again.

The place was empty. That's where the car would usually stand; you could see ghost tire treads on the dusty floor, but it was gone now. And there was still nobody around.

There were no windows in here, but an overhead light had come on when he'd opened the door, and by it he saw what had to be the door to the elevator. He went over there, pulled on that door handle, and another light went on, this one inside the elevator, which was right here.

Should he take it? He was in here now; there was nobody around; the penthouse up there was guaranteed to be empty, so why not?

Stepping into the elevator, he pressed the *Top* button and felt a moment of uneasiness as the elevator slid upward. But there was nobody around; there was nothing to worry about. Up there, he should be able to tell if the others had been through already or not. If they had, he'd just leave. If not, he'd wait for them, surprise them when they arrived, tell them he was just here to help carry stuff. If he was already in, they wouldn't throw him out, would they?

The elevator slowed, and stopped. Judson waited for the door to open, but it didn't, so he finally realized he'd have to push it open himself. As he did so (although he didn't know this), the elevator at the front of the penthouse was just closing on the last of the police as they vacated the crime scene.

Judson walked through the place, admiring the furniture, the carpets, the view. The living room was fantastic.

But it was also very empty. The walls were dotted with hooks where paintings once had hung. Pedestals stood around with nothing on top of them.

The gang had been here. They were so efficient, they'd walked right in and cleaned out everything they wanted and gone away again, and all before lunch.

They don't have to know I was here, Judson assured himself. I don't want to be some pest hanging around, like some little kid yelling, "Wait for *meee!*" So I'll just leave, and they'll never know I was here. But those guys are good, aren't they?

Walking back down the hall, he noticed they hadn't taken any of the few pictures hanging along here. They'd only taken things from the living room and dining room, probably figuring this stuff back here was less important.

One of the pictures attracted his attention, though it was kind of dark and small, less than a foot wide and maybe eight inches high. But for its size, it had a lot of detail. It was kind of medieval, with two guys his own age, in peasant clothes, and they were carrying a pig hung on a long pole, each of the guys having an end of the pole on his shoulder. They were walking on a path on a hillside with woods around them, and down the hill you could see what looked like a lake, with a few very rustic houses and wagons beside it, and a few people chopping wood and stuff like that.

What drew Judson's eye to this picture was the expressions on the two young guys' faces. They had, like, goofy grins on, as though they were getting away with something and couldn't help laughing about it.

Judson looked at the guys and their mischievous eyes and

goofy grins, and he felt a kinship. He'd be one of those two, if he had lived then.

And all at once he got it: they'd stolen the pig.

Judson took the picture down off its hook on the wall, and studied it more closely. It was old, all right, done when those clothes were what you wore. It was painted on wood, and it was signed in the lower right with a signature he couldn't figure out.

The painting was in an elaborate gilded frame that didn't seem right for those two guys. There was also a sheet of nonreflective glass. Once Judson removed the picture from the frame, it wasn't heavy. It wasn't big. He liked it. He slid it under his shirt, tucked into the front of his pants, and headed for the elevator.

53

B Y THE TIME they got back to Arnie's place, he was a nervous wreck in a completely different way. At first, when he'd rushed from Fareweather's garage with Dortmunder and Tiny, Arnie had been convinced Fareweather was no more than six feet behind him, probably still in his jammies, coming on like the avenging angel, whistling up cops right and left. When Dortmunder, constantly looking back because Arnie was too scared to, assured him over and over that no one matching Preston Fareweather's description was anywhere on the sidewalk back there, nor were there any cops, nor was there anything that looked remotely like pursuit of any kind, it didn't matter. Arnie, jiggling and jabbering like a marionette with electrified springs, just kept rushing forward, ahead of Dortmunder and Tiny, barely ahead of the imaginary hounds.

Then he was too scared to take a taxi, because the cabbie would write on his trip sheet what neighborhood he'd picked Arnie up in and would be able to testify against him at the inevitable trial before the inevitable incarceration of poor Arnie Albright, who should never, ever have been in that place in the first place, and where could he go now that the law was waiting for him at home?

"They're not waiting for you at home, Arnie," Dortmunder told him. "You'll go home, if somebody ever comes around, you say, that wasn't me, I don't know what the guy's talking about, search my place if you want."

"Ooohh."

"All right, you'll clean out a couple things. I'll come to your place with you, I know I'm partly responsible for you being—"

"Partly!"

"Well, Preston Fareweather has to take some of the burden, too, you know. Come on, Arnie, I'll come with you."

"I won't," Tiny said. "Good-bye." And he walked off down Madison, headed for lunch with J. C.

"Here we go, Arnie," Dortmunder said, "here's a nice cab—"

"No cabs!"

So it wound up, Arnie did walk through Central Park that day, though not in the cool of the morning but in the absolute heat and glare of the midday sun, like something in *Lawrence of Arabia*. Arnie didn't so much walk across the park, though, as hop from tree shade to tree shade and, where there were no trees, scuttle on like something you might see when you switch on the kitchen light.

Eventually they did traverse the park, and some of the West Side as well, and reached Annie's building, in front of which there were no official presences. Arnie scrambled up into the vestibule, followed by Dortmunder, but then, instead of unlocking the door he rang his own bell.

Dortmunder said, "Arnie? You're not home, we know that."

"But is somebody else?" Arnie said darkly, and stared at

the intercom until it became obvious even to him that it wasn't going to say anything. Only then did he unlock the door and lead the way up to his apartment, where he looked around, grabbed his head with both hands in tragic despair, and cried, "How do I clean *this* place for the cops? You think I got *receipts*?"

"I'll wait with you, Arnie," Dortmunder said. "There isn't gonna be a problem, because if there was gonna be a problem, by now there'd *be* a problem, with how long it took us to walk across town."

"You're the one wanted to walk."

"Going that way, not coming this way. You got a radio?"

Arnie looked at him in disbelief. "You want music?"

"I want the news," Dortmunder said.

"Oh. Sure. Right. Lemme bring it out."

Arnie went away to the bedroom and came back with a white plastic radio originally given as a bonus for opening a bank account in 1947. He plugged it in and turned it to the local news station. "You give us twenty-two minutes," they threaten, "we'll give you the world," and then they give you mostly sports. They may not know this, but sports is not the world.

After hearing some scores, and some manager firings, and some commercials, however, they did actually get some news, and it began, "A Manhattan penthouse was robbed this morning of over six million dollars' worth of rare art. Julie Hapwood has this late-breaking story."

"A luxurious Fifth Avenue penthouse apartment in Manhattan overlooking Central Park was the scene this morning of a daring daylight robbery of over nine million dollars in rare art. The owner of the apartment, financier Preston Fareweather, fifty-seven, who had just returned from abroad last night, apparently slept through the entire robbery, as did an associate, Alan Pinkleton, forty-four, who was a guest in the

apartment. Quick thinking on the part of two members of the
building's security guard detail, José Carreras, twenty-seven,
and José Otsego, twenty-four, who grew suspicious of a truck
they spotted near the building and called police, put authori-
ties early on the trail of the daring bandits. Police hope to
catch the gang before they can dispose of their loot. This is
Julie Hapwood, continuing to stay on this breaking story."

"You give us twenty-two minutes, we'll give you the
world," and then they got more sports.

Twenty minutes later, while Dortmunder was trying to
decide whether to eat the omelet Arnie had made in his du-
bious kitchen, the radio said, "Arrests have been made in the
daring daylight penthouse robbery on Fifth Avenue in Manhattan this morning. Julie Hapwood is here with this late-
breaking story."

Arnie quick looked at himself to see if he'd been arrested,
while Dortmunder leaned closer to the radio and farther
from the omelet.

"Just moments ago, police on Eleventh Avenue in Manhattan intercepted the white Ford truck seen fleeing the
scene of this morning's daring daylight robbery at the Imperiatum, the deluxe high-rise apartment building at East Sixty-
eighth Street and Fifth Avenue in Manhattan. Early reports
are that arrests have been made and the loot has been recovered. Mayoral assistant Zozo Von Cleve, thirty-six, announced, 'This is the kind of immediate instant-response
activity we have come to expect from our New York Police
Department, rightly known as New York's Finest.' This is
Julie Hapwood, continuing to stay on this breaking story."

"I don't think I have an appetite," Dortmunder said, pushing the omelet away.

"We're doomed," Arnie announced, and the phone rang.
Arnie stared at it. "The cops!"

"Cops don't phone, Arnie," Dortmunder pointed out. "Cops make house calls."

Still, Arnie didn't want to answer it, so finally Dortmunder did, and it was Kelp, saying, "John? I thought I dialed Arnie."

"Andy? I thought they arrested you."

"Not us, wait'll you hear. Where are you?"

"I'm at Arnie's, you called Arnie's. I answered because he's having a little nervous breakdown over here. You wanna come over? Where's Stan?"

"Next to me on the sidewalk. We'll come over."

"Further developments in the late-breaking story of the daring daylight robbery at the Fifth Avenue penthouse of financier Preston Fareweather, fifty-seven. It now appears there may be some Mafia involvement."

Dortmunder and Arnie stared at each other. Dortmunder said, "Mafia?"

"Julie Hapwood has this late-breaking story."

"The six men arrested in the daring daylight robbery on Fifth Avenue's posh Gold Coast in Manhattan today all, according to police, have ties to organized crime. Several of the men have convictions in New Jersey for extortion, gambling, arson, and assault. Police are looking for any link between financier Preston Fareweather and known mob leaders in New Jersey. Mayoral assistant Zozo Von Cleve, thirty-six, announced, 'It is unlikely this was merely a random burglary, if mob figures are connected with it. No one thinks Mr. Fareweather, one of New York City's finer citizens, had any link to the crime, but his associates are undergoing scrutiny at this time.' This is Julie Hapwood, continuing to stay on this breaking story."

"The O.J.," Dortmunder said, and the doorbell rang.

"It's the cops!"

"Arnie, it's Andy and Stan. Let them in."

But Arnie had to call down to them through the intercom, and insist they both identify themselves and swear they weren't accompanied by any other person of any kind, before he'd let them in. Then they came upstairs, and Kelp said, "You won't believe this."

"We just heard it on the radio," Dortmunder told him. "It was the mob guys from New Jersey."

"Dammit," Kelp said, "you spoiled my story."

"But that was it," Dortmunder said. "Somehow they got onto us, they followed us around—"

"I never knew a thing," Kelp said.

"None of us did. This was their idea of payback for the O.J., only it didn't work out like they wanted."

Stan said, "Half a block later, it would have been *me* getting pulled over. I'd be washing ink off my fingertips along about now. I don't need anything closer."

Kelp said, "Is it too early for a beer?"

"No," everybody said, and made Arnie go out and buy some.

It was while drinking beer they decided Tiny should be brought into the loop. Arnie was still afraid the telephone wanted to bite him, so Dortmunder made the call, and it was the kid, Judson, who answered. "Oh, hi, Mr. Dortmunder," he said. "They aren't back from lunch yet. I'm back quicker than I thought, so I'm just taking care of things here, taking care of the mail, watching things here."

He sounds guilty, Dortmunder thought. What's *he* got to be guilty about? "Tell Tiny," he said, "we got developments, and we're all at this number," and he read it off the phone.

"I will," Judson promised. "I wrote it down, I've got it, I'll tell Mr. Tiny the second he comes in, don't you worry about that."

"I'm not worried," Dortmunder said, and hung up, and said, "That kid's a little strange."

"We got something," Kelp said, and pointed at the radio.

"—connected to the crime. Julie Hapwood has this late-breaking story."

"Michael Anthony Carbine, twenty-six, son of reputed New Jersey mob boss Ottavian Siciliano Carbine, fifty-one, has been taken in for questioning by officers of Manhattan's nineteenth precinct, on the posh East Side. Carbine was discovered in Central Park, just opposite the Imperiatum, the deluxe high-rise apartment building where this morning's daring daylight robbery of over fifteen million dollars in artworks took place. The six men arrested earlier this afternoon in Manhattan in possession of the looted artworks are said to be known associates of Mr. Carbine and his father. Detective Inspector Sean O'Flynn, head of the NYPD's Organized Crime Squad, said an agreement between the New York and New Jersey mobs not to poach on one another's territory appeared to have been breached, which could mean a mob war may well be on its way. This is Julie Hapwood, continuing to stay on this breaking story."

When Tiny called, Dortmunder had to answer the phone again, and Tiny said, "We don't have the stuff."

"No, we don't," Dortmunder agreed, "but there keep being developments. We're all over here catching this late-breaking story on the radio."

"I remember radio," Tiny said. "I'll be right over."

So when the doorbell rang again a quarter hour later, Dortmunder got to his feet and said, "Stay there, Arnie, I'll let him in. I don't wanna hear any more interrogations."

"Probably," Arnie said, though with some doubt in his voice, "the cops reeled in enough for today."

While Dortmunder buzzed Tiny in, Kelp said, "Seven

known mob guys from New Jersey, *and* all the swag? If they want more than that, they're very greedy."

"I think they are," Stan said.

Dortmunder opened the apartment door, and Tiny had brought the kid Judson with him. "I brought the kid with me," he pointed out as they entered.

"So I see," Dortmunder said.

"Hello," Judson said, and smiled at everybody.

"He was gonna get a piece of the profit," Tiny explained, "so he can get a piece of the sorrow and woe instead."

"Just so the other team was driving the truck when the game was called," Stan said. "As far as I'm concerned, I'm ahead."

"That's you," Tiny said, and said to Dortmunder, "This is because you wanted to be a hero and save the O.J."

"I'm afraid it is," Dortmunder admitted.

"Do we know yet how much you owe me?"

Dortmunder offered a sickly smile, and Kelp said, "Julie Hapwood says they're doing an inventory now at the Fifty-seventh Street police garage, and Fareweather's at his place making a list of what he thinks is missing."

Tiny frowned at him. "Who the hell is Julie Hapwood?"

"The woman on the radio's been telling us all this stuff."

Tiny looked at the radio, which was in the process of giving them twenty-two minutes of sports. "So let's see what else she has to say," he said.

But that was it for Julie Hapwood. All at once, without even a wave good-bye, the late-breaking story seemed to have broken. The news now broke in from other fronts, of less neighborhood interest.

So at five they switched to television, to see what the local news broadcasts might have to say. At first, almost nothing, but Arnie kept switching back and forth among the stations, and all at once he stopped, pointed the remote at the set, and said, "That's him!"

A rich guy, you could tell. He wasn't fat, he was portly, and only rich guys are portly. He was being interviewed by a blonde television reporter in the living room Dortmunder and the others knew so well, with some very obvious blank spaces on the walls behind him as he said, "One does feel assaulted, Gwen. One had not expected Cro-Magnons from New Jersey to beleaguer one in the supposed safety of one's home."

"That's a lotta 'ones,'" Tiny said.

The reporter asked, "Do you have a sense yet, Mr. Fareweather, of what they took?"

"The cream of the crop, Gwen. I must confess, one would not have expected that degree of taste and sophistication from fellows best known for breaking their enemies' knees. At least one of that cohort had an excellent eye."

"There you go," Arnie said. He was grinning from ear to ear.

"They were so good," Fareweather went on, "they even got the Brueghel."

Arnie, Dortmunder, Kelp and the girl reporter all said, "Brueghel?"

Gesturing to something off-camera to his right, Fareweather said, "It was the only thing they took from the hall. Everything else was from this area here. And it's true, most of the items in the hall are of perhaps a bit lesser quality, but I always kept the Brueghel there to protect it from too much sunlight."

"And nevertheless they found it," the reporter said.

"Yes, they did, Gwen. And I certainly hope the police find it among the things they are looking at right now in that truck."

Arnie said, "*What* Brueghel?"

The girl reporter said, "What value would you place on that Brueghel, Mr. Fareweather?"

"Oh, lord knows," Fareweather said. "*I* paid just under a mil for it, seven or eight years ago."

Tiny said, "Off the set, Arnie, we gotta talk."

Arnie killed the TV by remote control and said, "I didn't red-dot nothing in the hall. I didn't even *look* in the hall."

"Dortmunder and me," Tiny said, "we didn't take nothing unless it had a red dot on it. Right?"

"That's right," Dortmunder said.

Kelp said, "Stan and me were downstairs, so I don't know. What did this Brueghel look like?"

"Kelp," Tiny said, sounding just a bit dangerous, "none of us took it, so none of us knows what the hell it looks like."

"Well," Kelp said, reasonably, "somebody took it."

"Judson," Dortmunder said.

Everybody looked at Dortmunder, and then everybody looked at Judson, who was blushing and stammering and fidgeting on that kitchen chair with his arms jerking around—a definite butterfly, pinned in place. Everybody continued to look at him, and finally he produced words, of a sort: "Why would you— What would I— How could— Mr. Dortmunder, why would you—?"

"Judson," Tiny said. He said it softly, gently, but Judson clammed up like a locked safe, and his face went from beet red to shroud white, just like that.

Dortmunder said, "Had to be. He went there, wanted to hang out with us, we were already gone, he went in and up, looked around, decided to take a little something."

Kelp said, "Judson, what made you take *that*?"

Judson looked around at them all, tongue-tied.

Arnie, in an informational way, said, "Kid, you're one of the most incompetent liars I've ever seen."

Judson sighed. He could be seen to accept the idea at last

that denial was going to be of no use. "I identified with it," he said.

Everybody reacted to that one. Stan said, "You *identified* with it?"

Dortmunder said, "What's it a picture of, Judson?"

"Two young guys stealing a pig."

Tiny said, "That's what goes for just under a mil? Two guys stealing a pig?"

"It's nice," Judson said. "You can see they're having fun."

"More than we are," Tiny said.

Dortmunder said, "Judson, where is this picture now?"

"In my desk in J. C.'s office."

Tiny said, "I tell you what, kid. You were gonna get a piece of what we got, but we no longer got what we got, so now *we* are gonna get a piece of what *you* got."

"That seems fair," Kelp said.

Again Judson sighed. Then he said, "Maybe I can take a picture of it."

"Good idea," Dortmunder agreed.

Tiny said to Arnie, "Your guy paid a million for it. You'll deal with the insurance company, you'll get ten per cent, that means around fifteen grand for each of us, which isn't what I had in mind, but these things happen, and, Dortmunder, I forgive you, and I think we all agree it was a good decision to let the kid stick around."

"Thank you," Judson said.

"Still and all," Tiny said, "all that stuff in there, and we wind up with one picture."

Dortmunder thought of, but decided not to mention, the trinkets still burning holes in his own pockets. Some people know how to keep a secret.

54

THE INTERVIEW WITH Preston Fareweather had been taped forty minutes before it ran, and at the end of it, as the sound man and cameraman were packing and assembling all their plentifulness of gear, Preston said to the fair Gwen, "That was quite enjoyable. You make the thing just about painless."

"Well, that's the job," she said.

"When you finish your assigned tasks at your station," he said, "why not pop back here, we could have a lovely dinner *a due*."

"Oh, I don't think so," she said.

"I would rather take you to one of the better restaurants in the neighborhood," he said, smiling upon her, "but I'm afraid little legal problems, process servers and all that, are keeping me housebound at least until I can get a new car. But those restaurants know me, I think I'm probably considered a good tipper, they'll be happy to send over a little something from the menu." Chuckling, he said, "Not exactly your Chinese takeout. What do you say? A little penthouse adventure."

"I don't think so," she said.

Gesturing, he said, "That view is even more magnificent at night."

"I'm sure it is."

He gazed on her with a sad smile. "Would you really leave me here, Gwen, all alone, in my pillaged penthouse?"

"Mr. Fareweather," she said, "I researched you before I came up here, and I know all about your little legal problems and the process servers. You have a surprising number of ex-wives."

"Oh, ex-wives," he said, dismissing them with an airy sweep of the hand. "Spiteful little creatures, it's best just to ignore them. You know what they're like."

"I do," she said. "I'm one myself."

He couldn't believe it. "You'll take their *side*?"

"I won't take any side at all," she said. "Ready, boys?"

The boys, with cameras and cases and boxes and bags hanging from black straps off their shoulders, agreed they were ready, and rang for the elevator.

The snippy, self-sufficient Gwen directed a cool smile toward Preston. "Thank you, Mr. Fareweather, you gave a very good interview. My editor will be pleased."

"I'm so happy," Preston said as the elevator door opened.

"Sir," the sound man said.

"Yes?"

The sound man handed him a thick white envelope. "This is a service of court documents," he said, "in accordance with New York State law." And he U-turned and entered the elevator.

"RRRAAAGGHHHH!" Preston cried, and threw the envelope, but it bounced off the closing elevator door, leaving him the image of Gwen's surprised laugh as she turned to the sound man and said, "What did you—?"

Gone. Preston stood there, panting as though he'd run a

mile, and stared at the hateful envelope on his lovely oriental carpet. At last he turned away. "Alan!" he screamed. "Alan!"

And Alan appeared, as festooned with luggage as the sound man. "Oh, I missed the elevator," he said, and went over to ring for it.

Preston gaped at him. "What are you doing?"

"You don't need me any more, Preston," Alan said. "Our jolly days as island castaways are over. I've been on the phone, I've a couple of leads on a new position."

The elevator reappeared, and the operator, an uppity black woman, said, "Lotta traffic up here all of a sudden."

"Good-bye, Preston," Alan said, boarding. "It was all really very amusing. Thank you."

55

WHEN DORTMUNDER WALKED into the O.J. Bar & Grill at ten that night in mid-September, the regulars were all clustered at the left end of the bar, heads bent, gazing at money, as though they were playing liar's poker. Midway across the bar to the right, Rollo was pouring a drink, and a little farther on was the guy Dortmunder was here to see, one Ralph Winslow.

As Dortmunder approached the bar, it became clear the regulars weren't playing liar's poker after all; they were looking at the colors on the bills, because one of them, sounding aggrieved, said, "What are all these colors? Money is supposed to be green. People say, 'The long green. Pay me in green.' What is this, a paint-by-number?"

"There's still a lotta green in there," a second regular assured him.

"Yeah?" The first regular was not assured. Stabbing a finger at the bill, to the left of Jackson's head, he said, "What's this here?"

The second regular studied his own copy. "That's charters," he decided.

The first regular shot him a look of revulsion. "It's *what?*"

"Charters. That's a green with a lotta yellow in it."

Dortmunder and Ralph Winslow's drink, a rye and water in a squat thick glass, arrived at the same moment. "Whadaya say, Ralph?"

Ralph, a hearty, heavyset guy with a wide mouth and a big, round nose, was the fellow they were supposed to meet here way back in July, when it turned out he'd had to leave town for a while instead. Now he was back, and belatedly the meeting could take place, once everybody got here. In the meantime, he lifted his glass to Dortmunder, and the ice in it tinkled like far-off temple bells. "I'm glad to be back, is what I say," he said. "Cheers."

"Be right with you." Dortmunder said to Rollo, "We're gonna be six. I could take the bottle and Andy's glass."

"Sorry," Rollo said. "You can't use the room right now."

Dortmunder stared at him. "What, again? I thought those guys were too busy with the felony cases and the mob war."

"No, it's not them," Rollo said. "That's okay now, knock on wood," and he knocked on the copper top of the bar. "What it is, there's a support group uses the place sometimes, they're running a little late, one of them had a relapse."

"Sorry to hear that."

"I'll get you your drink."

"Thank you."

Over to the left, a third regular said, "This Hamilton's still green. He's still got the frame around his head, too."

"Really?" The second regular was very interested. "That's an older one, then," he said. "Whadaya suppose that's worth now?"

The third regular said, "What? It's a ten-dollar bill!"

The first regular said, "Who was Hamilton anyway? All the rest of them are presidents. He wasn't a president."

They were all silent. They all kind of knew the answer, but not precisely. Then the second regular lit up. "He got shot!"

"Big deal," the first regular said. "My cousin got shot, they didn't put *him* on any money."

The second regular, interested in everything, said, "Your cousin got shot? Who shot him?"

"Two husbands."

"*Two* husbands?"

The first regular shrugged. "He was unemployed at the time."

Rollo had just poured Dortmunder's bourbon over ice, with Ralph Winslow tinkling beside him, when Rollo looked up and said, "Here's two more of you."

Dortmunder looked around, and it was Tiny and the kid. "We aren't in the back room," Tiny said.

Dortmunder explained about the support group and the relapse, and Rollo came back with two identical-looking tall glasses of bright red liquid with ice, which he placed in front of Tiny and Judson.

Dortmunder, not sure he believed it, said, "Tiny? The kid's drinking vodka and red wine?"

"No," Tiny said. "Rollo won't let him."

"It's strawberry soda." Judson sipped, made a face, and said, "Yep, strawberry soda. That's all Mr. Rollo will let me have."

"Ever since the trouble with the Jersey guys," Rollo half-apologized, "the precinct has been keeping an eye on the place. I serve an underage drinker, you know what that means?"

Dortmunder said, "They close the place?"

"It means I get Otto back up here again," Rollo said, and Ralph said, "Whadaya say, Andy?"

"You're looking good," Andy Kelp told him, arriving,

reaching for his glass and the bourbon bottle Rollo had left on the bar. "Your vacation agreed with you."

"More than home did, right then. But what can you say about mountains? They're tall." And he tinkled as he sipped his rye.

"What's this?" Kelp asked, gazing off to his left.

It was the support group: seven people, some men, some women, a little blended together. They were all extremely thin and all dressed entirely in black. They seemed to be embarrassed about something and wouldn't meet anybody's eye. They moved through the room like an approaching low on the Weather Channel, and one of them peeled off to come to the bar and press an envelope into Rollo's hand without looking him in the face. "Thank you," he whispered, and rejoined his pod, and they faded into the night.

"The back room is open, gents," Rollo said.

They all thanked him, not whispering, picked up their drinks, and headed for the back room, Ralph gently tinkling along the way. As they rounded the end of the bar toward the hall, the regulars decided spontaneously to laud Rollo in song:

"For he's a jolly good *fell*-oh,
For he's a jolly good *fell*-oh,
For he's a jolly good *fell*-OH!
For he's a golly good fell."

"I don't think that's right," the second regular said. "I think the last line goes, 'For he's a jolly good elf.'"

So they tried it that way.